Some Other Child

by

Sharon Buchbinder

This is a work of fiction. Names, characters, places, and incidents are either the product of the author's imagination or are used fictitiously, and any resemblance to actual persons living or dead, business establishments, events, or locales, is entirely coincidental.

Some Other Child

Cover Art by *Kim Mendoza*

The Wild Rose Press, Inc.
PO Box 708
Adams Basin, NY 14410-0708
Visit us at www.thewildrosepress.com

Publishing History
First Mainstream Mystery Edition, 2014
Print ISBN 978-1-62830-411-4
Digital ISBN 978-1-62830-412-1

Published in the United States of America

Sarah wanted to throw the remote at the screen, but instead changed the station to a nice soothing infomercial for self-cleaning mops.

The next time she glanced at the clock, it was a few minutes after six in the morning. She must have dozed off. Something teased at the edge of her mind and haunted her, like the familiar scent of a perfume.

Winston ran to the door and began barking.

"Jeez, you must have teeny-weenie bladder syndrome." She threw open the back door. "Go! Get me a clue!"

He flew out the door, barking. She paused for a moment and raced after him, her bathrobe flapping in the cool early morning air. Winston ran along the edge of his invisible fence and barked. She arrived at the top of her driveway just in time to see a white van circle the cul-de-sac. She ran down the pine-tree-lined driveway, trying to catch sight of the license plate in the pre-dawn light. The Maryland truck plate began with the letter "M" and the numbers one and three. The rest of the numbers or letters were covered in dirt or mud.

"You son of a bitch!"

The van stopped, reversed, circled the cul-de-sac and came back toward her.

She froze in place. The van was so close, she could see the face of the driver, a shaggy-haired man with an expression of hatred. A pine tree stood between her and the curb. She leaped behind the tree, fell onto the ground, and rolled into Aunt Ida's yard. When came to a stop, she fumbled for her cell phone and punched 9-1-1. "Help me! Please! He's going to kill me!"

Praise for Sharon Buchbinder

~*~

"*SOME OTHER CHILD* grabbed me at page one and didn't let me go until the very end. Sharon Buchbinder has created a cast of compelling and relatable characters in a story filled with suspense, family drama, and carefully buried secrets."

~Sharon Saracino, Author

~*~

"*SOME OTHER CHILD* is a moving story of love in the face of painful family secrets. Buchbinder's storytelling is fast paced and addicting. The theme of forgiveness as a necessary part of family life is compelling."

~J.J. Brown, Author

Dedication

To my husband, Dale,
who fills my life with love and romance,
and to our son, Joshua,
who brings joy to our family.

Prologue

Chicago, Illinois

Exhausted after a long day of teaching classes and endless rounds of revisions on her dissertation, Sarah Wright opened the front door to the house she shared with her fiancé and was almost knocked down by the dog. Gandalf's scramble of paws and claws left a wake of mail scattered across the foyer and into the kitchen. Neferkitty, her spotted silver tabby, perched on arm of the sofa and eyed Sarah as if to say, "I told you he was bad news."

"Great." She shrugged out of her blazer, tossed it onto a chair, and began to play fifty-two pick up. Her neck prickled. Sarah looked up from the mail. A giant gray slobbering monster stood with his front paws on the glass door, the fog of his breath mixing with mud smears. More work. She edged the door open and forced Gandalf to sit while she wiped his filthy feet. "Gandalf, it's time we had a 'come-to-Sarah' talk about your behavior."

The gray beast turned his back to her, raised his leg and peed on her jacket.

"Fabulous. What else can go wrong?"

Moments later, her fiancé strolled in the door, whistling a cheerful tune.

Sanitizer barely dried on her hands, Sarah spoke

through gritted teeth. "Gandalf pissed on my coat. Get rid of that dog."

Dan Rosen leaned over and gave Sarah a bear hug. She buried her face in his shirt and breathed in a mixture of aftershave and masculine scent.

"That's his way of showing he likes you." Dan kissed her brow. "You should be honored."

"I'd hate to know what he'd do to shower me with love." The canine in question slunk behind the sofa. "Give him back to your ex-girlfriend."

Dan quirked a brow. "Jealous?"

"Absolutely not."

"Methinks the lady doth protest—"

Sarah put her fingers over his mouth, stood on her tiptoes, and gazed into in his chocolate brown eyes. She loved him from the top of his head at six feet, two inches, dark hair flecked with white, all the way down to his size ten shoes. His dog, however, was a different matter. "He gives me the evil eye. I swear he's laughing at me."

The ring of the phone interrupted her appeal.

"Sarah, please come," her mother sobbed. "There's been a terrible car accident.'

A chill slithered down Sarah's spine. Not again.

"What happened?" White knuckled, she clutched the phone and mouthed "my mother" at Dan.

"Some idiot slammed into me. The police say it's my fault."

Sarah shook her head. Same story, different day. "How much did you drink?"

A long silence. Sarah sighed. "How bad?"

"My legs are broken. Ida's too old to help me. I can't ask your brother. He has a wife and a child to support. Your sister won't talk to me." She paused. "You're a nurse without a job."

"I'm in a doctoral program, not unemployed."

"Don't make me beg."

Her mother began to weep, and Sarah's vow not fall back into her old ways began to waver. Arrows of guilt pierced her resolve. Who else would come to the aid of this difficult elderly woman?

"I can't walk, drive, or do anything for myself."

Sarah closed her eyes and sighed already regretting her next words. "Okay, Mom. I'll come." She placed the phone on the receiver and turned to Dan.

Dan stared down at her with an expression of disbelief. "DUI, right?"

She nodded. "She needs me."

He took her face in his hands. "Look at me."

She locked her gaze with his.

"This woman sent you away to live with your deaf grandmother and didn't visit you for years."

"A nasty divorce. An alcoholic husband. Three little kids. What was she supposed to do?"

"Hardly a loving mother. You have physical and emotional scars, Sarah."

Tears welled in her eyes. "That's history. She's changed. I heard it in her voice. She asked for me, not Matt, not Debra. She asked for *me*."

Dan closed his eyes as the muscles in his jaw worked overtime. Raised in a normal household, he'd never understand what it meant to be the adult child of an alcoholic. They came from different planets, not just different religions.

An idea occurred to her. "You grew up in Baltimore. Your mom still lives in the city. Visit your mom and me at the same time."

His eyes flew wide open. "You can't stand Gert."

Sarah shrugged. "I'll get to know her better while I'm in Baltimore."

"Don't do this, Sarah. Ethel's an alcoholic—a mean one. Stay here. I love you."

She glanced at Gandalf. He stared back, shooting doggy daggers at her.

Dan followed her gaze. "Well, okay, he is a pain in the ass."

She kissed the tip of his nose. "Thanks for that admission, at least. I love you, too, but if I don't go and something happens to her, I could never live with myself."

"You can't keep running to rescue her."

She shook her head. "I won't abandon her."

He threw his hands up. "Go. But mark my words: One of these days she'll get drunk and kill herself."

Chapter One

Baltimore, Maryland
One year later

Sarah pulled into the cul-de-sac in front of her mother's house and screeched to a halt.

"What in the world?"

Three Baltimore County police cars and an ambulance parked at crazy angles in her driveway. She rolled down her sleet-streaked window, and a grim-faced police officer greeted her. "Ma'am, this area is closed off for an investigation."

"That house with all the emergency vehicles—it's mine. I live here. What happened?" She spotted a familiar man standing a few feet away, chatting with another cop. "Officer Mike," she called, "do you remember me?"

He waved at her and picked his way across the ice-coated street. Her mind raced with possibilities. That morning, as usual, her mom was asleep when she got up. Sarah had left the coffee pot on a timer and a bowl of her mother's favorite cereal on the kitchen table.

When she called to check in on her mother around ten in the morning, she seemed fine. Sarah told her she was stopping at the grocery store after work and to call if she needed anything. She'd never called.

Sarah gripped the steering wheel until her knuckles

turned white. Had something happened to Aunt Ida? Had a neighbor stopped by and been injured in a fall on the ice? Or had her mother—

"Dear God," she prayed, "Please don't let it be Mom."

Just as Officer Mike reached the side of her car, she heard a dog bay. She'd know that howl anywhere. She clutched the edge of the open window. "What's going on?"

His expression grave, he pointed toward the house. "Detective Engelman wants to speak with you."

As she got out of the car, Mike grabbed her arm to help guide her across the patches of ice up to the house. As they rounded a corner, two EMTs rushed toward them with a laden gurney.

"What happened? Mom, can you hear me?" Sarah pulled away from Mike, lunged for the gurney, and fell.

Mike pulled her up to her feet. "Ms. Wright, let them do their job."

She wrenched out of his grasp and body blocked the paramedics. "Tell me what happened to my mother."

"She fell. She's alive—but barely. We have to get her to the ER," the EMT said and pushed past her.

Sarah caught sight of her mother's silver hair spread across a tiny white pillow. A green plastic oxygen mask covered her face. Wrapped in dark blankets, the motionless form drove a knife of guilt into Sarah's heart. If only she'd gotten home earlier. Maybe this wouldn't have happened.

"I'm riding with you on the ambulance."

Mike was at her side again. "You have to speak with Detective Engelman first."

Again, a howl rose into the frigid air. In the glare of emergency lights, she saw Winston, her mother's eighty-pound Weimaraner, in the back yard, tied to a tree. "At least let me get the dog into the house. I can't leave him out here in this bitter cold."

An EMT shouted, "Sinai's ER is on bypass. We're going to Baltimore Medical Center."

"I'll get the dog," Mike said. "You go in the house."

Fearful of what she'd find—knowing it could be most anything—Sarah climbed the back steps and opened the kitchen door. A stocky man with salt and pepper hair sat at the Formica topped table and glanced up as she entered. "I'm Detective Engelman. Who are you?" His voice conveyed an attitude that said, "And don't even think about lying to me."

"Sarah Wright," she said. "I live here. What happened?"

He nodded. "Here's what we know. Officer Corrigan responded to a noise complaint. He found your mother in the back yard, unconscious, with the dog next to her. We have no idea how long she was out there. If it hadn't been for the dog keeping her warm, she'd probably be dead. The EMTs say she has a head injury and hypothermia."

Taking a deep breath, Sarah struggled to make a recognizable pattern out the chaos of information.

The detective continued to stare at her. "Can you tell me your whereabouts today?"

"I was at work. When I spoke with my mother at ten this morning, she was fine, and I told her I'd be stopping at the store on my way home."

"You have proof of that?"

Why was he acting as if she was a suspect?

For the past year her life revolved around work, taking care of her mother, housework and sleep. She felt guilty if she had to work late or take the time to run to the store on the way home from the hospital. Was he trying to make her feel worse?

"Are you serious?" Her voice was sharper than she intended, but his questions were keeping her away from her mother.

"Can you supply witnesses for your whereabouts?"

She tried to tell herself not to take it personally, that he was just doing his job, but anger began to bubble up in her chest. She'd done nothing wrong and his tone was one she'd expect a cop would use with a hardened felon, not a worried daughter.

She spoke through gritted teeth. "Yes, I have witnesses from work."

"Do you have a time-stamped receipt from the store?"

"In my car. With the groceries. How about asking me these questions on the way to the hospital? I need to be with my mother."

"Ms. Wright, does your mother have any illnesses that would cause her to wander, say like dementia or something like that?"

Sarah stared at the man and swallowed hard. Had he no compassion? "She does not have have Alzheimer's if that's what you're implying."

She took a deep breath. The definition of insanity was doing the same thing over and over again, expecting different results. Since the cop wasn't responding to emotional pleas, she decided to change tactics, go with a nothing-but-the facts tone.

"What time did it start to sleet today?"

"When my shift began. Around three."

By that hour, Sarah thought, Mom and one of the "boys"—Jack Daniels, Johnny Walker, Mr. Bell, or Old Granddad—and would have been having themselves a jolly old time.

"She was probably drunk." Sarah blew out a long breath. "She's an alcoholic. Has been for years."

Winston burst into the kitchen. She bent to put her arms around the dog and buried her face in his velvety ears. "You saved Mom's life."

As he licked her face, she realized she was crying. She turned to the detective. So what if he was made of granite. She wasn't going to apologize for her tears. "If you don't mind, I'm going give him a warm meal. He's freezing and hungry."

He shrugged. "I'll take a look around while you're doing that."

With a brief knock on the door, Aunt Ida, a seventy-five-year-old Jewish Aunt Bea, let herself into the kitchen. "Sarahlei," she puffed, short of breath. "I just got home from my senior citizen self defense class and saw the police cars. *Oy!* You look terrible!"

"Mom's had a bad accident. It looks like she took Winston outside and fell on the ice." Or to hide her empties where I wouldn't see them.

Aunt Ida sat down hard in a kitchen chair, unbuttoned her coat, and fanned her face with her hand. "*Oy vey iz mir!* Where is she now?"

"On the way to the hospital. I was just getting Neferkitty and Winston fed. He's a hero. He kept Mom from freezing to death."

Winston leaned against her leg. "I would have been

home sooner if I'd skipped the grocery store."

Sarah sat in a chair next to Aunt Ida and held the older woman's tiny hand. Because the poor dear looked so fragile, Sarah forced optimism into her voice. "Remember when she totaled her car last year? If she survived that, she can survive this adventure. Mom's hard-headed."

Aunt Ida gave Sarah a weak smile. "Ethel's always done everything on her own terms."

Once again, Sarah wondered how Aunt Ida and her mother could be friends. Such an odd couple. Aunt Ida was a kind, generous woman. Her mother was mean and tightfisted. Aunt Ida was a Reform Jew and a political moderate. Ethel had a near-fanatical devotion to one Reverend Bobby Moore, a Harry Potter-hating televangelist.

Sarah felt a rush of affection for the old woman. "Why don't you come with me to the hospital?"

Aunt Ida dabbed her red eyes with a handkerchief. "When can we go?"

As if on cue, Detective Engelman entered the kitchen, wearing latex gloves and carrying an empty bottle of Jack Daniels. "I'll be asking for a blood alcohol level when we get to the ER."

Now that's a no-brainer, Sarah thought. "Of course you will."

He held out a tiny brown bottle with a stopper top. "I found this on your mother's nightstand, Ms. Wright. Any idea what this is? It looks like water, but we'll have to have it analyzed it at the crime lab."

Sarah shook her head. "No clue."

"If we examine this for fingerprints, will we find yours on it?"

Again with the accusations. The man had a one track mind. She was just about ask if she needed to call a lawyer when Aunt Ida spoke. "You'll find mine."

Detective Engelman stared at the elderly woman as if she'd just materialized out of thin air. "And you are?"

"Ida Mae Katz."

"You know what this is?"

"An anti-aging compound, great for insomnia. Ethel told me she had trouble sleeping. I had an extra bottle, so I gave it to her."

She squinted at the label and frowned. "I wonder if she spilled it. It was full last Friday so it shouldn't be near to empty if she's only taking two to three drops at night. I don't mind spending money, but it shouldn't go to waste. That little bottle cost fifty bucks."

Detective Engelman's voice took on a razor sharp edge. "Mind telling me where you got this?"

"From Shirley Rubenstein," Ida chirped. "We play Mah-Jongg together."

"Anyone ever tell you what this 'anti-aging compound' contains?"

"G-something." She tapped a red, heart-shaped birthmark on her left cheekbone, as she always did when she was trying to recall something. "Oh. Now I remember." Her neck and face flushed. "I think Shirley called it 'Great Hormones at Bedtime.' Yes, that's it. Everyone at Mah-Jongg laughed when she said it."

Detective Engelman wasn't laughing. "GHB. I'll be asking for a blood level on that, too."

Sarah's stomach cramped and knotted. Gamma-hydroxybutyric acid? As if alcohol wasn't bad enough, her mother had ingested an illicit, potentially deadly drug, too. Could it get any worse?

"Is there a problem?" Aunt Ida asked her bright blue eyes darting between the cop and Sarah.

"You may have purchased an illegal substance," Detective Engelman said.

Aunt Ida looked toward Sarah, her sweet face creased into a puzzled expression. "I don't understand."

The detective looked at Aunt Ida with a mixture of sadness and pity. "GHB is a substance some rapists use to make sure their victims will cooperate. Combined with alcohol, it can cause coma and death."

Well, Sarah thought, maybe this crusty guy had a shred of empathy, after all.

"Rape? Coma? Death?" Aunt Ida dropped her face into her hands and sobbed. "What have I done?"

"You didn't know." Sarah squeezed her hand. "Someone took advantage of you."

"Now what?" Aunt Ida asked. "Do you arrest me? I have to call my lawyer, Sol Weinstein. He'll know what I have to do. Will I need bail?"

"Whoa. Slow down." The detective put his palm out like a traffic cop. "Take some deep breaths. We really don't know if this is GHB."

The detective seemed flustered. Maybe he wasn't used to hysterical little old ladies.

"I want to see my mother." Sarah stood. "Can we go now?"

He seemed to soften even more. "If you're up to it, I'll take you both to the ER."

"I've been ready since I heard the news." Aunt Ida straightened her shoulders, buttoned her coat, clutched Sarah's hand and pushed herself out of the chair.

"Winston, guard the house," Sarah ordered. The poor creature could barely lift his head off his bed in the corner of the kitchen to thump his tail.

Light flashing, the detective blasted past cars on the beltway, making up for the delay at the house, it seemed. A short time later, he let the two women out at the ER entrance.

As soon as they were at the desk, Sarah asked a dark-haired receptionist where she could find Ethel Wright. The woman glanced up from her keyboard and frowned. "You related?"

"I'm her daughter." Sarah pointed to Aunt Ida. "This is her sister." What the hell, after tonight's events why not make her an official member of the family?

"They're working her up now. As soon as the doctor has a moment, I'll ask him to speak with you." She pointed at a row of orange plastic chairs. "Take a seat and wait."

Tears, brought on by anger, fear—and guilt— welled in Sarah's eyes. "Why won't anyone tell me what's going on? I have a right to know."

"Young lady, I insist on seeing my sister. Now," Aunt Ida shouted.

Detective Engelman walked over to Sarah. "What's the problem?"

Sarah's head throbbed. "They won't let us see my mother." It wasn't right. She needed to be with her.

The detective leaned over the desk and whispered something to the clerk. Her head jerked back as if she'd been slapped. Face beet red, the woman jumped out of her seat and hustled around the counter. "With me. With me."

Inside the treatment cubicle, Sarah found electric warming blankets covering her mother. Her lips were blue and her skin had a mottled, pale, yellow-gray tone.

Plastic intravenous bags hung from hooks overhead; clear tubes extending from them wormed beneath the blankets. Multiple monitors beeped at irregular intervals. The numbers blinking on the heart monitor varied between forty-five and fifty. Standing at her bedside, Sarah realized that she'd never seen her mother this close to death.

"Hang in there, Mom, you can make it."

A torrent of memories laden with love, anger, guilt, and shame reminded Sarah of how much of her life she had sacrificed to take care of her mother—even giving up the love of her life. What would Dan say if he knew what had happened? Would he even care? She shook her head, opened her eyes and forced herself back to the here and now.

Aunt Ida sat down in a chair beside the hospital bed and held Ethel's hand beneath the covers. Tears slid down her wrinkled cheeks as she whispered, "*Shema Yisrael, Adenoi Elohenu, Adenoi Echod*," over and over.

Usually the Serenity Prayer helped, but tonight it failed to bring Sarah the peace she craved. She wished for the comfort of Aunt Ida's direct pipeline to God.

A tall, handsome African-American in a lab coat and chart in hand entered the cubicle. His name tag said Dr. Johnson. "I'd like to ask Ms. Wright a few questions in private."

"Mrs. Katz," Detective Engelman said, "how about you and I go find a cup of coffee?"

Sarah had been so engrossed in her own thoughts, she'd forgotten the cop was in the room. She hoped he'd gotten over the idea that she'd somehow caused her mother's accident.

Still weeping, Aunt Ida kissed Ethel's hand before standing with the support of the bedrail. Detective Engelman took her elbow and guided her out the door. Sarah watched them leave, worried that a blow like this would crush her frail aunt. Without taking her eyes off the pair leaving the room, she asked, "What do you need to know, Doctor?"

"Age, medical history, medications, allergies, all that good stuff."

Sarah turned to focus on his dark brown eyes. "I'll tell you whatever I can. She's seventy-nine years old, retired from a federal government job. Moved to Baltimore ten years ago. Last year, she got drunk, had a car accident, and broke both legs. I moved home to take care of her. She just started to walk with a cane last week. Even when she's not drinking, she's pretty unsteady on her feet. After her car accident, she stayed sober—until recently."

He scribbled some notes on the chart and frowned. "What happened?"

"I got a job and Aunt Ida was out of town. I guess she got lonely. She missed her boys."

"She has sons?"

"One biological son—my older brother. The 'boys' are her drinking companions. Jack Daniels, Johnny Walker, Mr. Bell, those kinds of boys."

"I see." He nodded and made some more notations. "How many drinks would you say she has in a day?"

"Half a bottle. The regular size, not a gallon jug."

"*More* than eight ounces of liquor? *Each* day?"

"Give or take." Sarah felt as if Dr. Johnson was calling her a bad daughter. She had to make him understand. "Look, I've tried everything to get her to

Sharon Buchbinder

stop: watered down the bottles, hid them, emptied them, called the liquor stores and told them to stop delivering. Even disabled, my mother managed to stash bottles everywhere. She's wily."

Dr. Johnson handed her a box of tissues.

She wiped her eyes and nose. "What else do you want to know?"

"Ever heard of Al-Anon?"

"I've been going to AA and Al-Anon meetings ever since I started nursing school. I've accepted the fact that she's an alcoholic. I know I can't fix her. It doesn't mean I stopped caring about or for her." She knew she sounded defensive. She didn't care. No one understood what life was like with her mother—except her brother and sister.

The doctor nodded. "Then you know that more likely than not, she's physically dependent. We'll be watching her for signs of alcohol withdrawal. She could become tachycardic, with fast erratic heartbeats and have seizures. We want to avoid that because of her head trauma. I've ordered an MRI."

"Do whatever you think is necessary."

"Okay. As soon as we get the scan, we'll know better. When the EMTs first arrived, her core body temperature was eighty-eight degrees. Below eighty-six degrees, atrial fibrillation and death occur. Lucky the dog was with her. I'm sure he kept her alive."

Sarah dabbed at her nose and sighed. "What do I do now?"

"You and your aunt should go home and rest."

"I can't leave and I don't think my aunt will go either. She's pretty hard-headed." She managed a weak smile. "Just like my mother."

"Well, they are sisters." Dr. Johnson stood and headed out the door. "You're free to stay with your mother until they take her to imaging."

Sarah reached down and grasped her mother's cold hand. Tears ran down her face as she groped for the right words. "Hey, Mom. Sarah here. We'll get through this, just like we always do."

Ethel didn't move. Sarah thought of Dan's prediction a year ago and shuddered. "Hang in there. Please?"

****

"Did you hear me?"

Sarah jerked out of sleep, looked around, and tried to get her bearings. She was in the ER waiting room and Aunt Ida snored in the next chair. Dr. Johnson stood in front of her, a concerned expression on his face. "Your mother's MRI was normal. No signs of intracranial bleeding. They're ready to transfer her to the ICU. Do you want to go up with her?"

"Yes."

He had a brief conference with the clerk and called to Sarah, "They're taking your mother up to the ICU now. Good luck."

Sarah turned to Aunt Ida and found the older woman awake. "Did you hear the good news?"

The elderly woman stared at her with glassy eyes, her skin the color of talcum powder.

Sarah's stomach fluttered. She looked awful. Was she having a stroke? "Are you okay? You look like you've seen a ghost."

"You could say that." Aunt Ida gave herself a little shake. "What's the good news?"

Relief flooded Sarah. Aunt Ida was a little wiped

out, but okay. "Mom's MRI was normal. They're heading to the ICU."

"Thank God."

"You sure you don't want to go home? It's three-thirty in the morning. You must be exhausted."

"I'm sticking with you, Sarahlei. Let's get your mother settled, then we can talk."

When they found the unit, Sarah asked a nurse who would be taking care of her mother.

A dark haired physician glanced up from a computer. "I'm Dr. Merrill, the ICU physician. She'll be under my watch until morning, then another physician comes on duty. Why don't we go into this conference room over here, so we can speak in private?"

"I'll sit outside in the waiting area, Sarahlei. Come get me when I can see your mother."

Dr. Merrill closed the door. "We're concerned about the alcohol and the gamma- hydroxybutyrate your mother has in her system. Were you aware her blood alcohol level was point-two-one percent when she was admitted? Lethal levels are between point-three and point-five percent. That, combined with toxic levels of GHB, hypothermia, and your mother's age, makes for a poor prognosis."

A cinder block of despair pressed on Sarah's chest. Her jaw ached with the effort of clenching her teeth so she wouldn't scream. Decades of unresolved emotions about her mother threatened to crush her. "What are you telling me?"

"The next twenty-four to forty-eight hours are critical. She could regain consciousness and recover." The doctor paused. "If not, I'm afraid you're looking at either a funeral, or a persistent vegetative state."

Despite her nurse's training, hearing the two outcomes spoken out loud bowed her head. A black well of despair threatened to suck her down. Sarah put her face in her hands and sobbed. This should have never happened. What had her mother been doing outside? Winston had an electric fence. All she had to do was open the door and let him out. Something else must have caused her to go outside in the sleet and fall on the ice. But what? As soon as she got home, she was going to take a look in the yard. The whole scenario just didn't ring true.

"Ms. Wright, are you okay?"

"I'm overwhelmed. If she's in a persistent vegetative state, she could live like that for years." She shuddered and figured at this rate, spending time with "the boys" might be an option for her.

A nurse in blue scrubs poked her head in the door. "Mrs. Wright's vitals seem to be stabilizing. Her pulse is sixty, respirations are sixteen, and her temperature is up to ninety-two degrees." She gave a thumbs-up sign. "Looks like she might be coming out of the woods. You can go see her now."

The fact that her mother was getting warmer and breathing normally gave Sarah a weak flicker of hope. It was within the golden twenty-four hours. Maybe, just maybe, her mother would be okay. Or maybe it was just magical thinking on her part. Wave a wand and abracadabra, Mom, you are well.

She stood and felt much older than her thirty years. "Dr. Merrill, thank you for your time and candor. I'm sorry I was so edgy before."

"Everyone here knows the stress families are under

when they walk through those doors." She paused. "Now we have to wait and see."

Sarah found Aunt Ida and shepherded her into Ethel's room. A fluorescent light flickered overhead. Her mother's bruised and bandaged head rested on clean pillows, and a pale pink color suffused her face. Intravenous fluids dripped, and a monitor beeped at regular intervals.

Aunt Ida reached under the bedding, held Ethel's hand, and whispered in Hebrew.

Sarah whispered when the older woman paused. "Would you teach me that prayer?"

Chapter Two

Ida sat at her best friend's bedside and prayed for forgiveness. This was all her fault. She should have never given her friend that drug. She should have doled it out to her a few drops at a time, not given her an entire bottle. But Ethel was an adult, wasn't she? Shouldn't she have listened to Ida? How could she have known Ethel would have used so much of that GHB?

What had she been thinking, going out in the icy rain? If only she hadn't passed that drug along to her, maybe Ethel would be at home watching television and eating dinner.

Ida looked at her friend, so near death, sighed and closed her eyes.

****

"Mitzi, Mitzi, oh, Mitzala, my Mitzala," Ida sobbed and rocked on her bed. The dead kitten's head lolled with her movements.

The monster pounded on the door. "Open up! Open up right now!"

Glued to the bed, Ida could barely catch her breath. The doorknob rattled and the key shook in the lock. More pounding and the door crashed open. He staggered over to her, grabbed her hair, and yanked her head backwards. His large red nose touched hers. He glared at her with blood-shot eyes and breathed alcohol fumes into her face.

"Don't you ever lock this door again. Let that cat be a lesson to you. The next time you lock the door, I'll kill your mother."

Her whole body shook with fear. "I'm sorry. I'll never do it again."

A week later, half asleep under her beautiful eiderdown quilt, Ida enjoyed the afterglow of her twelfth birthday. It had been a wonderful day. Buoyed by morphine, her mother had come downstairs for the party, a pale consumptive wraith in a long black dress. There had been much celebrating, many good wishes and presents. So many gifts to open. Ida drifted to sleep on warm waves of happiness.

Without warning, her bedroom door crashed open. In the dim light of a half moon, she made out the figure of her stepfather. He stumbled to the foot of her bed. "Hello, girlchik."

He was drunk again; she knew by the slur in his thick voice.

"I left the door unlocked just like you said," she whined. "Please don't hurt my mother again—or me."

"Hurt you? Oh, no, *girlchik*. I'm going to give you a very special birthday present."

****

An alarm went off. No, not again. He was dead. She jerked her head up and looked around the room. She was in the hospital with Sarah and Ethel. Nerves jangled, Ida's whole body trembled.

Sarah pressed the call buzzer and called to the nursing station. "I think my mother's IV is infiltrated. The alarm is going off."

A nurse rushed into the room and inspected Ethel's ballooning arm. "I'll get this restarted."

Still shaken from her dream, Ida turned to Sarah. "Remember the day your mother called and asked you to come back to Baltimore to help her?"

Sarah gave a short, humorless laugh. "How could I forget? She told me she called me because I didn't really have a job. As if getting my PhD in public health wasn't a full-time occupation."

"She was never good at asking for help," Ida said. "I really couldn't take care of her. She had so many problems."

And so many secrets. With Ethel so close to death, Sarah needed to know some of them. But which ones?

Sarah shook her head. "Her timing was terrible, too. I was in the middle of an argument with Dan when she called."

"What were you fighting about?" Ida asked.

"His dog hated me. Peed on my jacket."

"That's a naughty dog." Ida would have been angry, too.

"When Mom called, Dan told me not to go, that she must have been loaded. He was right, of course."

"She wanted you here." Sarah had no idea how much she was needed. "I did, too."

"Dan said she'd get drunk and kill herself one day." Tears rolled down Sarah's cheeks and her shoulders shook with sobs. "He was right."

"I'm so sorry." Ida clutched Sarah's hand. "I didn't mean to ruin your relationship with Dan. I wish I could make it up to you."

Ida had to do something. It wasn't fair. This poor girl had suffered and sacrificed enough. She deserved a life with a man she loved and who loved her.

Sarah shook her head and tears flew off her cheeks.

"I tried to get him to move to Baltimore. His mother lives here, for heaven's sake! You'd think he'd want to be close by. But every time we talked, we argued." The older woman reached over and wiped Sarah's cheek with a tissue. "Have you thought about calling him?"

"Every. Single. Day. I don't have the nerve to call him. Especially now. He'd probably just hang up on me. I guess it just wasn't meant to be. That's why I returned the ring." Sarah looked around. "Where is that nurse? She needs to restart this IV."

"What your mother did, sending you away when you were little, leaving you there for years," Ida said. "I'm sure it seems unreasonable." How could she ever explain? Make her understand Ethel better so Sarah could get on with her own life?

"She said she needed help then, too. Couldn't manage me plus my brother and sister. At least that's the official story."

"It's the truth."

"I'm a pediatric nurse, Aunt Ida. I understand family crises and foster care. Sometimes it's all a family can do just to hang in there." She paused. "What I have trouble forgetting is the abuse."

Ida whispered, "She was young. Had no guidance, no one to help her."

"I forgave her." Sarah shook her head. "God help me, I still love her."

"She has good moments," Ida said, trying to come up with Ethel's attributes so Sarah could see her through her eyes. "She's nobody's doormat. She has a good sense of humor."

"Yeah, Matt saved us from a lot of whippings by getting her to laugh," Sarah said and smiled. "It's a wonder he's not a stand-up comic instead of working in child protective services."

"Your brother rescues children. And your sister's a nurse, too. Ethel must have done something right."

Sarah turned away from staring at her mother and locked gazes with her. Funny, how had she never noticed before that Sarah had her mother's eyes?

"We went into these professions, in part to fix what our mother did to us." Sarah pursed her lips. "Aunt Ida, how can you be so loyal to someone who's so difficult?"

"It's a long story." A very old, long story. Did she have the courage to tell it to her best friend's daughter?

"All we're doing is sitting around and waiting. We've got time." Sarah stood up. "Speaking of which, it's been twenty minutes since the nurse left the room. Maybe she forgot. I'm going to go find her."

Ida fell back in her chair, exhausted. She looked at Ethel, immobile, pale and silent. Was it finally the right time to tell their secrets?

****

Sarah awoke when a new nurse came into the room to check her mother's vitals. The shift had changed and a different ICU physician appeared at the door of the semi-private room. "Your mother's stable. Why don't you go home? You can't help her if you get sick."

On the way out a young woman approached Sarah. "Ms. Wright?"

"Yes?"

"I'm a Patient Financial Services representative. I'm sorry to bother you at this difficult time, but we need your mother's insurance information. Do you know her Social Security number? We can get her

Medicare information with that."

Social Security? Insurance? Sarah's head buzzed with the effort to recall the events at the house. In the rush to get Ethel to the ER, Sarah hadn't thought to grab her mother's purse. "I have no idea. I'll have to go home and find her cards. Is there a way I can reach you?" The paperwork had to be in her purse or on Ethel's desk in the "forbidden zone."

She handed Sarah a business card.

Aunt Ida was asleep in the waiting area just outside the ICU. Sarah looked at the older woman with affection. Sometime during the night, Aunt Ida must have taken a bathroom break and decided to get a nap away from the beeping monitors and shrieking alarms. Strands of hair fell out of her normally tight bun, giving her a softer look. Her glasses sat halfway down her nose, threatening to slide to the floor.

Poor Aunt Ida. Time to get her home.

"Aunt Ida?" No response. Sarah spoke a little louder. "Aunt Ida." She touched her wrist.

Ida flailed her arms, hands balled into fists. "No, no, please don't touch me."

Sarah jumped back. "I'm sorry. I couldn't wake you up."

"*Oy*, no, I'm the one who should apologize. I was having a bad dream." She focused on Sarah's face. "Are you okay? Is your mother better?"

"Her vital signs are close to normal. Funny. She just looks like she's passed out from drinking. As if she'll wake any moment and demand a cup of tea."

Ida nodded. "Knowing Ethel, she'd make everyone jump to get it, too."

A taxi took them home to their now less chaotic

cul-de-sac. With the temperature ten degrees warmer than the day before, puddles replaced the ice skating rink of the previous evening. Sarah's car, groceries still sitting in it, sat parked on the side of the street where the police had stopped her.

"If you don't like the weather in Baltimore," Aunt Ida said, "wait ten minutes."

Sarah helped the older woman out of the cab and up to her kitchen door. Her aunt pulled out her key but, before she could get it into the lock, the door was yanked open from the inside. Betty, Aunt Ida's housekeeper, stood in the entryway.

Sarah raised her voice and enunciated each word with precision. "We did not know you were here. You startled us."

Betty's eyes blinked owl-like through bottle-bottom eyeglasses. She smiled and asked, "Ooo otay, Ms. Idah?"

Aunt Ida had always had a housekeeper. She also had lawn, pond, and pool services. In contrast, Ethel hung her clothes outside on the line to save money on her electric bill, and used her daughter as lawn service, housekeeper, and laundress. Once again, Sarah wondered how they could be best friends.

Aunt Ida had hired Betty through WorkForce, a vocational training organization for citizens with disabilities. The housekeeper wore hearing aids in both ears and was also intellectually disabled. When they first met Betty, Ethel was surprised she read lips instead of using sign language. Although Sarah had spent her preschool years with her deaf grandmother, she'd forgotten more sign language than she remembered.

Her mother, however, was fluent. When she

attempted to sign to Betty, she received an intense stare at her lips instead of a response in hand signs. "My dog knows more sign language than she does," Ethel had said in a stage whisper.

Sarah leaned over and gave Aunt Ida a hug. "Thanks for being with me. Get some rest."

"I hope I can. I always have trouble sleeping. Now that I can't use that G-stuff anymore, I'm afraid it will just get worse." She shuddered. "*Gottenyu!* I have the worst nightmares. Maybe I'll have a bit of schnapps before I lie down. You get some sleep, too, Sarahlei."

Sarah moved her car to the driveway and hauled the groceries into the house. Winston ran to greet her and nearly knocked her over in his exuberance. Already beginning to smell ripe, the mayonnaise-based perishables hit the trash can. The last thing she needed right now was food poisoning. Yuck.

Afraid to listen to her own mental chatter and fearful thoughts, she turned the radio on. One of the few things she and her mother agreed on was that they preferred the oldies but goldies to the current music on most of the stations. She hummed along one of her favorite crooners. Just as she began to sing the chorus, Winston barked to be let in.

Instead of the dog, the "Heckler," her mother's nickname for the president of the neighborhood association, Jean Hecklenberg, stood on the back porch. The president, along with her posse of elderly do-gooders, were what Ethel termed Yard Nazis. If there was anything in a yard they didn't like—gnomes, donkeys, jockeys, long grass, shaggy bushes, clotheslines—they'd harass the homeowners until they gave in from sheer exhaustion. They wore everyone down, except Ethel, who gave as good as she got.

Today the Heckler wore a bright blue hat that sported a pom-pom. As she shook her fist and yelled, the pom-pom bobbed with the vigor of a blue ping-pong ball. "I've been trying to call your house, but your phone's out of order. This is an official warning. One more time with that dog howling and the neighborhood association is taking you and your mother to court." The woman craned her neck in an attempt to peer into the kitchen.

Sarah took a deep breath. Despite the urge to scream, she kept her voice low. "Mrs. Hecklenberg, apparently you're unaware our dog was making that noise because my mother fell on the ice and was badly injured. My mother's unconscious, but alive. If it weren't for Winston, and your call to the police, she'd be dead. So thank you and have a nice day."

Sarah began to close the door but stopped at the Heckler's next words. "You mean she passed out because she was drunk, don't you? She's drunk all the time. You know it. I know it. The entire neighborhood knows it. She got what she deserved."

"Gee, Mrs. Hecklenberg thanks so much for your sympathy. I'll be sure to pass your wishes for a speedy recovery along to my mother. Oh, and there's one more thing."

She looked up at Sarah, her thin lips pursed, her ridiculous question mark penciled eyebrows raised.

"Go to hell." Sarah slammed the door and stared at her through the window.

The Heckler stomped down the steps and across the walkway to the driveway. Just inches before the spot where the electric shock of the invisible fence would stop him, Winston ran up and rammed his nose into her butt. The woman jumped, shrieked and practically flew down the driveway and out into the cul-de-sac.

Sarah burst into tears. "Just what I need. Now I'll be on her hit list for doggy assault and battery." She called Winston. "Are you trying to get me arrested?"

Winston tilted his head and stared at her as if he was trying to read her lips. Giving up, he flopped down on the floor and closed his eyes. Sarah abandoned her attempt to discipline him and went to bed. She was beyond exhausted.

At least things couldn't get any worse, could they?

****

Nightmares about her mother's accident plagued her sleep. She kept seeing her mother arguing with someone, then falling and hitting her head. Blood pooled next to her face as Winston howled.

Sarah sat up in her sweat-soaked bed, woken up by a thunderstorm. Winston threw himself onto the bed, whining and shaking. "Poor baby." She hugged and soothed him. "This weather terrifies you." He responded by shoving his huge head under her pillow.

The dog wasn't the only one having a hard time. Flashes of arguments and violence came back to her when she closed her eyes. She opened them and shook her head to drive away the visions. The visit from the Heckler must have prompted the nightmare. Maybe a long, hot shower would wash away the dream residue.

After the storm passed, she opened the back door to let Winston out. Aunt Ida was stood on the porch. "What's wrong?"

Deep wrinkles etched lines into the older woman's

brow. Her eyes were red, as if she'd been crying. "I'm worried about you, Sarahlei. Are you okay?"

"I'm fine." She pulled Aunt Ida into the kitchen and led her to a chair. Sarah had never seen Aunt Ida look so distraught. Her mother's accident was taking its toll on everyone. "You, on the other hand, look awful."

"Ach! I couldn't sleep. I tossed and turned. Must have been the storm. Are you going back to the hospital tonight?"

"First I have to find Mom's insurance cards. Do you want to come?"

"I'm trying to decide if I should head down to Florida this season. I have workmen lined up to fix the hurricane damage to the roof and the pool cage." She paused and pushed some strands of hair away from her face. "If I go, I need to get organized to leave early Monday morning. I'm not supposed to drive at night."

"I know Mom is your best friend, but unless her condition improves soon, she's probably going to be in a coma for a while." Sarah paused, and decided not to add, in a persistent vegetative state. She didn't want Aunt Ida to feel any worse than she already did. "You sure you're up for the drive? It's a long trip."

Aunt Ida frowned. "I'm getting older, but I haven't forgotten how to drive. I feel bad leaving you alone. What about Mitzi? She'll just be another burden."

"We'll be insulted if she didn't come here for the season. Who else will Neferkitty harass for fun?" Aunt Ida's six-toed cat, Mitzi, was a fur-covered bowling ball with legs. Sarah's cat, Neferkitty, spent hours leaping on her whenever the fat feline came to stay.

"I can't take her with me and she hates Betty. Those hearing aids turn her into a wildcat." Aunt Ida nodded. "You're right. I'll go to Florida. I'll take a break from packing in a little while and come with you to the hospital."

As the elderly woman clutched the banister to pick her way down the stairs, Sarah worried if she was really up to the trip. Part of Sarah wanted to beg her to stay; the other part didn't want to impose on her any more. The dear old lady had always been there for Ethel, but this time, she could do nothing for her best friend.

****

Ida sat in her cozy den, photos of her dead husband surrounding her. "What should I do, Jack? Should I tell Sarah or wait to see if Ethel comes out of her coma?"

Jack smiled back at her in a dizzying array of black-and-white and color snapshots, some candid, some posed. He wasn't very responsive tonight. Usually he had a lot of good advice for her. But tonight, no words of Jack's wisdom sprang to her mind. She needed him. Had never stopped needing him, even after all these years.

"Jack, you gotta help me here. Sarah needs to understand, to know, everything. I'm afraid for her. And, I'm afraid for Ethel." She yawned hard enough to feel her jaw crack. "So tired. If only I could catch a few winks of sleep"

****

"Forget about the baby," a man shouted. "We have to control the mother's bleeding."

"The baby is blue, Doctor. We'll lose her if we don't do something."

"Put her in the bassinette. Help me with the mother."

"Yes, Doctor." Footsteps scurried across the room

32

and back.

"Massage her uterus while I call for anesthesia."

Strong hands kneaded Ida's belly. "Doctor, why do we need anesthesia?"

"If we don't do a hysterectomy, right now, the mother will die."

A man appeared at her right side, his face half-covered with a white mask. Brown eyes filled with concerned peered down at her. "How are you doing?"

"You tell me," Ida whispered.

"We can't save the baby. We have to save you."

"Let me hold her. Please."

"You'll see, there's no use." He returned, removed a leather wrist restraint, and thrust a blanketed bundle into her arm.

She stared down at the still face. Her eyes were closed. She had the tiniest nose, just barely there. Her lips were bow shaped. Ida pulled the blanket back and gasped. The infant had a heart-shaped birthmark on her left cheekbone. The baby was snatched out of her hands.

She reached for the child. "Don't take Mitzi."

Ida struggled to push the black mask away from her face, but the ether took her away.

****

Ida jerked herself out of sleep and looked around the room. She was in her own home, thank God. She had to tell Sarah the truth—but how much did the girl really need to know?

Chapter Three

Sarah sat at the kitchen table in the late afternoon sunshine with a steaming cup of coffee and a large piece of cherry pie. She stared at her mother's purse for five minutes while she sipped her coffee. At last, she flipped it over and dumped the contents out before her. Candy wrappers, liquor store coupons, and an abundance of lint scattered across the scratched and dented Formica. Ethel's wallet held her Social Security and Medicare cards. So far, so good. Now where was her supplemental insurance card? Sarah found it and looked at the dates. Expired. There had to be another one. She rummaged in the bag. No luck. Maybe it was on Ethel's desk.

Neferkitty protested being removed from Sarah's shoulder where she perched like a parrot. "Sorry, baby. Let's go see what's in her inner sanctum."

Ethel was so paranoid about money that she never allowed anyone in her office, much less near her financial papers. Sarah rolled up the antique desk cover and gasped as unopened envelopes fell out at her in an avalanche. It looked as if Ethel hadn't opened her mail in months. Sarah plopped into a chair and dragged a trashcan over in anticipation of a mountain of junk mail. Instead, nearly every letter was a demand for payment of an overdue bill. Now Sarah understood why Ethel had always made it to the mailbox first.

"For God's sake, Mom, why didn't you tell me? I would have helped out."

Sarah closed her eyes and took several deep breaths. Steady. No need to lose it. Hang in there. She continued to open envelopes. At last she found one with a return address from the health insurance plan. Her mother's supplemental insurance had lapsed. She was not eligible for reinstatement.

"Just freaking great. What's next in this mess?"

Sarah reached for another envelope with trembling hands, fearful of what she'd find. The letter inside was dated four months earlier.

Dear Mrs. Wright:

Thank you for your generous donation of five-hundred dollars to the Florence Crittenton Services of Greater Washington. Your gift will be used to provide services to adolescent girls, low-income pregnant women, and teen mothers in the Washington, D.C. metropolitan area. Our mission is to provide women with the knowledge, skills, and support required for their physical, emotional, economic, and social well-being. Your gift will assist us in these endeavors. Thank you.

Sincerely,
Eudora White
Director of Giving

There had to be some mistake. Her mother never donated money to anyone, regardless of the cause. She believed charity began at home. Ethel had worked for a living and so had her deaf, non-speaking parents. She always said, "If they could do it, anyone could."

Sarah had heard the lecture a million times. If

someone on the street attempted to ask for donations with an "I am deaf, please help" card, Ethel yelled and signed at them, calling them liars, cheats, and beggars. They ran away from her.

But here, in front of Sarah, was written proof her mother had made a donation to a charity. She hadn't paid her bills, but she had given money for "low income pregnant women, and teen mothers"? Sarah set the letter aside and made a mental note to ask Aunt Ida about it.

Even if her mother had donated five hundred dollars to a charity, that shouldn't have bankrupted her. Ethel owned her house free and clear. She retired from the federal government after twenty-five years with an excellent pension automatically deposited into her bank account. Ethel had always paid her bills the morning after they arrived in the mail, then celebrated in the afternoon by getting drunk. Yet it appeared she hadn't paid bills in at least three months. This was beyond strange.

Sarah grabbed an unlabelled manila folder to organize the bills, opened it, and found a stack of letters. The oldest one was dated five years before, the most recent one from the month before. Each letter said:

Dear Sister Ethel:

Thank you for your generous donation of one thousand dollars to the Reverend Moore Theological Institute. Your gift will be used in the war against Harry Potter and his Cult of Satan Worshippers. We will use it to work with parents to teach them how to fight Harry Potter and the Forces of Evil.

By allowing your monthly donation to be automatically deducted from your checking account, you have demonstrated the highest level of devotion. You are now a member of my Inner Circle of True Believers. Be sure to tune in daily for special messages during my radio and television broadcasts. Through your donations to our ministry, you will be saved from the Forces of Evil when the End Days are upon us.

Humbly,
The Very Reverend Bobby Moore

Autographed photos of the Very Reverend Bobby Moore adorned the walls of the family room and Ethel's office in various poses of preaching hellfire and brimstone, thoughtful concern, and smarmy smiles.

Ethel had "met" the televangelist while hospitalized from her DUI and continued to watch him after she returned home, attributing her "miraculous" recovery to his prayers for the sick.

One afternoon, a drunken Ethel shared with Sarah that she felt the Reverend's power when she laid her hands on the television. When Sarah burst out laughing, Ethel smacked her with her cane. They had never discussed the Reverend and his miracle healings again.

Well, at least she had discovered why her mother hadn't paid her bills—and why the phone had been disconnected. Over the past five years, Reverend Bobby Moore had swindled her mother out of sixty thousand dollars. Sarah wondered if each of those eight-by-ten color photos of the televangelist represented a thousand bucks. The five hundred dollar donation to the Florence Crittenton Services paled by comparison—and there were no photos of pregnant teens to be seen in the house.

She decided to table that item for discussion with Aunt Ida. More importantly, how could she get this con man to stop taking money out of her mother's checking account? Anger and frustration bubbled up, defeating the usual breathing techniques.

She clutched the letters, balled them up, and hurled them against the wall. "The thief! How could he do this to old people and get away with it?"

She leaned on the desk, tears dripping onto the mountain of bills. Sarah whirled, throwing papers, pens, and envelopes around the room, creating a downpour of creditors' demands. Despite Aunt Ida's support, she felt so alone. If only Dan were here, he'd know what to do.

"Dammit, Mom, why didn't you tell me?"

An hour later, eyes aching from crying, she grabbed a flashlight and headed across the yard to Aunt Ida's house. The only illumination in the yards came from the corner streetlight and floodlights on the corners of Aunt Ida's house. Ethel had never bothered to add more lighting, claiming it wasn't necessary. Sarah's mother had made no improvements to her property, unless you counted the clothesline. Aunt Ida and her husband, Jack, on the other hand, had added a garage with an elaborate workshop, a large blue swimming pool, a separate hot tub for up to six people and an enormous fish pond.

After Sarah knocked at the back door, Ida appeared in the doorway, eyes wide. "Ready so soon?"

"No," Sarah said, "I need to use your phone to call my brother and sister to let them know what's going on."

Sitting in Aunt Ida's den with the door closed, she was surrounded by photographs of Aunt Ida's deceased husband, Jack.

"When's the funeral?" her brother, Matt, asked.

"I didn't say she was dead. I said she fell on the ice and is in a coma. She's broke. Gave all her money to a televangelist, hasn't paid bills in over three months, and her Medicare supplemental insurance was terminated. I'm drowning in bills. Do you have any words of wisdom?"

"Yeah. Get a lawyer, and call me when she's dead."

She called her sister, Debra. After hearing her out, she spoke in her calm, non-judgmental tone common to psychiatric nurses. "You know I haven't talked to her in over fifteen years. Maybe now you can hear what I'm saying: You're entitled to your own life."

Sarah couldn't respond. Her sister was right. Her mother had never wanted her around until no one else came when she called.

"Are you there?"

"Sorry. I drifted off. What did you say?"

"Put yourself first, for a change. I bet you haven't eaten a decent meal, taken a shower, or washed your hair since this all happened."

"Not true. I got a very long shower, and I shampooed my hair today."

"You need to get a lawyer."

"That's what Matt said."

"He's right. Find out how you can protect yourself and your assets. Did Mom have any kind of advance directives or a living will? Did she give you power of attorney at any time?"

"Are you kidding?" Sarah guffawed. "She thought everyone would rob her, including me."

"As an adult child, you're her de facto Surrogate Decision Maker. A lawyer should be able to tell you if there's some way to stop those donations. I can't believe she gave away all that money. Remember what she did to people who approached her with those 'I am deaf, please help me' cards?"

"Vividly." Sarah remembered the other letter. "Have you ever heard of the Florence Crittenton Services of Greater Washington?"

"No. What's that have to do with Mom?"

"She gave them money, too, but only five hundred dollars. It was a one-time donation." She recounted the details of the letter to Debra. "Do you recall her mentioning anything about that place?"

"No, none at all. What would she have to do with unwed mothers? She was married and divorced. She must have really been losing it."

Sarah agreed.

"I have to get ready for work," Debra said. "Take care of yourself. I love you."

"Love you, too." Sarah hung up the phone and looked at the clock. It was seven in the evening, Eastern Standard Time, six in Chicago, Dan Rosen Time, as she liked to think of it. She picked up the phone, pressed three-one-two, thought better of it, and hung up. She needed words of reassurance, support. She didn't need to hear him say, "I told you so."

Instead of calling Dan, she called the hospital to check in on her mother. Since her condition remained unchanged, the ICU charge nurse suggested that Sarah visit the next day, rather than this late in the evening.

Brahms' *Requiem* played while she was transferred to Patient Financial Services. How appropriate, Sarah thought. A financial services representative interrupted the funereal music.

After providing her mother's Medicare information, Sarah gave her a brief overview of her mother's financial mess. "Since she allowed her supplemental insurance to lapse, I'm concerned I'm going to be responsible for the balance of her bill."

"If Medi-gap insurance isn't available, then the family is responsible for the remaining twenty percent. We take credit cards, if that's any help."

Sarah's laugh sounded like a sob when it came out. "Not really. Do you have some kind of payment plan?"

"You'll have to call Patient Accounting tomorrow. When you return, be sure to bring her Medicare card."

Sarah hung up, reeling from the conversation. Conscious, Ethel had run up bills she'd be scrambling to pay just to keep the lights on. Unconscious and in a coma, she managed to create even more bills.

Sarah pulled up a stool in the kitchen while Aunt Ida made a pot of tea. "I'm not going to the hospital tonight. I spoke with Patient Financial Services. Talk about depressing."

She told her about the mountain of unpaid bills, the monthly thousand dollar donations to Reverend Bobby Moore, and the conversation with the Patient Financial Services representative.

Aunt Ida pursed her lips and put her hand over Sarah's. "Sarahlei, I have some money put away and no family. I'd like to help."

"That's very generous, but I have no idea what this will cost. Mom could be in a coma for a very long time.

I can't let you take this on."

In a firm, strong voice Aunt Ida said, "I have lived a long, and at times, very difficult life. I was extremely fortunate to meet and marry Jack."

Sarah knew the story. Jack had been a self-made man. When he and Ida met, he had only twenty-five dollars in his pocket. Full of dreams and willing to work, he grew a home building company, learned about real estate, and amassed a large fortune. At one time, he owned most of the land in Pikesville.

"My Jack worked himself to death and died of a heart attack before he could enjoy his wealth. The only leisure time he took was when I talked him into going to Florida on vacations. Even then, he turned the visits into real estate deals. We bought land and built a house in Punta Gorda when it was a sleepy little town. Now, it's one of the top one-hundred places to retire in the United States. He had the Midas touch with money."

"My mother has the reverse. She touches money, it turns to shit. She's so deep in debt I have no idea of how I'm going to dig out and take care of it all. I appreciate your offer, Aunt Ida, but it isn't right for me to take your money. I do need a couple of things from you, though, before you go."

"Anything." She removed her hand from Sarah's and poured two mugs of tea.

"I need a good lawyer to help me sort things out."

"Sol Weinstein is my lawyer. His specialty is Family Law and Estate Planning. He'd be perfect for this. I'll give you his number. What else?" She held a bottle of amaretto and poured a generous amount into Sarah's mug.

"Have you ever heard of the Florence Crittenton

Services of Greater Washington?"

The bottle slid out of Aunt Ida's hand, struck the granite counter, and exploded. Shards of glass and amber liquid shot in every direction. Sarah grabbed a roll of paper towels, and noticed blood on her wrist.

"*Oy*, what a mess!" As Ida held her hands up, a crimson thread trickled down one arm.

"You're hurt. Let me take a look at that."

"I'm fine." She waved Sarah away, pulled a handkerchief out of her pocket and pressed it to the cut.

Sarah picked up shattered glass until she could no longer see glittering shards, then mopped up the sticky fluid. She put a paper towel on the cut on her own wrist until it subsided, then tossed it in the trashcan along with the rest of the mess. They tried for another cup of tea and switched to ouzo, with Sarah pouring this time.

"So, have you heard of the Florence Crittenton Services of Greater Washington?"

Aunt Ida's face reddened. "Why do you ask?"

"Mom donated five hundred dollars to them. I think they have services for unwed mothers. She was married and divorced, not an unwed mother. I can't figure out why she'd give money to them."

"I had no idea she was giving money to that con artist, Reverend Bobby Moore. Why should I know about this charity?"

"You guys were close. I thought she might have mentioned it to you. I wasn't trying to upset you, Aunt Ida. I have a pile of bills, a sick mother, and more bills on the way. I'd just like to know why she did it."

"Yes, of course. I'm sorry. We're both upset." There was a long pause in the conversation. At last, Aunt Ida shrugged, nodded her head, and broke the silence. "Things aren't always what they seem, Sarahlei. Sometimes we can't bear to share our secrets, even with those we love.

"She's not good at showing it, but your mother loves you—and your sister and brother. She stayed with your father because she loved him and kept thinking the next day would be better. When he began beating your brother, she packed you up and put you on that plane to Connecticut. She was terrified your father would kill you. It took tremendous courage for her to leave him."

There was a long silence, punctuated by sniffles and nose-blowing. Sarah stomach felt as if it was in free fall. Her mother didn't send her away out of hate. She'd done it out of love, to save her youngest child's life, doing the best thing she could at the time. Tongue-tied for once in her life, at last her mouth worked and she was able to speak. "Thank you for this gift, Aunt Ida."

"That reminds me. I have something for you for your birthday. I know it's early, but I want you to have it now."

"With everything that's going on, how could you remember?"

"How could I not? You're the daughter I never had. I can't wait to see the look on your face when you open it." She went into the dining room and returned with a gaily-wrapped package. "I hope you like it."

Tearing the paper, Sarah smiled when she saw the photograph on the box of a cell phone, perfect for pocket or purse. "Aunt Ida, this is wonderful. I really appreciate it, but I can't afford the monthly fees."

"Ha! That's the best part." She whipped out an identical phone from her pocket. "I bought one for me, too, and it's on the same account, so you can't turn it down. I got us the nationwide plan and unlimited evenings and weekends. I can call you every night on the road and from Florida."

"You're too much." Sarah laughed and hugged her. "Pretty tech savvy for a little old lady, aren't you?"

"Not quite. I need you to figure out how to set up the voice mail and program important phone numbers for me. The instructions are in such small print, I can't read them."

Over the next hour, Sarah waded through the instructions and programmed numbers into the phone. "What access code do you want, Aunt Ida? It has to be four numbers that are easy for you to remember, but other people won't guess."

"That's easy. Use 1-1-2-7. It's a very special date to me. I won't ever forget it." As her eyes brimmed with tears, she blew her nose. "Oh, what a silly old lady I've become."

"You picked my birthday." Sarah stood up and hugged her, tears brimming in her eyes as well. "You're not silly. You're sweet, kind, and generous. Thank you for telling me that my mother loves me and sent me away to save my life. That's the best gift I've ever received."

Aunt Ida dabbed at her eyes and gave the younger woman a sly smile. "So, Saralei. Now that you have a new phone, don't you think it's time you called Dan?"

Chapter Four

Elizabeth Woods lay awake in her bed in her nursing home room and stared, unseeing, into the dark. She wondered when Bernice was bringing Mitzi for a visit. It had been at least a week, maybe longer since they had come in. She missed her daughter and her sister-in-law. No matter that Elizabeth was a nearly blind old crone now, waiting for death, no one could ever take away the memory of Mitzi's birth. As the noises of the nursing home slowed down into the whispers of the midnight shift, she heard her roommate stir.

"Clarice, are you awake?"

A grunt, her usual response, came back. A stroke victim, Clarice could see and hear, but not talk. A diabetic, Elizabeth could hear and speak, but not see. Elizabeth whispered all her memories to Clarice, glad to be able to speak them aloud to someone who always listened, never judged, and kept secrets.

"Did I ever tell you about my daughter's birth? It was a close call. We almost lost her," Elizabeth said. "It was different then. We didn't really know how to save babies in distress. The doctor ordered me to put her back in the bassinette, to focus on saving the mother. I did what I was told."

Clarice grunted twice. Elizabeth took that as a sign to go on. "The mother, just a child really, could hardly speak. She said 'Don't take Mitzi away from me.' and then they put her under and took out her uterus—just like they did to me."

A trickle of hot tears ran down the side of her face. As she reached for a tissue to wipe her nose, another grunt that sounded like a question came from the other bed. Clarice was eager to hear more. Elizabeth could tell.

"Oh, it was a mess in that room. Shouting. Cursing. Blood everywhere. But we saved the mother. Pale as the sheets." She paused. "The doctor told me I did a good job. I was so proud, I cried. He ran out the door with the mother and the anesthesiologist, leaving Mitzi for dead, and me to clean up."

She paused recalling the next moments with exquisite clarity. Her voice quavered with emotion. "I was all alone. The whole reason we were there lay in the bassinette. I said, 'Poor little Mitzi. You never had a chance.' I reached for the baby to take her to the morgue. She moved. I was so startled, I jumped back."

More grunting, a faster pace. Clarice was hanging on her every word. Elizabeth continued, eager to share, to get her secret off her chest, at last. "I put her in the crook of my arm and she rooted at my breast. Mitzi was alive and hungry. Tiny girl. So helpless. Needy. That little girl, only twelve years old, just a child. Near death. But the baby, the beautiful, sweet baby girl was alive."

Elizabeth's voice cracked. She grabbed more tissues to wipe her eyes. Clarice was awful quiet. Did she disapprove? She thought they were friends.

"You must understand. Let me explain. I was an adult, twenty-one years old, a trained nurse. Married to a physician with more than enough money to care for an infant in an empty house. My husband was off to war and I was so lonely." Bitter memories surfaced, bringing the taste of bile to her mouth. "He was the reason I couldn't have children. I had a miscarriage. I had a bicornate vagina, cervix, and uterus—two of everything a woman needed to make a baby. You'd think I'd get twins. But, no. The specialist told us that if I became pregnant again, I could hemorrhage to death. John forced me to have surgery."

Clarice grunted loudly.

"Shocking, isn't it? Then a miracle. An answer to my prayers." She smiled in the darkness, joy swelling her chest. "As far as the hospital was concerned, the baby was dead. So I wrapped her up, took the blank birth certificate and walked out of the delivery room, toward the morgue. And I kept walking, right out the back door."

Her roommate was making strange sounds. "Clarice? Are you okay?"

When no response came, Elizabeth pressed the call bell and yelled for a nurse.

****

Barking invaded Sarah's sleep. She opened one eye. "Okay, okay, I'm getting up. Give me a minute."

She staggered to the kitchen, let Winston out, and made a pot of coffee. The taupe colored dog ran around the yard while she watched him through the kitchen window. "You're not a greyhound, Winston."

He raced to the edge of his electric fence and ran back and forth, hurling himself at the invisible wall. Was he was barking at deer? In the past, as many as ten females and a buck with a huge rack grazed in the front

48

yard. Hostas, daylilies, tulips, and thornless bushes were full course banquets for the deer, enraging many of her neighbors. Sarah went outside to where Winston was bounding back and forth and peered at the front yard in the pre-dawn light. Not a single deer, but a white van idled in the cul-de-sac.

Why would a truck be parked in front of Aunt Ida's house at this hour? She could see no sign on the side, nor could she read the license plate from where she stood. The driver's window was cracked open and a thin line of smoke curled out through the gap.

Sarah walked across the front lawn to see what the driver wanted. As she got within five feet of the vehicle, the driver put the car into gear and took off.

Odd. Shrugging, she whistled for Winston and headed toward the back yard, scanning for anything out of the ordinary. Something about her mother's fall wasn't making any sense. A branch stuck out of the bushes but the color was different from the test of the branches.

"Wait. That's not a branch. It's Mom's cane with the dog head handle."

Brushing off mud, she picked the walking stick up and examined it. The rope Winston had been tied with was still on the tree. Where had that come from? One of the three lines of rope for the clothesline flapped in the breeze. It had been cut.

Had the police done it? She'd ask Mike the next time she saw him. Right now, she needed to check on her mother's condition and speak with her sister.

The ICU nurses informed her that her mother was the same, looking rested and warm. The staff at her sister's office said she was with a patient and unavailable to talk.

Sarah opened the refrigerator, hoping to find something to eat, instead she found wilted lettuce, limp carrots, and an ancient jar of dill pickles. They joined the groceries she'd had to toss out from the night before.

Sarah's phone chirped. "Did I wake you?" Aunt Ida asked.

"No, I've been up since five-thirty."

Aunt Ida sighed. "Me, too. I tossed and turned all night. Are you hungry?"

"I thought I'd lose my appetite with everything that's gone on, but I'm starving. Unfortunately, my cupboards are bare."

"How about we go to the deli for breakfast?"

"I'll pick you up in ten minutes."

The traffic was only slightly backed up going into the parking lot, but she had to stop. An enormous Cadillac had parked at the end of the row, and someone was being dropped off at the back door. Sarah watched as a young black woman climbed out of an ancient Toyota and assisted an elderly woman with plum colored hair. The older woman looked familiar to Sarah, but she couldn't place her. Then it was Sarah's turn to block traffic as her elderly passenger disembarked.

She found Aunt Ida sitting on a cracked vinyl banquette in a booth across from the woman with the purple hair. The smell of toast filled the restaurant. Sarah's stomach growled. As she sat down and grabbed the menu, the woman called across the aisle. "Is that you, Ida Mae Katz?"

The gravelly voice and hacking smoker's cough

clinched it. Sarah suppressed a groan. The woman with the plum colored hair was Dan's mother. Sarah had meant to call Gertrude when she moved to Baltimore, but with everything going on in her life, she'd forgotten. Well, maybe repressed was a better word.

Aunt Ida waggled her eyebrows at Sarah and turned in her chair to face the other woman. "Yes, it's me. How are you, Gertrude? How's the Whispering Willows Retirement Community? Have you won any Mah-Jongg games lately?"

"The only thing they whisper about at The Willows is the food. It stinks. No flavor. Bland and blah. That's why I'm here. And, no, I haven't won any Mah-Jongg games lately. Have you?" She fixed a piercing gaze on Sarah. "Nu, do I know you?"

Sarah felt like a deer surrounded by hunters at a salt lick. "Hello, Mrs. Rosen. We met once a while ago when I was dating your son, Dan."

She would kill her aunt for this one. "Gee, Aunt Ida, why didn't you tell me you knew Mrs. Rosen?"

"Slipped my mind. We just started playing Mah-Jongg together on Tuesdays at the Senior Center."

"Ahh." She whispered, "You knew she was going to be here today, didn't you?"

Aunt Ida winked, and continued her conversation. "So, Gertrude, how's your son?"

Gert hacked again. "Do you see any grandchildren with me?"

"No."

"That's how he is. No grandchildren for me and I'm not getting any younger. I'm beginning to wonder if he'll ever get married. I sure hope he's not gay. Wouldn't that be a kick in the ass?"

Sarah's mouth opened and closed. She could personally attest to his sexual preference, but didn't think this was the time or place to announce it.

"Tsk, tsk. That would be a shame. But, Gert, I thought he had a new girlfriend."

"Bobbi the Bitch? Phooey!"

"Oh, I'm so sorry to hear that. Perhaps we could get him back together with Sarah."

Sarah almost fell out of her chair. What was Aunt Ida doing? In the midst of all the craziness surrounding her mother's accident, the little old lady had been matchmaking.

Gertrude looked Sarah over like a side of beef and said, "You've gotten a little *zaftig*, haven't you?"

Sarah couldn't remember what that word meant, but she knew it wasn't a compliment.

Aunt Ida said, "Not *zaftig*—*gesund*."

"She's very *gesund*."

"And your son, he's perfect?"

"*Oy*, the abuse I take from you." Gertrude slapped her palm on the table and turned her piercing gaze on Sarah. "So, Sarah, I can't remember so good. What's your age? You're not Jewish, are you? You don't look Jewish."

On all but one brief occasion, Sarah had avoided meeting Dan's family during their short engagement because she feared this question. What exactly did Jewish look like? She never understood the expression. To her eyes, Jews came in all sizes, shapes, and hair colors. Yet to Jewish eyes, she looked alien, non-Jewish, goy.

"I'm thirty. You're right. I'm not Jewish." She decided not to add that she had planned to convert when she was engaged to Dan.

"Hmph. *Macht's nicht zu mir!* Doesn't matter to me. So, have you ever been married? Any children?"

Sarah wondered if the next question would be if she'd ever been arrested, or convicted of a misdemeanor or a felony. She made a pre-emptive strike.

"Never married. No kids. I'm a nurse and I finished my PhD in Public Health. I work at Hopkins in Pediatrics Research. I live with my mother, but she's in the hospital because she had an accident. She's in a coma. I have a dog and a cat. Have I missed anything?"

"*Oy!* You're a feisty one. I like that!" Gertrude shook a well-manicured index finger at Sarah. "Give me your number. We'll meet for bagels and lox. I'll bring Dan when he comes into town for a visit."

Sarah gave her the cell number.

"Hey," Gertrude bellowed in the direction of a passing waitress. "How about some service here?"

Sarah leaned over and lowered her voice. "God will get you for this, Aunt Ida. You set me up. Why'd you do that? Do I look desperate? And by the way, I just figured it out. She called me fat."

"*Zaftig* means 'plump.' I said you were healthy." Her mischievous smile made Sarah laugh.

The whole thing was absurd. Sarah was certain the probability of Gertrude calling her for bagels and lox with Dan was zip, zero, zilch, and *bubkes*.

A server arrived, and Gertrude was mollified with a cup of coffee. The only noise coming from her side of the aisle was an occasional sigh and a rattling smoker's cough. Aunt Ida shook her head when Sarah glanced in Gertrude's direction.

"Don't look at her, or we'll be here the rest of the day. She sighs when she wants attention. She's been very lonely since she lost her husband. When she's in a mood like this, she'll talk your ear off."

"By the way," Sarah said, "there was a white van in front of your house early this morning. I thought it was odd."

Wrinkling her forehead, Aunt Ida said, "Betty's brother, Patrick, he's an electrician with a white van. He's done some work around the house for me. Sometimes he drops Betty off, but it's not her day to work. Must have been some other contractor."

Sarah looked down at the joke paper placemat labeled "Dictionary of Basic Yiddish." She was struggling with *kloppen kop on vant*, which they translated as "asking the landlord to paint" when the steaming omelet arrived, the aroma of onions tantalizing her nose and putting her appetite in overdrive. "My taste buds are singing, Aunt Ida. Can you hear them?"

"Mine, too."

The server kept the hot coffee coming. After a leisurely meal, Sarah went to get the car while Aunt Ida paid the bill.

A white van pulled into the parking lot as Sarah turned the key in the ignition. The driver's side door opened and a man in a maintenance uniform climbed out. A sign on its side panel read "Jacob's Heating and Plumbing."

As she drove around the block past the old Maryland State Police Crime Laboratory, she spotted another white van. When she took a right onto Sudbrook Lane, there was another one, and yet another when she pulled up in front of the restaurant. White vans everywhere. They must breed like rabbits, she thought.

"Is there anything I can do to help you get ready?" Sarah asked when she walked Aunt Ida at her door.

"You could put some boxes in the trunk of my car. Look in the kitchen."

Sarah followed her into the house. "Do you have a list of all the hotels you'll be staying at, just in case?"

"It's next to that *Gee-chazerei* for Detective Engelman." The bottle sat on the kitchen counter next to the telephone, with a note attached: "GHB. Give to Det. Engelman." No mistaking that for almond extract.

"Look at the time. Aunt Ida, I'm heading over to visit Mom. I know you have a lot to do, so if you don't want to come, that's okay. I'll take those boxes on my way out."

"As long as I'm still in town, I'm coming with you. Before we go, could I ask you to do one more thing? I'm concerned the CD player in my car might not be working. I haven't used it in a while and I have to be able to listen to my audio books. Could you check it for me?"

"Sure." Sarah went outside and put the boxes in the trunk. A new bumper sticker was taped to the rear window. She stopped to take a closer look. It read in large, colorful, pseudo-Hebrew print, "Mah-Jongg Maven."

Sarah played with the CD player and cued up the first chapter of a murder mystery. She pressed the play button and listened to the actor's resonant voice. Despite her heavy jacket and scarf, she shivered with an unexpected chill. Her heart raced and for a moment she had an ominous feeling, as if something bad was about to happen.

Not possible. Her mother was in a coma and her finances were in the toilet. What else could possibly go wrong?

Chapter Five

Exhausted, despite having caught some shut eye for a few hours, Sarah stood in the doorway to her mother's room, listened to Dr. Merrill and waited for the other shoe to drop. "Your mother's vital signs are stable. We've ordered an EEG to see what her brain activity looks like. If she'd wake up, then we could say she was on the road to recovery."

"And, if she stays in the coma, then what?"

"We transfer her to a medical unit or a nursing home." She paused. "But, we're getting a little ahead of ourselves. Let's see what the EEG shows. Any other questions? No? I'll see you later."

"Well, Mom, this is a fine mess you've gotten us into," Sarah said in a weak imitation of Oliver Hardy. She sank into a chair alongside Aunt Ida.

The older woman stared at Ethel as if her friend would wake up and ask where her damn tea was. Beeping and occasional overhead pages punctuated the silence. "I don't know what I would have done without your mother when I was younger. I was so alone," the older woman whispered, not taking her eyes off Ethel.

Sarah held her breath, half-afraid Aunt Ida would stop speaking and half-afraid of what she would learn. She knew they went back decades, but neither Ethel nor Ida had ever spoken of their earlier days together. Sarah had always thought it was odd. Most good friends will say, "Remember when…?" and then amuse listeners with a funny story from youth. Not a single naughty or nostalgic tale had ever been shared with Sarah. Not one.

"You asked me a question, and I wasn't honest with you, Sarah." She spoke louder. "Ethel, if you can hear me, I'm sorry."

Her mother's pale face nearly blended in with the pillowslips. She didn't move or make a sound, but the heart monitor beeped as if to say, "Please go on. I'm alive. I can hear you."

Sarah didn't want to push Aunt Ida—nor did she want to push herself. Maybe it was better to leave things in the past. Now was not the time for a shocking revelation "Aunt Ida, if you don't want to—"

"Let me finish."

That was a command, not a request. Sarah snapped her mouth shut.

Aunt Ida pulled a handkerchief out of her handbag and blew her nose. "My stepfather—got me pregnant." She spoke in little bursts, between sobs. "Sent me away. The Florence Crittendon Home. DC. Met your mother. We were young, teenagers. She was like my sister. She—she looked out for me."

Sarah squeezed Aunt Ida's hand and glanced at her mother. No response. "We went outside for a walk. My stepfather showed up. Said he was going to kill me. Like he killed my kitten. And my mother." The elderly woman took a deep breath.

Despite her fear of shattering, Sarah couldn't take her eyes off Aunt Ida. Riveted by the older woman's words, Sarah swallowed hard and whispered, "What happened?"

"Ethel stepped between us. Hit him on the chin. He

fell. Hit his head. Blood everywhere. We ran."

"She saved your life." Sarah looked at her mother with a mixture of newfound awe, respect, and shock. Ethel had never been an easy woman. Her mouth mean whether sober or drunk. Yet her loyalty to Ida was absolute. Her mother had killed a man to protect her best friend. Did Ethel have other secrets? What could be worse than that?

"Sisters forever," Aunt Ida whispered and broke down in tears.

Sarah leaned over and hugged her dear, sweet Aunt Ida and wept with her. "Thank you."

After a while, Aunt Ida regained control of herself. Her voice was firmer when she spoke.

"I helped her escape from the home. It was like a prison. She was unhappy. She wanted to be with your father." The older woman sighed. "We lost touch. I met Jack. Love at first sight. A handyman." She smiled. "Who knew he'd become so wealthy?"

Fresh tears rolled down her cheeks, and she dabbed her paper-thin skin with her crumpled handkerchief. "Your mother married an abusive drunk. She wrote to me, but he sent all my letters back. 'Return to Sender.' Beneath all my happiness was this great sorrow that she was suffering. I hoped to see her again before I died."

"What happened?" Sarah knew her father had been a mean drunk. She heard the stories over and over from her mother.

"She found me when Jack passed away. She was working for the federal government, living in Washington, D.C. Saw the story on the news."

Aunt Ida waved at the television in the room. "They showed our wedding photo and she recognized me. When she came to the memorial service, she told me she'd been looking for me for years."

Aunt Ida dabbed at her nose. "One of the happiest days in my life. She said it was an amazing coincidence. I said, 'There are no coincidences.'"

Aunt Ida turned and gripped Sarah's hands with surprising strength. "Sarahlei, never, never, ever give up hope. I almost gave up on ever seeing your mother again, and she reappeared in my life just when I desperately needed her. I was grief-stricken when my darling Jack died, and no matter how awful your mother's behavior can be, she's my best friend, my sister forever. She loves you. Don't give up on your mother, don't give up on yourself, and, for God's sake, don't give up on the love of your life, Dan."

Sarah stood up and hugged Aunt Ida. "Thank you for sharing this story with me." She was crying, too. She turned toward her mother. "Mom, you have a hell of a good friend here. I hope you know that."

The heart monitor attached to her mother began to beep louder. It had been registering seventy beats per minute, but now showed ninety beats per minute. Just as Sarah was about to call for a nurse, Ethel's heart rate dropped back down to seventy-five.

Hearing was the last sense to go. Somewhere, deep inside, Sarah knew her mother had heard everything. Did she approve? Or did the heart rate monitor reflect her internal agitation?

Aunt Ida looked exhausted. "Sarahlei, do you mind taking me home, please? I have to get up early and I need some rest."

Sarah went to her mother's bedside and smoothed Ethel's hair away from her brow. At one time, her mother had been young, healthy, vibrant. And she'd accidentally killed a man to save Aunt Ida.

Troubled youth, troubled adulthood. Was that all coming to an end soon? Sarah hoped not. Despite her bad girl days and drunken debacles, her mother deserved compassion. "Stay out of trouble. Don't go out drinking with the nurses after work."

As she rose, Sarah could have sworn she saw Ethel's lips turn up in a smirk. She stopped and looked again. It was only a trick of the fluorescent lighting.

****

Back at home, Sarah reviewed her to do list: pick up Mitzi; call Baltimore Gas and Electric; get to work and tell everyone what was going on in her life. A sign flashed in her mind: Proceed with caution: Ugly Monday ahead.

She let Winston out, fed the whirling dervish, Neferkitty, and set the timer on the coffee pot for five in the morning. Then she remembered she hadn't heard from her sister. A tiny envelope appeared on her cell phone. She pulled out the instruction manual and read, "Occasionally, there will be areas where your cell phone will not be accessible."

Great. The ICU must have been a "dead zone," like the pediatricians always complained about at Hopkins' Pediatric ICU.

Her sister answered on the second ring. "Are you okay? I worried when I couldn't reach you."

"I was with Mom and Aunt Ida." And boy, did she have a story to tell her sister.

"How are they?"

"Aunt Ida's fine. We had a nice brunch this morning at a deli. Mom's the same. She's having an

EEG tomorrow. Guess I'd better put 'shop for a nursing home' on my list of things to do." Sarah paused. "Are you sitting down?"

"Yeah. Is another shoe about to drop?"

"A whole shoe store." Sarah told her sister about Aunt Ida's surprise disclosures. As she repeated the story, the emotions she'd attempted to keep in check flooded her, choking her up. She wept softly at the end of the tale. If she'd known this before, she would have seen her mother in a different light. Would she have behaved differently toward her? Would she have thought less of her mother for it? Would she have stayed in Chicago when she received that fateful call? Would she still be with Dan?

"Oh my God," Debra said. "We never knew. They've kept this secret for what—sixty years?"

"Longer. I'm still trying to wrap my head around this." She sighed. "It's as if we have Mom Version 2.0. I have to rethink all my feelings for her and put them in this new framework. On the one hand, I respect her for protecting her friend. On the other hand, it makes me wonder if she's more resilient than I gave her credit for. Perhaps she could have handled her recovery from that car crash on her own, without disrupting my life and destroying my relationship with Dan."

Despite the fact Debra had the grace to remain silent and to withhold "I told you so," Sarah still heard it echo in her mind. "I do have a new sense of respect for Mom. She stuck up for Aunt Ida. No wonder they're such good friends."

"What happened to the babies?" Debra asked. "Did Aunt Ida lose her baby? What about Mom? Do we have a brother or sister out there looking for us?"

"I didn't ask," Sarah said. "I was so overwhelmed, and Aunt Ida was so distraught. "

"It's going to take time for me to digest all this," Debra said. "I'm great with other people's psychological issues, but it's different when it's my family. Is there anything I can do for you?"

"Be my sounding board. If you could help me get some sleep that would be good."

"You've had a hell of a couple days."

She could say that again.

"Oh, on a lighter note, you'll never guess who Aunt Ida and I ran into." Sarah recounted the "accidental" meeting with Gertrude Rosen at the deli.

Debra agreed. It was a set up.

"Aunt Ida, Match-Maker to the Pathetic," Sarah said with a little laugh.

"Do you think Gertrude will come through and bring Dan to the deli? Or are you going to call him?"

Sarah cringed at the thought. "What would I say to him? 'Hi, Dan, guess who? Oh, and guess what, you were right about my mother.' Besides, his mother said he has a girlfriend."

Debra snorted. "It didn't sound like she liked Bobbi."

"Gert's not dating her," Sarah said.

"Well, at least you haven't started adopting stray cats, like all the old maids."

"Me-ow. Very funny. I'll just keep hanging around clinics and hospitals. That way, I'm sure to meet another doctor."

****

Sarah stared at the face of her alarm clock and wished the Everly Brothers would shut up and leave her alone. Instead, they continued to tell Little Susie to wake up at the top of their lungs. Time for the morning routine: dog out, cat fed, coffee sucked down in large quantities.

Winston barked and refused to return when she called him. She went outside, coffee mug in hand. Once again, the dog ran back and forth in front of the invisible shield. Once again, no deer. Once again, a white van sat in the cul-de-sac. Was it the same one? They all looked alike.

Not needing the Heckler's harassment today, she yelled and signed at Winston to be quiet. He ignored her. She grabbed his collar and dragged him back into the house, spilling coffee down the front of her robe. Even when she shoved him through the kitchen door, he continued to bark. "Give it a rest. It's just another white van. Have a cookie."

The clock indicated half past five. Time to see if Aunt Ida was ready to go.

Sarah crossed the wet lawn, saw the white van, and approached it. The driver started the engine and drove away. She shrugged, headed up Aunt Ida's back steps and rapped at the door. "Do you have anything left to put in the car?"

"No, but I have something for you to take to Sol Weinstein." She handed Sarah a bulky manila envelope. "He's expecting it. You're making an appointment with him, right?"

"Yes." It felt like a book, it was so heavy. Sarah hoped Sol didn't charge by the page.

Aunt Ida gripped Sarah's hand. "Do you think you might have time at lunch to take it over to him? I want him to have it as soon as possible."

"Sure. Maybe he'll have time to see me today."

The older woman smiled. "Excellent. You have no idea what this means to me."

A soft meow came from the cat carrier on the kitchen floor. "Mitzi, baby, you're coming home with me. Winston and Neferkitty can't wait to see you," Sarah said. She set the envelope on top of the cat carrier and turned to Aunt Ida. "Okay, lady, this is it. I'll walk you out to the car."

Aunt Ida buttoned up her jacket and hoisted her purse onto her shoulder. Sarah lifted Mitzi's carrier and the envelope, then spotted the bottle of GHB on the counter. "I'll come back and get that bottle later."

They made an odd little parade to the car. As Sarah bent down to hug Aunt Ida, a sense of déjà vu came over her. Love, anxiety, and sadness swirled together squeezing her heart so hard, she wondered if she'd ever catch her breath.

She worried about Aunt Ida making it to Florida safely, but didn't want to voice her concerns for fear of insulting the older woman. She was a competent adult, quite capable of making her own decisions. And she wasn't ready to have her car keys taken away.

"It feels like we've been doing this for a lifetime," Sarah said, her voice thick with emotion.

"It's a good feeling." Aunt Ida gave her a fierce hug. "You're the daughter I never had, Sarahlei. I love you. You know that, don't you?"

"Yes, I do. I love you, too." Sarah hugged her back, and then pulled away, her vision blurred with tears. Soon she'd be left to look after her mother and to make some gut-wrenching decisions. Part of her wanted to say "Don't go, stay, I need you here." The other part said, "Go. Take care of yourself. Have fun. Be safe."

Sarah was alone and on her own. Her childhood hadn't been great, but her adulthood really was a bitch. She waved good-bye to Ida and watched her turn the large white Cadillac around in the cul-de-sac. It reminded her of a ship heading out to sea.

Safe passage, Aunt Ida.

****

Ida sighed and thought about the long journey ahead as she drove toward Stevenson Lane. Sarahlei was going to have her hands full with all those pets. Such a good girl. Ida thought of the daughter she gave birth to, the one she never got to know. "Oh Mitzi, even though I knew you would have been different, I wanted you. I wanted you more than life itself."

But Mitzi had died at birth. The nursing supervisor told her the baby had been buried in the hospital rose garden. With the hysterectomy, all of Ida's future children had been left behind, as well.

Don't go there. Think about happy things.

She looked forward to catching up with her neighbors in Florida. She'd been going to Punta Gorda for over twenty years, and it was truly her second home. Yet, the strong ties in Baltimore kept her from moving south full time. And, with Sarahlei back home, there was no way Ethel would ever consider moving to Florida with her.

Ethel. In a coma, for God's sake. What was she thinking?

She'd always been there for Ida, keeping her spirits up when they met at the Florence Crittendon Home, looking out for her, making sure Ida always got the best piece of meat, the softest bed, first in line at the bathroom. Then the ultimate act of courage: protecting her from her drunken, violent step-father.

"What am I doing?" Ida pulled the car over to the side of the road, took a deep breath, and looked at herself in the rearview mirror. "Shame on you, Ida Mae Katz! Go home and take care of your friend. She needs you!"

Putting the Cadillac in gear, she began to make a U-turn. As she crossed the street, a white van roared up and pulled alongside her car. A man in a mechanic's overalls, ski mask, and gloves jumped out of the van and ran over to her car door. Ida reached to put the car in reverse, but the thug smashed her side window and yanked the door open before she could escape.

"Who are you?" Ida used her fists to beat at his hands. "What do you want?"

He reached over and grabbed the car keys.

"If you want the car, take it. Just leave me alone!"

He dragged her out of the car and pulled her to her feet. "Let go of me! Somebody help me! Please, for the love of God, help me!"

The side door to the van slid open and a short man clad in the same mechanic's overalls, ski mask, and gloves hopped out, holding a rag.

"I have money," Ida sobbed. "Look in my purse. There's six hundred dollars. Take it."

The first attacker held her arms and the second one pushed the cloth in her mouth, then duct taped it in place. She struggled and bucked as they forced her into the van. One taped her wrists and ankles while the other held her down. Then they blind-folded her. Ida heard the door slide shut, the Cadillac's engine rumbled and she passed out.

When she awoke, Ida found herself on a metal frame bed, covered with a ratty quilt. The tape had been removed from her hands, ankles, and mouth, but when she moved her feet, she found she was shackled. She sat up with care, rubbed her tape-burned wrists, and touched her hurting face with care. When she pulled her hand away, her fingertips were bloody.

Why didn't they kill her?

Chapter Six

The sun rose as Sarah slogged across the wet grass to her house. She struggled with the weight of the cat carrier while inside the box, Mitzi danced and emitted a steady stream of soft, plaintive mews. "Don't worry baby, just one more minute and we'll be in the house."

Once inside, Winston raced over and head butted Mitzi's carrier. Sarah put the cat and her belongings into her bedroom and locked the happy dog out of the room. Winston banged his head against the door and Neferkitty stood behind him.

"Go lie down. She's not ready for either of you."

The dog flopped down on the floor, his body conveying the loud message of "Spoil sport."

After throwing on black slacks and a purple sweater, she grabbed her backpack with the envelope for Sol Weinstein and headed out for her car. "Groceries, must get new groceries on the way home."

She sipped her black coffee, listened to public radio, and chortled with glee when she found a whole row of good parking spots. Why didn't she do this more often? This was a new personal best. She'd be in the office before eight o'clock in the morning.

She loved her job and felt honored to be affiliated with the Johns Hopkins School of Medicine. In addition to working on child abuse research, she taught epidemiology, research methods, and she mentored the

Pediatric Academic Fellows' projects. Since she'd been a pediatric nurse before going to graduate school, Sarah knew the territory and loved working with the eager physicians-in-training.

After she sifted through the pile of requests for help from the residents, she checked her email. She had a message from Dr. Kirby. Marian Kirby had returned to medical school and become a pediatrician after teaching high school biology for several years. Her round, sweet face, blue eyes, and mild manner were deceiving. Years of working in a neighborhood riddled with gun violence had transformed her into a vocal advocate for gun control.

"Marian, this is Sarah. Do you have a few minutes? I need to speak with you."

"Yes, I just finished up an early meeting. I'm free for the next thirty minutes."

Swiping her ID card at the security device, Sarah walked through the corridor to Marian's office. Marian set down a sheaf of papers. "What can I do for you?"

"It's my mother. There's been an accident." Sarah gave her the short version. "Right now, she's stable. I wanted you to know, just in case there's an emergency."

"Don't even give it a thought. You're way ahead of schedule on all your work, not to mention that stunning discovery you made when you helped Peter re-analyze his data. The Baltimore City Police said they'd send someone around today to interview you."

Mindful of her boss's time, Sarah provided a run down on the residents' projects and her availability for the day. She stood to leave. "Thanks, Marian."

"Sarah?"

"Yes?"

"I'll say a prayer for your mother," Marian said. "And for you."

"Thank you." Sarah turned her face away, afraid her boss would see her cry. Emotional displays were not welcome here. The job required objective analyses and data interpretation, not guesswork and sensationalism. She needed to stay strong, not fall apart, even now when she felt as if a steam roller had flattened her.

Back at her desk, she called BGE about the overdue bill. The woman she spoke with didn't care if Sarah owed five, fifty or fifty thousand dollars. You can't pay? Too bad. You should have thought about that before you were born.

After an argument with a supervisor, Sarah paid the bill on the phone with her credit card. She wanted to slam the receiver against the wall, but needed it to call about the water bill. They informed her that she was lucky the bill was under two hundred and fifty dollars or they would have turned off the water. Still more creditors to call, to pay something, anything to keep the gas going, the phone on, and her life going.

If it weren't for bad luck, she wouldn't have any luck at all.

Could things get any worse?

****

Ida surveyed the basement. Unadorned cement walls, narrow windows up too high for her to reach, a naked light bulb. It was the perfect prison. Wooden stairs appeared in a corner, rising up dim in the gloom. Toilet to the right of the bed. Left of the bed, a nightstand. Plastic pitcher of water. Disposable cups. A

71

sandwich. Her purse. A note that said: "Eat and drink. You'll be here a while."

"Hello? Is anyone home?" she called out. No answer.

Ida picked up her bag, dumped it on the bed, and searched for her cell phone. Gone.

She collapsed on the bed and cried herself to sleep.

****

Sarah watched the screen saver of tropical fish swimming across her computer monitor, the phone receiver glued to her ear. After five rings, someone picked up. "Law office of Solomon Weinstein. How may I help you?"

"This is Sarah Wright. Ida Katz referred me to Mr. Weinstein. I have an envelope she asked me to deliver. I'd like to set up an appointment."

"Oh, yes, Ms. Wright. Mr. Weinstein told me you'd be calling today. Ida called him at home last evening to give him a heads up. Will eleven-thirty work for you?"

"Perfect."

Taps sounded at her office door: "shave and a haircut, two bits," the secret code she used with co-workers. Sarah got up from the desk. "May I help you?"

"You might say so." Peter Lassiter, one of the Pediatric Fellows, stood in the hallway, holding a large cardboard tube.

At the sight of the cylinder, Sarah couldn't resist a feeble joke. "Is that a poster in your pocket or are you just glad to see me?"

"Correcto-mundo! It is a poster and I'm happy to see you. Want to come around to the wall of fame and give me your feedback?" Peter's grin faded. "You look awful. What's wrong?"

Sarah filled him in on his mother's accident and financial woes. She kept the other secrets to herself. "But, hey, I spent only half of my paycheck on my mother's overdue utility bills with a bit left over to to eat, drink coffee, and be merry. But enough about me and my woes. What about you? How about a latte?"

"I'll have a little."

Sarah groaned and weaved through the crowded corridors. Medical students, nursing students, runners, orderlies, clergy, nurses, physicians, researchers, administrators, patients, and visitors all walked purposefully toward their respective destinations. Mandatory badges identified everyone, faculty, staff, students and other employees, including contractors. Security required all others to wear self-sticking visitor labels dated to prevent unwanted overnight guests.

Even without a nametag, a visitor was easily identified by the fact that he was often found turning slowly in a circle, a piece of paper in hand and a puzzled look on his face. This morning was no different. A chaplain walked past her, explaining to a lost man that his destination was three buildings away. The medical complex was so extensive, that an employee could take a two-mile walk every day without going outdoors.

Sarah ordered at the coffee stand and offered to get Peter something to eat which he declined. "Just a coffee, thanks. I really want to show you my poster."

The year before, Peter had decided to conduct a five-year retrospective study of newborns treated in the clinic. Using data on children seen in the newborn clinic, he wanted to see if there were any differences between mothers of babies with congenital sexually transmitted infections, such as syphilis, gonorrhea, herpes, HIV, hepatitis B and chlamydia, and those who did not. It had been his wife's idea to include church affiliations when he had collected the information from the charts.

The last time Sarah had met with him, the counter-intuitive finding of a high number of congenital syphilis cases among girls with religious connections had shocked and intrigued her. When she re-analyzed the data, she found the Jerusalem A.B.E. Church carried a disproportionate number of cases. The mothers were all very young—some only eleven years old at the time of conception.

Sarah hypothesized that a sexual predator was victimizing these girls. She had informed Marian of the findings and the police had been notified as part of mandatory child abuse reporting.

"You have tape or push pins to put this up?" She asked between dodging wheelchairs and nurses' aides.

"I have both. I used to be a Boy Scout."

She grinned. "Somehow, I'm not surprised."

They arrived at the door to the corridor leading to the Pediatric Department offices. Sarah swiped her ID card and entered the hallway. Peter selected a large, clean space, unfurled the six-foot by four-foot roll of paper, and pinned it to the wall. Sarah stepped back across the corridor to survey his work. The poster was easy to read with colorful pie charts, but was about as interesting as thumbing through a telephone book.

"How do you feel about the poster?" Sarah asked between sips of latte.

Peter shook his head. "B.O.R.E.D."

"What can we do to make this un-boring?"

"Pictures," Peter said. "Photographs of babies and young children with syphilis. This is a horrible disease, and it's not going away. In spite of antibiotics, Baltimore in the top tier for congenital syphilis, thanks to sex-for-drugs. These kids are damaged for life."

"We can search the Medical Archives for photographs of patients followed in the Pediatric Clinic in the 1900's, before penicillin," Sarah said. "What do you think about using their photos to punch it up?"

A few minutes later, Marian granted permission to access the archives. The pediatrician gave her a memo for the Medical Archivist and gave Sarah an update. "I have the head nurse in the Outpatient Clinic pulling all the files we have on children born with congenital syphilis to see if there's any connection to that church." Her face wore a grim expression. "If there's a sexual predator in that congregation, I hope we get the bastard."

"What's your schedule look like?" Sarah asked Peter as they headed down the hallway.

"I'm free until noon. I have to cover the Outpatient Pediatric Clinic."

"I have until about eleven. I have an appointment with a lawyer." She looked at her watch. "Two hours to get to Medical Archives and dig through the photos. Let me grab my backpack, so I can leave directly from there and go to my appointment." She paused and looked at the poster. "Why don't you put a 'Give Me Your Comments' sheet up next to the poster? That way if the other Fellows have suggestions, you'll have them in writing."

"The last time we did that, all we got was jokes.

Let's hope we get more useful feedback this time."

****

A large underground tunnel led to the Medical Archivist's warren of dust-covered filing cabinets and cardboard boxes. Water oozed from a wall, and Sarah's nose itched from the smell of mildew hanging thick in the air.

A pale-skinned, elderly woman with a dowager's hump sat at a desk at with a nameplate that said, "Miss Taylor, Archivist." She looked up as Sarah and Peter approached her desk. "Yes, may I help you?"

She spoke in a paper-thin voice. Her thinning gray hair was pulled back in a severe bun. Something about the woman reminded Sarah of her mother. She felt a pang of sorrow and wondered how she would get through the day. Focus on work, Sarah. If you don't, you'll be overwhelmed. Think happy thoughts. Dan. Yes. Think about Dan and the possibility of seeing him again.

"We have an archival request." Peter handed the memo to the archivist.

Miss Taylor stared at the paper, as if examining it for authenticity. "Well, this grants permission from the Department, but you need to complete a request for access form and a confidentiality agreement. It's the privacy law."

Sarah and Peter rushed through the forms and handed them back to Miss Taylor. "Okay, let me see where the Pediatric Archives are. I have an index of all the major collections. Just give me a minute." She turned and clicked away at a keyboard. The computer and her desk were the only areas not covered in dust.

"Ah. Here we are. Come with me." She stood and

motioned for them to follow.

Sarah walked through what seemed like a mile of narrow rows of rusted filing cabinets and mildewed cardboard boxes. Rivulets of water ran down the basement walls, making the surface look as if it had been slimed by a giant garden slug. Afraid to touch anything for fear of getting filth on her clothes, she began to wonder if they were entering the waiting room to Hades. The thought was in a bubble over her head when Miss Taylor stopped, and waved her hand over a row of filing cabinets.

"The files you want begin here in 1900 and go to here in 2000. If you find what you need, we can discuss the next steps. Be cautious when you handle the files. These materials are irreplaceable. Good luck."

Sarah and Peter started at opposite ends of the row, and began pulling out the drawers, looking for anything resembling files on syphilis. The enormity of the task gave new meaning to the expression "looking for a needle in a haystack." From time to time, Sarah glanced up and looked at Peter. She didn't have to ask how he was doing. Dust streaked his face and shirt, and sweat trickled down his brow. She wondered how Miss Taylor could work in the moldy gloom and had a newfound appreciation for her windowless office.

An hour and half, a major sneezing fit, and zip, zero, zilch and *bupkes* later, Sarah approached the fourth filing cabinet with trepidation. Halfway through the third drawer down, she saw the file. In flowing old-fashioned script, one word appeared: Syphilogy. The study of syphilis. She opened the file and saw a close-up photo of an infant.

She waved the photo in the air. "Bingo."

"Thank God, I was about to give up." Peter replaced the folder he was holding in the file cabinet in front of him, closed the drawer, and dusted his hands. He came over and stood next to Sarah as she flipped through the pages. Photo after photo showed infants with closed eyes, scrunched faces, and wee little noses. Names and dates were written in ink on the back of each picture.

The babies transitioned to children at different ages with glassy stares, thick eyeglasses, slack jaws, and flat, "saddle" noses, as if they belonged to an elementary school boxing club. This was the classic, flat, hypoplastic nose of congenital syphilis. The intellectual disability, deafness, or other functional disability could not be discerned directly from the photos. That information was written on the back, along with a name, date of birth, and the date of the photograph.

"It's the mother lode." Peter looked over Sarah's shoulder as she thumbed through, turning each photo over to read the comments. "Really. What a find."

With her heart hammering in her chest, Sarah stared down at the face of a little girl with dark, curly hair. Her head was turned to the side, as if the camera had clicked as she looked away. She had a flat nose, bow shaped lips and a heart-shaped birthmark on her left cheekbone just in front of her ear.

"Whoa. You don't look too good." Peter grabbed Sarah's elbow as she teetered. "Maybe you should go home and get some rest."

Sarah shook her head. "I just got a little lightheaded. Guess I should have eaten something today."

Miss Taylor appeared beside them. "Any luck?"

"Yes!" Peter crowed. "The good news is, we found

some great photos."

"The bad news is if you want to use photos of deceased persons, you'll need to get permission of the heirs and then the approval of the Privacy Board," the archivist said.

Peter looked stricken. Sarah looked down at the little girl's image in the photo she clutched. Okay, I know it's probably a long shot, but let's start with this one." She turned the photo over and read the notes out loud. "Her name is Bessie M. Woods, date of birth, November 27, 1942, and the date the photo was taken was November 30, 1945. This indicates she's deaf, 'feeble-minded,' and has very poor vision. She's a poster child for congenital syphilis with all the consequences."

And, Sarah thought, she has a birthmark like Aunt Ida's. A wave of melancholy washed over her and tears sprang to her eyes, as she thought about Aunt Ida. She would have been a wonderful mother. She hoped she was having a nice drive to Florida.

"If this Bessie is still alive," Peter said, "she's over sixty. I wonder if we'd be able to find any relatives."

He looked up at Sarah, brow furrowed. "I don't know how we can get this done on time. I'm in the clinic and on call for the Pediatric ER all week. Do you feel like doing a little detective work?"

"If she was seen at this clinic, it's likely she was from this area. I'll start with the telephone book and make some calls."

Sarah knew she had a long list of things to do, but she felt compelled to find out what had happened to Bessie Woods. Besides, she needed something to take her mind off her mother. She handed the photograph back to Miss Taylor.

"By the way," the archivist said. "Did you know there's one other place you could look for images of congenital syphilis?"

Sarah glanced at Peter. He shook his head.

"Go to the National Library of Medicine's Web site and look for the link for the History of Medicine Division and Images. I have no idea if they have any photographs of congenital syphilis, but it's worth poking around online. You should use it as a backup. Really, what's the likelihood of you finding this child's family after so many years?"

Chapter Seven

Elizabeth Woods lay in her bed and sighed. "I miss Clarice," she said to the woman bathing her.

"What is?"

The woman's heavy Haitian accent sounded like "Wassis?" to Elizabeth. "My roommate. I miss her."

"Ahahahaha."

What was this woman's name? Elizabeth couldn't recall. No matter. The aide's hands were gentle as she washed her face and neck with warm water and scrubbed her arms and hands. Elizabeth missed long soaks in the tub and reading a book.

Books on audiotape were a good substitute for reading, but nothing could replace the relaxing sensation of leaning her head back on a pillow and floating in a tub full of bubbles. Nowadays, she was lucky when the nurse's aide who bathed her had kind hands. "You have nice hands," she said.

The woman grunted.

"My husband had good hands, too. Gentle, like yours. He was devastated when he had a heart attack and the army sent him home from the frontlines. He had a hard time getting used to being a civilian again."

The aide sighed. "Ahhhhh. Army good for men. Make them strong."

"He loved my daughter, Mitzi, but he didn't show it very well. He had a hard time getting used to having a child. He kept asking where she came from. Isn't that silly? He was a doctor, for heaven's sake. He knew where babies came from."

A grunt and the soft hands moved down her right side with a warm washcloth.

"We were a happy family," Elizabeth said to the nurse's aide who hummed as she bathed her. "We left Washington, D.C. and moved back to Baltimore, where we had friends and relatives. John went into private practice as a general practitioner and was very successful. I stayed home to raise our lovely daughter. Our neighbors had small children and the mothers would meet at each other's homes for coffee, apple cake, and gossip while we watched our children play."

After covering her right side with a flannel blanket, the aide crooned a hymn and moved to the other side. "Mitzi was different. When the other babies were walking at twelve months, Mitzi was crawling. When they said their first words, Mitzi was blowing spit bubbles and crying. Her wee little nose was too small, all out of proportion with the rest of her face as she got older. Flat. Not pretty. The other mothers made snide comments on her looks and her behavior. They were so proud of their perfect children."

The Haitian woman said, "Ahahahaha, women tongues can cut. Bible say we must be good. Not all read the good book."

"I was angry at the other mothers. They were mean-spirited. Then I became concerned my baby might have polio. Why, in 1943 alone, the newspapers reported over twelve thousand cases of polio in the United States. Anyone could get it, even Presidents!"

The nurse's aide tsked and began to hum another

hymn. "John said I was being ridiculous and should know better. If she had polio, she'd have a fever, muscle spasms, and paralysis. He told me not to spend so much time with those other mothers and their children. He said I just kept comparing Mitzi to them and making myself sick with worry. He was right, they were hurtful. I stopped the visits, but her progress was too slow. The final straw was potty training. At three years old, she was content to sit in a full diaper all day long and play. Well, enough was enough. I wanted some answers, and by God, I was going to get them."

"Ahahahahaha. Yes, I hear you. Babies must learn to use the toilet."

"While John was at work, I bundled the baby up and took the red, white and blue streetcar downtown. Mitzi sat on my lap and sucked her fingers."

Elizabeth recalled the posters overhead in the streetcar. "The more women at work the sooner we win!" "Women in the war—We can't win without them!" Someone had hummed the tune to "Rosie the Riveter."

The posters and song made her feel guilty for not being a war worker, but Mitzi needed her at home.

The nurse's aide sang snatches of songs in a language Elizabeth didn't understand.

"We spent the whole day at the Johns Hopkins Clinics and went back the following day. A different specialist, a man who dealt only with nervous disorders in children, examined Mitzi, conducting test after test. He even had a photographer take pictures of her. I could hear Mitzi crying in the next room, but I wasn't allowed go in. They told me I'd only be in the way. I waited and prayed."

"Ahhh. Pray good," the aide said. "Pray very good."

"At last the doctor came out of the examining room and motioned for me to enter. I can still see the scene in my mind, as if it were a snapshot embedded in there forever. The room was cold and sterile, with a big white examining table. He motioned to me to sit in the chair. In his formal suit and long white laboratory coat, he looked like a giant. I was in awe of him, the room, and being at Johns Hopkins." She laughed, but it became a dry cackling sound that ended in a cough. "My daughter was unimpressed. Mitzi sat on a nurse's lap, sucking on a toy."

"Hmmmmm." The woman continued to work her way down Elizabeth's body, scrubbing at her legs.

"The doctor said, 'I have some difficult news for you.' I begged him, please say it's not polio," Elizabeth said. "He said he had conducted extensive tests on Mitzi. He told me she was deaf, nearly blind, and feeble-minded."

"Ahahahaha." The aide washed between each toe with care. Then she put soft socks on her feet and helped her into a flannel nightgown.

"Doctor, I said, how could this be? Tell me it's not from polio. He looked directly into my eyes. I held my breath and stared back at him waiting for his next words. I remember hearing Mitzi fussing. Then he said, 'It's not polio.' I wept for joy and clutched his hands."

The woman hummed and brushed Elizabeth's hair. "Good hair. Much hair."

She couldn't speak the rest aloud. Not even to this kind woman who spoke so little English.

The doctor was despicable. His vile accusation still

rang in her ears all these decades later: "Tell me, Madam, when you were pregnant, were you treated for syphilis?"

Sputtering with rage, Elizabeth had jumped up, snatched Mitzi out of the nurse's hands and shouted: "I am a good woman, a married woman, and a trained nurse. I'm not some fallen woman you can insult. I trained right here at this very institution. How dare you make such an accusation? My husband is a highly respected physician in the City of Baltimore. I trust you will keep your outrageous slurs and obscene thoughts to yourself, and I trust you and your nurse will never speak of this matter again to anyone."

As she had run out of the room, clutching her wailing child, he had called after her, "Madam, I mean you no harm. It's time you faced up to this matter. We're not living in the dark ages. Now we can treat syphilis with penicillin. If you haven't been treated, you should be, and so should your daughter."

"Missy Lizabeth, you done," the aide said.

Elizabeth heard the woman gather up her tools and the squeak of her rubber-soled shoes on the floor as she left the room.

"Yes," she said. "What had I done?"

****

Solomon Weinstein looked like one of the Muppets' curmudgeons who sat on the balcony, making wisecracks during every show. Well over six feet tall, even with stooped shoulders, he had a large pouch of a chin that looked as if it might puff up like a gecko when he made an argument in court. Two hearing aids explained why he yelled when he spoke. Gray and black eyebrows resembling large caterpillars wiggled over his wire-rimmed glasses and rheumy red eyes.

He stared across the desk, appearing to focus on every movement of Sarah's chapped and bitten lips. After she finished a lengthy recitation of the facts about her mother's accident, hospitalization, and subsequent discovery of her perilous financial condition, he looked at Sarah for a long time, as the clock on the corner of his desk ticked loudly.

"Well, Ida was right about you," he yelled. "You do need help and fast."

"Yes," she yelled back. "Can you help me?"

He lifted a sheaf of papers and a white business sized envelope with a shaky hand, and appeared to be oblivious to her question. Sarah looked at the clock, wondering how soon she should repeat the question.

"You need to petition the Court to be appointed your mother's Guardian of Property and Person. Guardianship is a legal procedure by which a court seeks 'to protect those who, because of illness or disability are unable to care for themselves.' Your mother meets the criteria. She's incapacitated and unable to make medical or financial decisions for herself. There are no other alternatives. She has no spouse or other legally appointed guardian. Although she has two other children, you're living with her and you're already acting as her surrogate."

He stopped, pulled a large white handkerchief out his breast pocket, blew his nose like a trumpet and replaced the handkerchief in his pocket. He continued to yell. "The court needs evidence she's disabled before they will grant you guardianship. She has the right to be at the hearing, but in this case, she's in a coma and unable to attend. You'll need to get two doctors to certify she's unable to make a health care decision and to manage her property. Any problem with getting the documentation?"

"I could get two dozen physicians to certify she's in a coma. She isn't even responding to my bad jokes."

He smiled and displayed a bright white set of perfect teeth. Sarah grinned back at him.

"Okay. Give me the names of the doctors caring for her. I'll have my wife get in touch with them for documentation. I'll see if we can expedite this."

Sara stared at him.

"What is it? Was there something you didn't understand?"

"Who's your wife?"

"You met her on your way in. Her name is Molly. She's my receptionist, paralegal, secretary, and wife. I like to keep things in the family."

"Oh." Sarah almost fell out of her chair.

Molly, his receptionist/paralegal/secretary/wife, was a beautiful, willowy blonde with enormous breasts and big, blue, dewy eyes. Hers had been the pleasant voice on the phone when Sarah called Sol's office. She appeared to be close to Sarah's age. Sol, on the other hand, seemed to be three days older than dirt.

He guffawed and slapped his knee, enjoying Sarah's reaction. "I love the looks on peoples' faces when I tell them. It makes me feel ten years younger. Molly, come on in, honey, we've got a new client."

The door opened and Molly walked in holding a tray with cups of coffee and a plate of rugelach cookies. She turned to Sarah and said, "Did he just tell you I'm his wife?"

Molly set the tray down on Sol's enormous desk,

Sharon Buchbinder

stood in front of him, and shook her index finger. "Sol, you keep telling people that whopper and I'm gonna make you marry me. Now stop it. She looks like she's about to have kittens."

"But, Molly, you know how much I love a good joke." Tears ran down his cheeks, and he slapped his thigh as he guffawed and snorted.

His humor was contagious. She hadn't laughed this hard since her mother's accident. Wiping tears from her eyes, Sarah asked, "Molly, is there a public rest room I might use?"

"Let me show you." She pointed one long finger At Sol. "You behave, mister!"

Sarah could hear him chortling as she went out of the office and into a hallway. "Does he do that to everyone?"

"Only with clients he thinks have a good sense of humor. You're a friend of Ida's, so he must've figured you'd like a good joke." She pointed at an open door. "There you go, hon. If you need anything, just holler!"

Looking in the mirror, Sarah realized why he thought she could take a joke. She looked like a clown. Dust was smeared across her cheeks and forehead and some spots of what appeared to be mildew decorated her sweater. She washed her hands and face and finger combed her shoulder length blonde hair. She should have put it in a pony tail before they went to the archives.

"You want some coffee, hon?" Molly was at her side, escorting Sarah back to Sol's office.

"Yes, I'd love some. Why didn't you tell me my face was covered with dust?"

"I thought it was Ash Wednesday or something, so

88

I didn't want to be insensitive. Besides, I knew Sol wouldn't care. He can hardly see your face, much less what's on it. He's real near-sighted."

"Do me a favor. If I ever come in here looking like that again, please tell me. I just left a dusty, moldy medical archive and there were no mirrors."

Sarah sat back down in the client's chair. Sol was engrossed in reading the documents she'd seen him holding earlier, his nose practically next to the paper. She sipped her coffee, nibbled at a rugelach, and waited. Even upside down, the handwriting looked familiar. Where had she'd seen it before? It was almost half-past noon. She wondered how much longer this would take, and looked out the window at the traffic.

"Well," he yelled, startling her. "Ida is quite fond of you, young lady."

That explained the familiarity of the handwriting on the paper he was reading.

"I'm quite fond of her. She's a wonderful person."

They nodded at each other.

"What do I need to do now? Do I give you a retainer?"

He waved his hand. "Not to worry. Ida asked me to take care of this matter for you. I'm her lawyer and financial manager, so there's no need for you to pay."

"Is that legal? I thought I had to give you a dollar at least. That's what they show in all the legal thrillers."

He grinned at her. "You want to give me a dollar?"

"Yes."

"Okay!" He put his hand out and Sarah placed a bill on his palm. He waved it at her, then placed it on the desk. "Now we shake on it!"

They shook hands and while he began to laugh

again, Sarah had a feeling she was going the one who be laughing all the way out the door. "Goodbye, Mrs. Weinstein. Have a nice day!"

"You, too, Ms. Ash Wednesday!"

A cab sat at the curb with the motor running. Sarah tapped on the glass and asked if he was available. "Yes, ma'am. I've been waiting for you."

Sarah glanced back up at the office window. Molly waved and smiled. Sarah thought she could hear laughter, too, but that was probably just her imagination. A short ride later, she climbed out in front of the main entrance to the hospital. "What do I owe?"

"Nothing. It's on Mrs. Weinstein's account."

"Can I give you a tip?"

"Nope. She said not to take any money from you. Have a good day."

Did Molly think she was too poor to afford a cab ride? Sarah had enough money for cab rides—just not to pay all her mother's past due bills. She took a deep breath and reminded herself to have an attitude of gratitude. Molly was being generous, not throwing Sarah a pity party.

A wall of payphones by the hospital entrance reminded her to check in on her mother. She pulled out her cell phone and leaned on a corner of the ATM.

"ICU. This is Debbie."

"This is Sarah, Mrs. Wright's daughter. I think I met you the night my mother was admitted."

"Yes. Your mom looks great."

Practically dropping the phone in a rush of excitement, Sarah yelled into the receiver. "Is she talking?"

"Sorry, I meant her color and vital signs were

normal. She looks like she's sleeping."

Disappointment slowed her pulse. "Oh. Same as yesterday. Yeah, she has better color now than she's had in the past five years. Must be the lack of alcohol in her system."

"Is there anything else you need?"

"Did she have the EEG yet?"

Sarah gazed at the parade of employees and visitors hustling, strolling, and sauntering by and did a double take. From the back, one of the men in a white lab coat looked like Dan. Her heart lurched, but when the physician turned his head to speak to a colleague, she realized she was mistaken.

"Hello?" Nurse Debbie asked. "Are your there?"

She shook her head to clear the nostalgia. "Sorry."

"I said, yes, she did, but the results haven't been interpreted yet. That could take a day, depending on how busy the doctor is."

"I'll be in later this evening. Tell her I called. I think she hears everything and just isn't letting on. I'm beginning to think this is her idea of a practical joke."

"That would be quite a joke."

Sol Weinstein, might feign a coma as a practical joke, she thought, now, there's a fix-up. Her mother and Sol. Perhaps they could run off to Elkton, the "Las Vegas of Maryland," and get married in one of the little chapels. Sarah smiled at the thought. She was punchy from fatigue and being on the edge twenty-four/seven. She should eat something, try to recharge her batteries. Forgoing the temptation of a freshly baked chocolate chip cookie, Sarah picked up a chicken Caesar salad and a latte at the coffee and snack bar. As she set the food down on her desk, she noticed the red message light blinking on her phone.

She put it on speaker so she could unwrap her lunch and eat while she listened to Peter's excited voice. "I found an image we can use from the National Library of Medicine Web site. It's an 1886 etching of a toddler with a facial malformation caused by congenital syphilis. I printed it out, and I'm going to go put it on the poster when I get a break between patients."

Way to go, she thought. That should help put a little punch in his poster.

A second voicemail. Peter, again, but this time his voice shook. "Sarah, when you get in, come over to the Pediatric Clinic right away. I have something to show you. Marian needs to see it, too."

So much for lunch.

Peter was with a patient when Sarah arrived moments later at the clinic. Surrounded by mothers, babies and toddlers, she sat in the waiting room. Two boys fought over a bright yellow toy truck while a little girl with pink bows in her curly pigtails sat on her mother's lap and sucked her fingers. A ceiling mounted television blared cartoons day and night.

Sarah was sipping her coffee, watching a show about a dog with a badge chase a rascally cat burglar when Peter emerged from the exam room, looking pale and drawn.

"What happened? Bad diagnosis for a kid? You look ill."

"When you see this, you will, too." He held a manila folder in his hand. He led the way to Marian's office and passed by the poster.

"Any response to your 'Comments?' sign?"

He gave a grim little laugh and shook his head.

"You could say that."

"What's the emergency?" Marian asked when they entered her office.

"This." He lay the folder down on Marian's desk and opened it. On the white column, marked "Comments?" someone had written "Satan pretends to be an angel."

The sight of the reddish-brown letters made Sarah put her hands behind her back. "I hate to be all CSI, but doesn't that look like dried blood?"

"Where and when did you find this?" Marian asked.

Sarah related about the placement of the poster, her suggestion to put up the comments sheet, and their two hour expedition to the archives. "It's a little after one now," she continued, "that hallway is secured with a swipe card from both the main corridor and the clinic side. Only employees, faculty or students can enter that area."

Marian asked, "Peter, do you feel this is targeted at you or the poster?"

After an exchange of glances with Sarah, Peter said, "I think it's about the poster and the investigation we're doing in the Clinic."

Marian nodded. "Agreed. We've found more cases of congenital syphilis associated with that same church. I'll have to make another call to the police."

Back in her office, Sarah tossed the wilted salad in the trash and pulled out her marked-up to do list. She started to write "Call Dan," then scratched it out.

She drummed her fingers on her desk, yanked out the Greater Baltimore telephone book, and started looking up "Woods." Perhaps one of the hundreds of

"Woods" on the three pages of fine print would be related to the Bessie Woods in that photo. She gave the same spiel with each phone call:

"Hi, this is Dr. Sarah Wright, calling from the Johns Hopkins School of Medicine, Department of Pediatrics. May I please speak with Bessie Woods?"

The responses ran the gamut of possibilities—none good.

"What? Who? Nobody here by that name."

"Lady, you got the wrong number!"

"Is this another telemarketing scam? You people are unbelievable."

"I don't owe you money, so just go away."

One particularly vile stream of profanity ended with "Drop dead."

She called Woods, E., of 4555 Pecan Hollow Court, Baltimore. A recorded message in a quavering, elderly woman's voice picked up after three rings. *"You have reached the home of Dr. John and Elizabeth Woods. We are unable to come to the phone right now, but your call is important to us. Please leave a message at the tone."* The machine beeped.

Sarah opened her mouth to leave a message when a tinny, machine generated voice said, *"Mailbox full"* and clicked off.

When she looked up the address online, she was surprised to find it was less than a mile from where she lived. Well, that was convenient.

Someone, not using the usual code, tapped at the door. "Baltimore Police, ma'am. May I come in?"

When Sarah opened the door, a leprechaun of a woman with short red hair, fair skin, and freckles looked up at her. Sarah half expected her to start Irish step-dancing. The imp flashed a shield and introduced herself. "I'm Detective O'Grady, of the Child Abuse Unit, Special Investigation Section. Tell me about this research you and Dr. Lassiter have been doing."

She gave the woman a rundown on the project and her hypotheses about the results of the data. Then she told her about the events of that morning. O'Grady took copious notes, asked if she could call on Sarah in the future, shook hands with an iron grip, and left at a brisk walk. The cop was professional, speedy, and strong.

As she opened and closed her hand, still wincing, Sarah's cell phone rang. She rushed to get it. Maybe it's call from the ICU, she thought. Nope. Wrong area code. Where the heck was it from? "Hello?"

"Sarah. How are you?"

"Dan?" Her breath whooshed out of her and she plopped into her desk chair, grateful for the soft landing. "How'd you get my number?"

"You gave it to my mother. She said she saw you at the deli." His voice filled with concern. "What's going on with Ethel? Are you okay?"

She felt as if she was breathing through a straw. Heat rushed up her neck and face and her thighs trembled. Holy. Moly. If the sound of his voice could do this to her after all this time, she could only imagine what his scent would do to her. Good grief. She was doomed to love this man forever, but could he ever love her back again?

Voice cracking, she whispered, "She told you about Ethel?"

"My mother said she's in a coma. Is that true?"

"Oh, Dan, it's been terrible." Hot tears rolled down her face. "I don't know where to start. I couldn't get into everything with your mother. Things are a mess." She took a deep breath and began the saga from the time she found the police cars on her lawn. By the time she was done, he'd been quiet for so long, she thought he'd hung up. "Are you there?"

"Yes, I'm here. I'm so sorry. How are you holding up under all this?"

"I have lists of things to do as long as my arm. Debra's been supportive, but Matt's been a curmudgeon. Told me to call him when she's dead." Sarah understood her brother distancing himself from Ethel's insanity, but sometimes he could be a jerk. Even if he didn't want to help Ethel, the least he could do was extend some support to her.

"Is there anything I can do for you, Sarah?"

Dan, the man who predicted Ethel's demise, was more compassionate than her own brother. Fresh tears blurred her vision. "Your phone call's the high point of my day. I really miss—"

"Hang on. Another call's coming in."

Sarah smacked her forehead. She'd been about to tell him how much she missed him and still loved him. Stupid move. He had a girlfriend. What was she thinking? Get a grip, Sarah.

"Okay. I'm back. What were you about to say?"

"Oh, I was going to tell you about this case I'm working on." She described the poster, the note, and her conversation with the police detective. She played up how closely she worked with Peter and omitted the fact that he was married. No need for Dan to think she was pathetic, even if she was.

"You've got a lot happening in your life," he said. "I won't keep you. I just wanted to touch base and see how you were."

"Thanks for calling. That was very kind of you."

"Call me if you want to talk. I'm still your friend, Sarah."

She sat and stared at the cell phone, replaying the conversation and her body's responses in her mind. She willed him to call her back, to tell her he was through with Bobbi and ready to hop on a plane to be at her side. Given that the circumstances were similar to those that led to their break up in the first place, that was probably too much to ask of anyone, even someone as forgiving as her ex-fiancé.

Everyone had their limits, the place where they threw their hands up and said, "Enough. This isn't working." She'd passed that boundary a year ago. No point in wishing for what she could never have again. They were friends. Nothing more.

Chapter Eight

Doctors, nurses, patient families, and dietary staff crowded the ICU. Hair-netted workers delivered dinner trays for those patients who could eat by themselves, and aides attempted to feed those who couldn't.

Debbie was right, Sarah thought as she approached her mother's bedside. Ethel looked wonderful with her silver hair flowing over the pillow in an elderly version of Sleeping Beauty. She'd never thought of her mother as a physically attractive woman until that moment. In this state of suspended animation, with Ethel's mean mouth stilled and her cheeks with a blush of pink color, she looked relaxed and—dare she think it—happy.

"Mom, you look great." Sarah held her hand. "This place is like a spa for you. Maybe we'll get a manicurist up here to do your nails."

She took a deep breath. There would never be a better time to have this discussion with her mother. She began in a soft voice, just above a whisper. "Aunt Ida told about how you sent me away to save me—"

Ethel's hand twitched, then jerked. "Ohmigod." Sarah jumped out of her chair. "You moved!"

Skidding around the nursing station, Sarah launched herself into the small, glassed-in conference room where Dr. Merrill sat, sipping coffee and reading a book. "My mother's coming to. She pulled on my hand while I was talking to her!"

"Hold on a second." Dr. Merrill pointed to a chair. "Have a seat."

Sarah jiggled on her feet in the doorway. "Come with me. Now. She's moving!"

Dr. Merrill shook her head. "Let me pull up her Electronic Medical Record and see what her neurology reports say." She turned to the computer behind her and began tapping at the keyboard. "Here we are. Looks like she passed the hearing test with flying colors."

"No kidding. She jerked her hand because I was telling her something important."

"Sometimes comatose patients can have non purposeful movements," Dr. Merrill said in a sympathetic tone of voice. "It's good you talk to her. She needs to hear your voice, know you're there with her. Lots of patients who recover recall conversations they heard while in the coma."

Sarah shook her head, "No. She understood me and she responded."

"Hold on. Here's the EEG report." Dr. Merrill scanned the screen. "I'll cut to the chase and read the interpretation to you. 'Abnormal EEG. This activity differs in appearance from alpha rhythm, which occurs with normal background in its lack of reactivity. Compatible with alpha coma. Although this pattern indicates a poor prognosis, instances of recovery have been reported on occasion. Clinical correlation is recommended.' " She looked up from the computer and locked gazes with Sarah. "I'm sorry."

She heard me, Sarah wanted to shout.

No matter what Dr. Merrill quoted, she knew her mother had heard her. But that didn't matter if no one else believed her. She had to think about the future and about getting her mother the best care she could afford. Throat tight, mouth dry, she swallowed hard and tried to speak. Tears ran down her cheeks. At last she whispered, "Would you please help me find a good nursing home?"

"The Social Work Department coordinates discharge planning and skilled nursing facility placements, or SNFs." The doctor handed Sarah a box of tissues. "A few here in Maryland have traumatic brain injury programs. I think there may even be one in Pikesville. Sensory stimulation programs for comatose patients are considered experimental, aren't covered by Medicare or Medicaid."

"Do you happen to recall the name of the facility?"

The doctor's brow furrowed. "Shady Rest? Something like that."

At six in the evening, Sarah doubted she'd reach anyone in the nursing home admissions office. First thing tomorrow, she'd call them, arrange a visit. Right now, she needed to head home, take care of the animals. As she headed out to the parking lot, she realized she hadn't heard from Aunt Ida. She should have called by now. Sarah checked her cell phone for missed calls.

The battery was dead.

"Dammit." Unused to having the gadget, she'd forgotten to recharge it. She gave herself a mental smack on the forehead. Shaking her head, she pulled out the directions to 4555 Pecan Hollow Court, and with any luck, the elusive Bessie Woods or her relatives.

"Groceries first, detective work after."

Traffic was relatively light on the highway and in

the Old Court Giant grocery store. Debra and Dr. Johnson were right. It was time to take care of herself. She grabbed some eggs, egg substitute, sugar-free low fat yogurt, skim milk, apples, baby carrots, and a bag of salad for the new healthy shelf she'd be creating in the refrigerator. Then she saw a store clerk putting out freshly baked pies.

Pies equaled comfort food. God knew she needed some comfort. Just one last hurrah. Then she'd get right on her new diet. They were fruit pies. Wasn't fruit healthy? Which would it be? The cherry pie was always good, but tonight they had apple, too. She toyed with the idea of getting both, but decided she didn't want the cashier to ask her how many people were coming for dessert. On the other hand, if she did the self-serve checkout lane, there'd be no questions asked. Yes, two pies. Worst case scenario, she'd take one to work. Problem solved. Monster sweet tooth satisfied.

She checked the time. It was about a quarter after seven in the evening. If Dr. and Mrs. Woods were home, perhaps they wouldn't mind if Sarah tapped on their door and asked a few questions. She sat in the grocery store parking lot and practiced her approach.

"Yes, I'm looking for Bessie Woods. She was a patient at the Johns Hopkins Clinic in the forties, and we're doing some follow-up research."

Ewww. That didn't sound good. Visions of guinea pigs break danced in her head. She'd have to appeal to Dr. and Mrs. Woods' sense of helping other people and contributing to a greater good.

"We're hoping our work will help other kids and prevent this disease. We need your help." That was better. At least she didn't sound like Dr. Demento on a mission to experiment on humans. "Ready, set, go before you chicken out, Sarah."

A secluded cul-de-sac, Pecan Hollow Court branched off Birch Hollow Drive. The red brick house with white siding and a carport appeared to be well maintained. Sarah pulled a sales brochure out of a plastic tube hanging in front of the house. Built in 1946, the Stevenson rancher sat on an acre of land, with five bedrooms and three and a half bathrooms, all totally redone in the last ten years. It also had a workshop, storage room, recreation room, and a completely renovated kitchen with a Sub-Zero refrigerator, Wolf double oven, gas range and grill, and a five hundred-bottle wine cellar in the basement, all for only $489,999.

The real estate flyer starred "Rivah the Realtor." A color photo showed a blonde, overly made up, truly *zaftig* woman in a low cut, gold sequined sweater exposing generous cleavage. She appeared to have believed the photographer when he said, "The camera loves you, baby!" because the expression on her face belonged in X-rated videos. Under the leering lady's mug shot, the caption proclaimed, "Call Rivah and She'll Make You a Believah!"

A believer in what?

The carport was empty.

Sarah knocked at the door and peeked through the kitchen window. No furniture. Not even a kitchen chair. The lawn was mowed, and no newspapers lay on the driveway. The mailbox was empty, devoid of even a pizza flyer.

Sarah considered knocking on the neighbors' doors to ask them what happened to the Woods, but couldn't come up with a good cover story on the spot. She tucked the real estate brochure into her purse, climbed into her car, and headed home. When she was able to use her cell phone again, she'd call Rivah the Realtor. Maybe she'd tell Sarah where to find the Woods. More likely she'd try to sell her a house.

A pile of bills sat in Sarah's mailbox. "Enough already." She shoved the mail into a grocery bag, and put the key in the deadbolt lock, but before she could turn the knob, the door swung inward. "Hello?"

What you were supposed to do in case you discover a burglary? Should you go inside or stay out and call the police? Her cell phone was dead. Panic rose in her chest, quickly followed by relief. She hadn't locked the deadbolt when she rushed off to work that morning. The doorknob was loose and the latch didn't line up properly. That was all.

"Settle down, Sarah. Don't let your imagination go into hyper drive."

She set the bags down on the kitchen table. No Winston to jam his nose in her crotch, nor was Neferkitty twirling on the counter. Where were the animals?

Pins and needles prickled her skin. She looked around for a weapon and grabbed a butcher's knife out of the wooden block next to the range. Sarah crept down the hallway, slammed her bedroom door against the wall, and shrieked like a banshee as she leaped into the room with the knife held on high. For a split second, she beheld a strange tableau.

Winston was on his back in the middle of her bed, all four feet in the air, and his head on her pillow. Wrapped around his head, like a fat, brown, furry boa

103

constrictor was Mitzi. At his side, curled in a ball, was Neferkitty.

All sound asleep.

Until she awoke them with her Tasmanian Devil-woman-with-knife-routine.

Winston jumped to his feet on the bed and barked. The bed shook with the force of his fear. Neferkitty leaped at Sarah's shoulder and landed on her chest, making her lose her grip on the butcher knife. Mitzi bolted between her legs, threw Sarah off balance and knocked her on her butt. Claws firmly attached to Sarah's chest, Neferkitty held on for dear life as Sarah fell like an axed tree. A brown blur that had to be Mitzi blasted past and flew to parts unknown.

When Sarah sat up, weak with laughter, Neferkitty relented and climbed onto her shoulder. The next hour consisted of apologizing to Winston verbally and in sign language as he kept shooting her hurt looks. She fed both animals, petted, and soothed them. Mitzi had to be hiding somewhere in the house. When she settled down, she'd come out for food. Sarah plugged in her cell phone, grabbed a bite to eat, and called Aunt Ida.

Voicemail kicked in immediately. "Hi, Aunt Ida. It's just me, trying to track you down. Hope you had a good day. I'll try the hotel now. Love ya."

Calling the first hotel on her itinerary in North Carolina, Sarah asked to be connected to Ida's room. "One moment please." Keys clicked on a computer. "She hasn't checked in yet. May I take a message?"

"Are you sure?" Sarah stopped sipping her tea. "She can't drive after dark. Do you have a restaurant?"

"We do, but it's after ten in the evening, Sugar. The kitchen closed at nine."

This was odd. Totally out of character for Aunt Ida not stick to her schedule. "Is there any place nearby she might have walked to or taken a cab for dinner?"

"We're next door to a bank and a hospital, no restaurants."

The ER receptionist was absolutely certain no Ida Mae Katz had come through their doors. "Perhaps," she suggested, "you should call the State Police."

The North Carolina State Police had no report of any accident involving a large, white Cadillac with a "Mah-Jongg Maven" bumper sticker on the window, much less a woman named Ida Mae Katz.

"Since she can't drive after dark," the dispatcher suggested, "maybe she stopped at a hotel sooner rather than later."

"I hadn't thought of that," Sarah said. But why hadn't she called? It was unlike Aunt Ida to be so inconsiderate. Where the heck was she?

Unbidden, Dan's Chicago telephone number leaped into her mind. Dan hated whiners. She took a deep breath, and worked on being cheerful and upbeat. She was just calling to keep him informed of her mother's status. Hadn't he told her to call if she wanted to talk?

"Hello?"

"Dan, it's Sarah."

"Hey, how are you? Hold on a sec while I turn the TV down."

He sounded happy to hear from here. She'd read people could hear you smile on the phone. She grinned so hard her face hurt.

"I'm back. What's up?"

"I just thought I'd give you an Ethel update." She

described her visit to the ICU, the hand jerk, and the doctor's response. He made listening noises at all the right times.

"What do you think? Part of me thinks she's having a good laugh at my expense, the other part thinks she's never coming out of it."

"It's not my specialty, Sarah, but you never know with comas. There was a man who came out of a coma after nineteen years. He thought Nixon was still President."

"Rip van Winkle."

"Pretty much. How are you holding up?"

"Work is keeping me from thinking about my mother every minute of the day and freaking out. I'm trying to track down someone who was seen at the Children's Clinic in the forties." She described the project, and let him know that Peter's wife had suggested including church affiliations in the study.

"How's your Aunt Ida doing?"

"I'm not sure. I haven't heard from her since she left for Florida. I'm getting worried." She gave him the short version of her efforts to reach Aunt Ida.

"I'd give it another day before I'd call in the police. You wouldn't want to embarrass her, and make her feel she wasn't capable of taking care of herself. Older people aren't children. They deserve to be treated with dignity."

"You're right. She was annoyed with me when I questioned her driving all the way to Florida by herself." There was a lull in the conversation. "I'm sorry. I must be boring you to tears."

"It's nice to hear your voice, Sarah. I'm very glad you called."

She happy danced around the kitchen. "So, what's new with you?"

"I'm moving."

Sarah stood still. "Where are you going?"

"I've accepted a job with a vascular surgery group in Towson. I couldn't say anything before because I didn't have a signed contract, but it's official now."

Sarah sat down hard on a kitchen chair. Was the room spinning? "Towson, as in Maryland?"

"As in Maryland. My mother is ecstatic."

She's not the only one.

"It will be nice to have you in town." She decided to take the bull by the horns. She cleared her throat. "Will your girlfriend be relocating with you? And Gandalf, too, of course." Can't forget the canine from Hades, she reminded herself.

Silence stretched on too long for comfort. She wondered if the phone was dead. She pulled it away from her ear and looked at it. Nope, still lit up. Sarah swallowed hard. She'd gone too far.

His patient sigh sounded over the line. "That must have been some breakfast at the deli. If you mean Bobbi, that's over. It's just me. As for Gandalf—well, shortly after you moved away, I gave him to a family on a farm."

Sarah looked at Winston and opened her mouth in shock. "You gave him away? Why?"

"Because you were right. His behavior was outrageous, and he got worse after you moved out. He needed more attention than I could give him. And lots of space to run."

Sarah could scarcely believe her ears. He gave up his dog. And he said she was right. She would have to mark this on the calendar. In permanent marker. Could a re-do be on the horizon? She tried to remain calm, taking deep breaths before she spoke again. She felt terrible that he'd given up his dog. "I'm so sorry, Dan. I know you must miss him."

"I do, but the family has six kids. They love him and told me he's become a perfect gentleman. Said I could visit him. But that would be too hard."

He cleared his throat. She knew that sound so well. He was trying not to cry. Poor baby. "I know I made the right choice," he mumbled.

Maybe you could teach old dog new tricks. Breathless with excitement, she could barely speak. "Call me when you get into town, I'd love to see you."

Phone at her ear, she waltzed around the room, feeling happier than she had in months. Sarah caught sight of her reflection in the kitchen window. Yup, that's me, the one with the huge, goofy smile.

"How's this weekend look for you?" he asked. "My mother's trying to fix me up with some strange woman she met at the Essen Deli and I thought I'd humor her."

Sarah laughed. "We could always pretend it was all her idea."

There it was. So terribly clear.

All she could think of was how she wanted to stroke his cheek and touch his hair, lean on his chest encircled by his strong, protective arms and stay there for the rest of her natural life. She whispered goodbye and realized it sounded like a prayer. In the midst of all the angst and sorrow over her mother's situation, she'd almost forgotten what real joy felt like.

"Welcome back, Dan the Man," she said, then

added a few bars from "My Boyfriend's Back" for good measure. She raised Winston's front paws and boogied around the kitchen with him, singing at the top of her lungs.

The dark clouds had parted; the sun now shown on her life. No one and nothing could drag her back down into that deep, sucking well of despair.

Chapter Nine

At half past five in the morning, Sarah woke, still tired. She removed Mitzi from her head and Neferkitty from her crotch. Both made annoyed little mewing sounds, but went back to sleep. Winston continued to doze. She must have worn them all out the night before with her home defense routine.

Sarah's back and butt ached from falling on the floor and her shoulders hurt. Other than that, she was fine. She hadn't told Dan about her Tasmanian Devil Woman routine. There were some things best kept to oneself, especially embarrassing stories. She threw some water on her face and headed to the kitchen for some strong coffee. On her third cup, she decided it was time to wake up Winston and call Aunt Ida.

Voice mail, again. "I hope you remember to re-charge your cell phone soon. If I don't hear back from you, I'm sending out the dogs." She ended the call and set the phone down.

Winston was waiting at the door with something white in his mouth. She could just see the tail end of whatever it was. "Drop it."

He just stood there, mouth closed, tail wagging like a flag in a brisk wind. She opened the door, let him in and made him sit in the kitchen. As she yanked on the white thing, she yelled at him to "Let go!"

He finally released it when she waved a biscuit

under his nose. It turned out to be a handkerchief, slimed over with saliva and covered in dark smears.

"Yuck. Where did you get this?" She held the edge of it with two fingers. He just wagged his stubby tail, as if he had given her the greatest gift of his life. She tossed it into the garbage pail, then rushed to wash her hands.

Maybe she'd lose some weight and shape up a little before Dan moved back to town. Yeah, that was a good plan. Take her mind off her mother for a bit. Think happy thoughts. Dan. Back in town. Dan. Back in her life, back in her arms, back in her bed.

She'd better take both pies to the office. Time to find the slimmer, sexier inner Sarah. She knew she was in there, somewhere. She fed the cats, and rummaged in her closet for sneakers and a sweat suit. Tunes, earpieces, leash, dog. Ready for a jog. The sun was just beginning to push away the dark night sky when she pulled up the hood to her jacket.

They walked the tenth of a mile from the house to where the sidewalk began on the main drag, near the elementary school. Dozens of people were out walking, jogging, and strolling with and without dogs. Who knew the neighborhood was such an exercise friendly place? She should have started this ages ago.

A heavyset man with a gray beard stood at the edge of the school baseball field with a fat yellow Labrador. He called and waved at Sarah to come closer. Probably just some harmless retired guy, but caution restrained her from getting to close to him. For all she knew he was homeless, or worse, a serial killer.

"What's your dog's name?"

"Winston." Then it occurred to her that she should

probably ask his dog's name. She didn't want to be in violation of some sort of doggy etiquette. "What's your dog's name?"

"Polly. Does your dog want to play with her?"

She looked down at Winston. He glared and growled at Polly. No. He did not want to play with Polly. He wanted to eat Polly.

Sarah had to lean backwards in order to control Winston. "I don't think so."

"Why don't you let him off his leash so they can play together?"

"He'll run away." At this point, she was hoping to keep Winston from ripping Polly a new throat.

"Would he stay and play if you brought a wiener with you?"

A wiener? Did he really say *wiener*? This was getting creepy. "He'd still run away. I have to go. Bye."

The man started toward the sidewalk where she stood with Winston.

Sarah yanked at the leash and hauled Winston away from Polly and her weird owner. She vowed not to speak to anyone else on morning walks. She'd be pleasant, nod her head, smile, but there would be no more conversations, especially about dogs and wieners.

Winston rushed to greet and groin each person they approached. She finally got off the sidewalk and headed down a side street away from the crowd. She was tired and hadn't even walked a mile.

A large, green SUV passed by with a German shorthair pointer's head and neck poking out of one of the rear windows. The dog yapped non-stop. Just what they needed: a drive-by barking. For once, Winston didn't respond. She had to try this a different time of day, when fewer people were out and about with their pets. This was nuts. Time to go home.

The maple trees were on fire with gold and red leaves. The dewy grass soaked her sneakers. As the sun began to heat the lawns, steam rose as if fires smoldered deep beneath the surface. Black mailboxes smoked like chimneys, and tree trunks, leaves, and bushes gave off a hazy mist. The world looked magical, mystical, and marvelous. Too bad she didn't have a camera with her. Dan would have appreciated the moment.

"Well, Winston, that was interesting, wasn't it?" The Weimaraner gave her a big doggy grin. Yeah, he wanted to go back and have a wiener with a side order of Polly.

They approached a blind curve banked on both sides with pine trees and undergrowth. The disco music segued to a love song and her walking slowed down, too. A large red fox shot across the street in front of them and ran into the thicket. The dog yelped and lunged after the fox, dragging Sarah with him. She felt a blow to her back and was airborne. When she hit the ground, she lifted her head, saw a white van race past—

And the world went black.

****

Somewhere in the distance, a dog howled. Sarah opened her eyes and winced at the bright light. The lined face of an elderly woman swam into sight. Her head was turned at an odd, bird-like angle, looking past her. "Easy. Let me help your owner. She needs help."

Winston was lying beside Sarah, howling. She grunted, and Winston turned his head in her direction. She signed to him it was okay.

"Thank God, you're awake," the voice said. "Someone went to call the police. What happened?"

Sarah struggled to push up from the cold, wet ground. "Don't get up," the elderly woman ordered. "You might be injured."

Sarah found her voice and recounted the fox running across the road, being dragged by Winston, and the van zipping by. "I saw one flying by like a bat out of hell just a little while ago, heading toward Greenspring Avenue. I wonder if it's the same one?"

The sound of sirens approached from the direction of the school. "Here they come," the woman said. "They'll know what to do."

The sirens stopped. Officer Mike Corrigan squatted down next to Sarah, his wholesome face a welcome sight. He reached over and patted the dog on the head. "Hey, pal. What'd you and Ms. Wright get into now?"

Sarah repeated her story, feeling a little silly talking to him from the ground. She was fine. Just needed to sit up and show them, but he insisted she stay down. "Did you see it happen?" he asked the elderly woman.

"I found her passed out. She just opened her eyes a few minutes ago. I did see a white van speed by."

Officer Mike motioned to two paramedics who approached with caution. Winston allowed them to take Sarah's vital signs and check for broken bones. While they poked, prodded, and felt where she had no complaints, Mike scribbled in a small notepad, stopping only to ask for details.

"If it hadn't been for Winston chasing that fox and dragging me into the trees, I think I'd be dead."

"Aside from the van being white, do either of you

recall anything else about it? A license plate number?"

"No. I just saw it racing off," Sarah said. "I wonder if it's the same one I saw yesterday morning."

"Do you remember the Sniper Shootings? I must have stopped about a hundred white vans during that investigation. If you don't have a plate number, or another distinguishing characteristic, it'll be impossible to find."

A young paramedic with greasy hair, a pockmarked face and garlic breath broke into the conversation. "We gotta take you to the hospital."

"Do I have any broken bones?"

"We didn't feel anything, but that don't mean nothing. We'll take you to Randallstown Community," the second paramedic said and spat out a huge wad of chewing gum.

These guys made Sarah's skin crawl. "I'm not leaving my dog. I'll sign a waiver."

The paramedics exchanged glances. The Greaser shrugged and said, "Suit yourself. I'll get the form."

The elderly woman had waited throughout the exchange. "Is it okay for me to go now? I need to get home."

"Could I get your name, address, and telephone number?"

"Woods," she replied. "I live on Pecan Hollow Court."

Heart racing, Sarah almost sat bolt upright. "Woods? Elizabeth Woods?"

"No. Bernice. Elizabeth is my sister-in-law." The woman's brow furrowed. "Why do you ask?"

"I've been trying to reach her about a medical matter." Fearing she'd alarm the elderly woman, Sarah decided not to tell her the nature of the investigation.

Bernice shook her head. "Elizabeth had to go into a nursing home a few months ago."

Officer Mike cleared his throat. "The paramedics need Ms. Wright's signature."

A few yards away, the Greaser waved a clipboard with a piece of paper. Sarah motioned for him to come over. Despite her freezing butt, she wasn't eager to stand up until after the paramedics left. No need to give them reason to toss her into the wagon.

The sketchy EMT handed her the clipboard and a pen. She signed it and thanked him for his understanding. "No problem." He snatched it out of her hand and stomped off.

Officer Mike returned and stood over her. "I can't find any tire tracks in the grass. Is it possible you got dragged by the dog and tripped over a tree root and that's why you 'flew' through the air? Maybe it's just a coincidence the van was driving by at the same time."

"I guess it's possible, but why would I have felt a blow on my back if I wasn't struck by the van?"

"Our minds can play tricks on us. Happens all the time when an accident occurs. Adrenaline is rushing around. People get confused."

"Usually I'm not confused." She wavered a bit under scrutiny, doubting her memory. Had the shock of hitting the ground and passing out scrambled her perceptions? "Usually I'm very accurate in my observations."

"Always a first time."

This wasn't getting anywhere. Sarah decided to change the subject. "Any possibility you could give Bernice, Winston and me a lift home? I drank two cups of coffee before I left the house."

Officer Mike smiled. "I'll give you a ride home if you promise not to wet the seat."

"I'll do my best."

"Give me your hands. Let's see if you can walk."

After he pulled on her hands and she stood up on wobbly legs, Bernice gasped.

"What's wrong?" Sarah croaked. "Did I wet my pants already?"

"Officer, look at the back of her jacket," Bernice indicated with a nod of her head.

"Turn around, Ms. Wright." He whistled. "I stand corrected."

"Why do you say that?" She winced from painful muscle spasms and gave up on turning her head.

"Unless your jacket had the outline of something about the size and shape of a headlight in dirt on it when you left your house this morning, then it appears you were, indeed, struck by a van."

Rubber legs betrayed her. She teetered and Officer Mike grabbed her elbow. "Okay. Let's get you in the car. You and Winston can ride in the back. Ms. Woods, why don't you ride up front with me?"

Winston leaped into the back seat, and Sarah crawled in behind him. A metal cage divided the front and back, and the door closed with a heavy thud. With Officer Mike's assistance, Bernice climbed into the front passenger seat. "I'll take Ms. Woods home first, okay?"

"Fine by me."

When he stopped, Sarah remembered her manners. "Bernice, thank you for all your help. Is there some way I can thank you? Can I take you to dinner?"

"That's not necessary. It's what anyone would have done."

"Sorry I messed up your day."

"It's okay, I can go see her later. She's happy whenever I get there."

"At the nursing home, you mean?"

"What?" Bernice looked at Sarah with a puzzled expression. "Oh. No. I saw my sister-in-law yesterday."

It was Sarah's turn to look puzzled.

"I meant my niece. She lives in a group home for adults with disabilities. We had to move her there after they closed the Rosewood Center."

****

Officer Mike drove Sarah and Winston home at about ten miles an hour, scanning the neighborhood. His radio crackled in the background. Dazed, Sarah stared out the window at passing cars. As they inched down her street, a car approached and then passed them on the opposite side of the street.

The Heckler locked eyes with Sarah, did a double take and smirked. Sarah was certain the harpy thought she'd been arrested. Perfect. Just perfect.

The police car turned into the cul-de-sac. Officer Mike climbed out of the driver's seat and released them from the cage. Sarah invited him in for a cup of coffee. She thought it was the least she could do for him.

"No, thanks, I have to get going." He handed her a gray brochure. "This is a crime victims' pamphlet. That's your complaint number. You'll need it if you want a copy of the police report." He fished in his shirt pocket. "Here's my card. If you see the van again, call me. Any questions?"

"No. Thanks for everything."

"Take care." He reached down and patted Winston's head. "You, too."

The cats stared at Sarah as she entered the kitchen. Mitzi had commandeered a dishtowel from the front of the range. Neferkitty stood on the kitchen counter, poised to leap. The thought of the cat landing on Sarah's shoulder was too painful to bear. She hobbled to the bathroom as fast as she could, turned on the hot water, peeled her clothes off, and assessed her naked body in the mirror.

At one time, she had been slender, almost svelte, and sexually attractive. Dan had loved her body. He had even loved her breasts, although she thought they were too small. "They're perfect. When you're old, your breasts will still be above your waistline, unlike women with melon-sized breasts."

Dan and Sarah had made love on their first date. Progress had been slowed down by the snap in the crotch of her body suit. After fumbling for what seemed to be an eternity, he yanked it apart, yelling, "I got you at last!"

They fell back on the couch, laughing and lusty, paired in perfect union until she was sore and he was limp from exhaustion. The chemistry between them was so intense, fatigue didn't last long. They invented places to have make love, even pulling off the interstate one night to do it in his tiny sports car. The stick shift had added an interesting dimension.

She smiled at the memory of their tearing at each other's clothes like sex crazed teenagers, heedless of the headlights passing by. He had made Sarah feel like Venus. Today, however, she was feeling old, fat, beat up, and un-goddess-like.

Her reflection showed a myriad of scratches on her face, with a pattern of dark blue spots blooming under and around the scrapes. No doubt about it, she was going to have a black eye.

Even her breasts were beginning to show bruises. As she turned her neck with difficulty, she saw a large curved blue spot on her flank. That must have been a huge headlight, she thought. She stepped into the shower, adjusted the water temperature, and tried to clear her mind while shampooing her hair and soaping her battered body.

Her thoughts skipped to her conversation with Bernice Woods. "*I meant my niece. She lives in a group home for adults with disabilities. We had to move her there after they closed the Rosewood Center.*"

Toweling off, she mused over her incredible, dumb luck at finding the Woods family. Here she'd been looking for Elizabeth Woods and it turns out there were not one, but three Woods: a mother, sister-in-law, and a daughter. Aunt Ida's favorite phrase ran through her mind: "There are no coincidences."

Aunt Ida. Sarah padded into the kitchen and dug her cell phone out of her jacket pocket.

No messages. No missed calls. She tried calling her again, got the voicemail again, left a message again, and had the feeling something was terribly wrong.

Chapter Ten

After muscle spasms seized Sarah's neck as she dressed, she accepted the obvious truth that she'd have to go to the ER. She skipped the make-up because no amount of foundation would cover the bruises and scratches.

Before she left the house, she pulled Ida's itinerary off the kitchen cabinet door and began calling all the places in North Carolina she had called the night before. Once again, no one knew anything about Ida Katz. She called all the other places on her itinerary and all the state police along the way. No sign of Aunt Ida and no reports of accidents involving large a white Cadillac bearing her license plate and "Mah-Jongg Maven" bumper sticker came from her inquiries.

She called Sol Weinstein's office, but he was out. Molly said she'd leave him a message. She, too, was concerned that Sarah hadn't heard from Aunt Ida. Molly agreed it was out of character. Sarah was getting zip, zero, zilchand *bupkes*.

Where the hell was Aunt Ida?

"Dammit, dammit, dammit!" She slammed her palm down on the kitchen table. The cell phone bounced off the table and landed on the floor with a clatter. It rang and she snatched it up. "Where the hell have you been?"

"That's a fine hello," yelled a gravelly smoker's

voice with a strong New York accent.

Sarah grimaced and pulled the phone away from her ear. "Sorry, Mrs. Rosen. I thought you were Aunt Ida. I've been trying to reach her since last evening. She's not answering her phone, and she's not in any of the hotels where she said she'd be staying."

"She's a big girl. She can take care of herself. You young people think you're the only ones who can be in charge of your lives. We crossed the streets long before you did, *girlchik*."

Sarah felt a chill go down her spine and shuddered. The stress must be catching up to me, she thought. Maybe I'm overreacting. "You're right, I'm sure. With my mother in the hospital, I worry a lot. How are you?"

She wondered if Dan had told her they'd spoken. She glanced at the clock on the stove. Nearly ten o'clock. No great parking space today. Mrs. Rosen said something to her. "I'm sorry, what did you say?"

"I asked if you were available to meet my son this Sunday for bagels and lox at Essen Deli? He's coming into town for a visit." She began to cough like she was hacking up a piece of lung.

"This weekend?" Sarah felt panic rising. She wanted to see Dan but not looking like this. She needed an excuse.

"*Vot* other time of the week would this Sunday be?"

"Well, you see, um, I ah, I'm, um." She couldn't think fast enough.

"*Vot? Vot* is it already?"

"I was hit by a van this morning. I look like I had a fight with a truck and lost."

"Now that's an excuse I've never heard before."

Sarah heard the older woman take another drag on the cigarette. "Come anyway, he's seen worse."

"Well, thanks very much, but—"

"Okay, so we'll see you on Sunday at nine in the morning at the deli. We gotta beat the crowd coming out of religious school or we'll never get a table."

"Okay, see you then. Thanks for calling."

Mrs. Rosen coughed and hung up.

Panic bubbled. She wanted to see Dan but not when she looked like a battered woman. "What am I going to do?"

The clock edged toward eleven. She had to call the office and let them know what was going on. She didn't want to bother Marian so she called her Grants Administrator, Arlene Brown.

Arlene was a strikingly beautiful, God-fearing, intensely private African American woman. She was so modest, she always wore long sleeve blouses and dresses, even in the summer. She had grown up in the tough neighborhood surrounding the Hopkins Medical complex. At twenty-two, she was one of the smartest people Sarah had ever worked with.

One time, Arlene had reviewed the monthly printouts for the child abuse and neglect prevention grant Sarah worked on and found an unexplained equipment expense of $3,500.

"Sarah, what was this big purchase for?"

Flabbergasted, Sarah pulled the print out over and stared at it. "I have no clue. I haven't bought anything that expensive since the project started. Are there any purchase orders to go with this?"

"I can't find any," Arlene said.

An unsettling thought occurred to her. "Does

anyone else have access to this account?"

"Yes, there are a few people. Let's keep quiet and see what happens."

Two weeks later, Sarah saw Arlene examining a stack of new computer boxes in the hallway. "What's up?" Sarah asked.

"Seems these items just appeared. No one's claiming them. They've been stripped of their paperwork."

Just then, Diane, an extremely overweight administrative assistant appeared. She wore a denim Western skirt and blouse, silver and turquoise jewelry, fancy black and red cowboy boots, and way too much blush on her pale white cheeks. Sarah wondered if Diane was going to a country and western singers' audition.

With a major claim to fame as the control freak in charge of supplies, Diane put faculty and staff through an inquisition before unlocking the supply closet of pens, pencils, and pads of paper. She waved a piece of paper. "Here's the purchase order."

"Let me see that," Arlene said.

Diane handed Arlene the sheet of paper. "Remember when we hired that new faculty person and then she decided not to come?" Diane's speech was pressured, almost breathless. "Well, I had already ordered her a PC and printer. You can tell it's a faculty computer because it has an Ethernet card to access the Internet. You know, we administrative staff aren't allowed to have that. It must have been put on the wrong account number, don't ya think?"

Arlene looked up from the sheet of paper. "This is a photocopy. Where's the original PO?"

Diane flushed. "Oh, sure, no problem." She returned with the original purchase order and handed it to Arlene.

After holding it up to the light to inspect it, Arlene turned to Diane. "This PO has been altered. Do you want to tell me the truth now, or shall I call the Baltimore coppers about your attempted theft?"

Diane burst into tears. "You owe me, dammit! I'm getting married and moving to Arizona and all you people gave me was a crummy platter, a book and a card. Ten years and you didn't even give me a decent going-away party. Deli platters? I deserved a dinner and drinks and a band. I deserve this computer and printer and anything else I can lay my hands on."

"Diane," Arlene said.

"What?"

Unfazed, Arlene said calmly, "If you attempt to touch anything, I will have you arrested. Sarah, please stay with Diane while I call Security."

"Okay."

Diane stamped her red and black cowboy boots. "You can't do this to me. I've been here longer than either of you. How dare you treat me this way!"

She was still stamping when Security arrived to escort her out of the building.

Arlene could smell trickery, fraud, or deceit at a mile away. She was a watchdog without being a control freak, an unusual combination of traits. When Sarah called to tell Arlene what had happened, the voicemail picked up with instructions to "Press zero if this is urgent."

"General Pediatrics, this is Jazmin Bedford. How may I help you?"

"This is Sarah. I just wanted to let you guys know I was hit by a van this morning while I was out walking the dog. I think I'm okay, but I need to stop by the Adult ER and be seen."

"It's been one terrible day. First Arlene. Now you."

Sarah clutched the phone tighter. "What do you mean? Is she hurt?"

"She's okay, but her Mama had a stroke. Arlene's pretty torn up about it."

"I'm so sorry. Where's her mother now? Any word about her condition?"

"She's in Randallstown Community. That's the closest hospital to them," Jazmin said.

"Arlene must be going crazy. If you speak with her, please tell her she's in my prayers, and give her my cell phone number if she wants to call me."

"You want me to tell Dr. Kirby what's going on?"

"Yes. I'll probably be in the ER for the rest of the afternoon. I just didn't want people to think I abandoned ship."

"I'll take care of it, don't you worry."

The outpatient parking lot was full, as were the surrounding flat lots and more distant garages. Sarah drove back to the outpatient center, pulled up to the valet stand, and asked them to park her old beater of a car. She limped away, leaving the valets flipping a coin to see who would be forced to drive it. The good news was no one would ever be tempted to steal it, regardless of where they parked it.

The Adult ER was rocking and rolling, another day in Charm City, home of drug dealers, gangs and random acts of violence. Sarah checked in at the front desk, grateful she'd brought her guilty pleasure with her: the latest novel from her favorite romance author. No sooner did she sit down, than her name was called.

"Sarah Wright?" asked a pretty young African American woman in blue scrubs. "Come with me, please."

Wincing at the assorted muscle aches and pains she was just discovering, Sarah pushed herself up out of the hard plastic seat and followed the young woman down a hallway, past a lineup of wheelchairs and gurneys. "Did I forget to complete a form?"

"Nothing's wrong with your paperwork." She flashed a blinding smile at her. "Come with me, and we'll get you seen as soon as possible."

Who had intervened on her behalf? It had to be someone with clout. Had Marian Kirby called down to tell them to see her immediately? Sarah knew waits in the ER for non-life-threatening emergencies were legendary. People sometimes sat for as long as twelve hours before a doctor saw them.

The nurse led Sarah into a four-bed room occupied by three other people. She pulled a long gray curtain around the one empty bed, and invited Sarah to sit on a chair. She held a pen poised over a clipboard. "Tell me why you're here."

Sarah described her not-so-healthy walk and pointed to the various places on her face, chest, and back where she had cuts, scratches, and bruises. She also told her about refusing to be taken anywhere by the two creepy EMTs. She finished with, "I wanted to come here, where I know and trust people."

"I know what you mean," the young woman said.

"I'm going to have a humongous bruise on my back, because that's where the van hit me. But that's not what's hurting me the most. My neck is killing me."

Gently palpating, the nurse asked where it hurt the most. Sarah shrieked in pain when she touched the sides. "I'm going to get the ER resident in here as soon as I can. You just sit and relax for a little bit." She looked down at the book in Sarah's hand. "What are you reading?" She held the cover of the latest New York Times best seller up for review.

"Is it the author's latest one?"

"Yes. I had it on pre-order for a month."

"Me, too. I'll see if I can track down the resident. While I go look for her, why don't you put on this very fashionable gown?" She handed Sarah the traditional blue and white Johnny coat that leaves the butt exposed and left in a swirl of gray cloth and jangling shower curtain rings.

Sarah decided she'd rather clutch the two seams together in front than have them flapping uncontrollably in back. She had just gotten to the second chapter in the book, when the curtain opened and an attractive, twenty-something, white woman with shoulder-length chestnut brown hair came in. She entered the curtained area with her head down, reading the clipboard.

"How are you doing?" The physician looked up and stopped in her tracks. "How's the other guy look?"

"A large white van, with one very clean headlight."

"Tell me what happened."

Sarah repeated the story while the doctor palpated and prodded. Then she had Sarah turn around and raise the back of the gown so she could see her injuries. More probing followed.

"You have so many hematomas, not to mention the

shiner you have on your right eye, I'm a little concerned you might become anemic. I want to do a hemoglobin and hematocrit to make sure you're not bleeding too much."

"Please tell me you're not talking about a blood transfusion."

"It's more likely you'll need to take iron supplements for a while until your numbers come up. What about your neck?"

She listened and then induced the same shriek the nurse caused. "You just won a trip to Imaging."

"You mean I get to spend time in out-of-the-way rooms with strange men? Then this is my lucky day. I haven't been in a dark room with a man in a really, really long time."

The doctor laughed. "Don't get too excited. It's mostly female radiologists and rad techs these days. Let me see how quickly we can get you in and out. In the meantime, we'll get you fitted with a cervical collar and get your blood work done." She parted the curtain from the wall, leaving Sarah alone with her book.

The same nurse returned with an assortment of soft cervical collars. "Which one of these accessories would you like?"

Few sights were more unattractive than cervical collars. Now, not only would she be bruised when she saw Dan, but also wearing this ugly foam neck brace. "Wouldn't you think someone would have designed a pretty one by now?"

The nurse agreed.

"If I wear the white one, I'll look like a roll of toilet paper. If I wear the Caucasian flesh tone one, I'll look like I have a really fat neck. I think I'll take the black one and make a fashion statement."

Five minutes later, her blood work was drawn, followed by a trip to radiology and back. They were working on some kind of land-speed record that day. In less than forty-five minutes, the MRIs were completed and Sarah was back in the cubicle with her book.

"I have good news," the ER doctor said a few minutes later. "Are you ready?"

"Hit me," Sarah said. "No, on second thought, don't."

"You have no broken bones. All soft tissue injuries."

"Now what?"

"Do you need anything for pain?" The doctor pulled out a prescription pad.

"Can't I take aspirin?"

"Not with those bruises. How about some Tylenol with codeine?"

"Will it knock me out?"

"You're not supposed to operate heavy machinery or drive when you take it. You probably want to keep it for bedtime. Get dressed and meet me out at the front desk. We'll get your paperwork and prescriptions all squared away out there."

Slow arm movements helped Sarah to avoid sudden jabs of pain. She hobbled out to the front desk, keeping her head straight and heard a familiar voice. "Look at you all decked out for a night on the town."

A tall young African American woman, with braids, lots of gold jewelry, high cheekbones, and expressive brown eyes, Jazmin was all smiles. Today she wore a purple dress with a long red scarf and red high-heeled shoes with pointed toes and sexy ankle straps. Sarah's feet hurt just looking at them.

"Were you the person who got me seen before the next millennium?"

"I told you I'd take care of it." She grinned at Sarah's surprise and pointed to the nurse who had taken care of Sarah. "I called my twin sister, Ayana."

Sarah teetered and Ayana ran over to Sarah's side. "Steady there, Dr. Wright."

"Twins?"

"Fraternal." Jazmin smiled. "She's three minutes older than me. Got all the brains, too."

"You're twin angels. I owe you."

"No, you don't. I'm just returning a few favors."

Tears welled up and dribbled down Sarah's cheeks. Damn, she was tired of being so emotional. "Thank you, Jazmin. You're too kind. I've been having a hell of a week. This is one of the nicest things anyone has done for me since my aunt drove away and disappeared." She stopped, stunned at her own choice of words.

"Hey now, Dr. Wright." Jazmin came over and took her arm. "Let me take you up to your office. Want some coffee?"

Afraid she'd be bawling like a baby in the middle of the ER if she opened her mouth, Sarah could only nod and allowed Jazmin to take the lead.

Jazmin held Sarah's arm and walked with her as if she was Queen Elizabeth. She guided Sarah to her desk chair. "I'll be right back. Sit and relax." She refused money for the coffee and left.

The computer moaned and groaned as it booted up. Sarah kept thinking about how she'd vocalized her worst fear. Aunt Ida had driven away and disappeared. She was not to be found anywhere along her route.

Should she go to the police? Or would they laugh at her and tell her "She's old enough to take care of herself," like Gertrude? She sat there and deliberated her options. A soft, scratching noise came from the door. Jazmin. Probably struggling with coffee and keys. Sarah shuffled a few steps, and a piece of white paper slid underneath the door. This one said, "Suffer the little children."

She knew enough not to touch it. By the time she got to the door and opened it the hallway was empty. "Is someone there? Do you want to talk to me? I'm here. Hello?"

No reply. Only the scent of a familiar perfume she couldn't place hovered in the air. Soon, even that was gone.

Chapter Eleven

Ida heard footsteps overhead and looked up. She had no idea of how long she'd been held captive. Her watch didn't have dates and her sense of time was distorted, thanks to the constant light of the overhead bulb. Sandwiches appeared and the water pitcher refilled. She slipped in and out of fitful sleep. Were they drugging her?

"Hello?" she called. "Anyone?"

A door creaked open and a wedge of light appeared. Heavy footsteps stomped down the stairs, followed by a lighter set. The two approached her, one carrying rope. They wore the same outfits as before, but this time, instead of ski masks, they wore stockings over their heads, distorting their features. She could see dark hair on the taller one, and light hair on the shorter one, but that was all she could distinguish.

"Ready to go for a ride?" the taller man asked.

"Where are you taking me?" Ida asked.

"We thought you might want to go home," the shorter one said in a husky voice.

"Home? Yes, I'd like to go home."

"Then, be a good girl. Don't scream, and we'll take you home," the taller man said.

Ida sat without resisting as one man tied her hands after which the other undid the shackles and led her up the stairs. She passed through a kitchen with dishes stacked in the sink. Large brown roaches crawled around the counters. She shuddered and wondered if she'd eaten any bugs in the sandwiches.

The van sat in a connecting garage. She was motioned to get into the van and sit in a lawn chair. The two thugs said nothing on the twenty-minute trip. When the door slid open, Ida wept with relief to see that she was indeed home, and inside her own garage. She staggered out of the van, helped down by the larger man. The smaller man dragged the lawn chair out of the van and dropped it in front of the workbench.

"Thank you," Ida said.

An automatic courtesy, but the big man snickered. "Oh, yeah, you're going to thank us a lot."

He pulled on her wrist, dragging her to the workbench. "Put your hands up here."

Ida stared at him. "I don't understand. What are you doing?"

"Hold on," the shorter man said. "I'll get something to help." He returned a few moments later with a small bottle. "Have a sip. You'll feel better."

"That's straight GHB!" Ida said. "If I drink that, it will knock me out. It might kill me."

The larger man turned around, holding a power saw. "Maybe you won't want to feel this," he said and clicked the on switch.

****

"Okay, let's see if I've got this right." Detective O'Grady reviewed her notes. "You're sitting in your desk chair. You hear a noise, like a scratching sound. You're injured, so you can't move fast. You go to the door and this piece of paper comes underneath. Is that correct?"

"Yes."

"Then what happened?"

"I glanced at the paper on the floor. I didn't touch it. I stepped around it and opened the door. The hall was empty. I even called to let whoever it was know that I was here if they wanted to see me."

"But you moved it to your desk. How did you handle it?"

With a nod toward her friend in purple and red, Sarah said, "Jazmin came along right after this happened to bring me coffee. She got a pair of latex gloves from the Pediatric ER so I could touch it as I didn't want it to be stepped on."

"Good, good." She made notes. "Anything else you can recall?"

"Yes, but it's probably irrelevant."

"Let me be the judge of that."

"There was a smell of perfume right when I opened the door. It's a scent I recognized, but I can't place it. I'm not sure how it helps."

"It may have been someone passing by wearing heavy perfume, or the person who put this under the door may have been wearing it. It's like a good jigsaw puzzle. Until we put all the pieces together, we may not see the picture." Detective O'Grady pulled a plastic evidence bag and latex gloves from one pocket, put the gloves on before sliding the paper into the bag.

"It's from the Bible."

Jazmin spoke for the first time since Detective O'Grady arrived. "Parents brought children to Jesus for a blessing and the disciples told them to go away. Jesus got angry with his followers. He said, 'Suffer the little children to come unto me and forbid them not: for of such is the Kingdom of God!' "

"Jazmin, how'd you remember all that?" Sarah asked. She was lucky she could remember the twenty-third psalm, much less anything else from the Bible.

"I was at the top of my Sunday school class with Pastor Black."

"Do you recognize this phrase?" Detective O'Grady flipped through her notebook. "Here it is. 'Satan pretends to be an angel.'"

Jazmin looked thoughtful. "I don't recall anything like that. Satan is mostly being told to get behind or out of someone."

"Well, it was worth a shot. Thanks." Detective O'Grady snapped her notebook shut and put it back in her pocket.

"I'll be going, then," Jazmin said. "You okay, Dr. Wright?"

"I'm fine, Jazmin. Thank you for everything." Gratitude flooded through her, filling her chest with affection for her friend. "I'd hug you, but I hurt too much."

"Don't worry," Jazmin said. "I got your back."

Sarah was still smiling after the door closed. "What a terrific person. We just never know, do we, Detective?"

"You're right about that. By the way, it was a good thing you didn't touch that paper."

"I've watched enough CSI to know better."

"That's true. But I was referring to something else."

"What?"

"The words on the last piece of paper were written in human blood."

Sarah had suspected as much when she first saw the note. "I was afraid of that. Does Peter know?"

"Fortunately, he watched the same TV shows."

Relief flooded Sarah. She knew the hepatitis virus could survive at least a week in dried blood. Anyone could be contagious.

"Well, unless you have something else for me, I'm going to go see doctors Kirby and Lassiter to give them an update."

"No, that's all I can think of right now," Sarah said.

"Here's my card. Think of anything, call me."

Almost four o'clock. Sarah needed to get her prescriptions filled, but she had other things she needed to do, too.

****

Peter and Marian stared at her with shocked expressions. Marian spoke first. "You look terrible. Why did you come in to work?"

"Sarah, do you need a ride home?" Peter asked. "I'm not on call so I can drive you."

"Hold on a minute," Sarah said. "I'm here because I wanted to be seen in our own ER. Much to my amazement, Jazmin has enormous influence over getting people seen quickly in the Adult ER. I had no idea her twin sister worked downstairs."

"Oh, yes. I learned early on when I moved to Baltimore that you never know who's a relative," Marian said.

"What'd they find?" Peter asked.

"Soft tissue trauma, lots of hematomas and many scratches. No broken bones though. Hence, this attractive cervical collar."

"When we heard you'd been hit by a van, we

thought you'd be in a body cast," Peter said.

"My dog jerked me into the trees in the nick of time. The van grazed me."

"I hope you gave him extra biscuits," Marian said, worry creasing her round face.

"You bet I did." Tired of being the center of all this unwanted attention, Sarah changed the subject. "I assume Detective O'Grady told you about the latest note?"

"Yes. I told her we found more recent cases of congenital syphilis connected with the same church. We gave her all the contact information in our records. My concern is that many of these families move three to four times a year." Marian played with a pen. "They get a few months behind in their rent, the sheriff's deputy shows up, and all their belongings get dumped on the curb. No forwarding address. We might see them here in the clinic once a year or never again. She has her work cut out for her."

"She's going to need an army of investigators to track these people down." Sarah shifted the weight on her feet, the only parts of her body that weren't sore. "Do you think they still attend the same church?"

Marian and Peter stared at Sarah as if she'd sprouted a horn out of the center of her forehead and sang a karaoke song.

"Why would a family whose daughter was molested by a sexual predator continue to attend the same church?" Peter asked.

"What if the daughter was afraid to tell them she was molested, much less who molested her? Most sexually abused children know their abuser. Or, what if the daughter told but her parents didn't believe her?"

"I'm sure Detective O'Grady has a good handle on this," Marian said. "Why don't we let her do her job, and we'll do ours. Okay?"

"I was just thinking out loud. I have no desire to play Nancy Drew."

Peter grinned. "I think you're a little old for Nancy Drew or Harriet the Spy. You're more like Abby in NCIS with that black collar."

She arched an eyebrow at him. "Does that make you Ducky?"

"Children, that's enough sassing each other." Marian shook her head. "Sarah, at the moment, you may feel okay, but by tomorrow morning you'll feel every bump and bruise. Go home, and do not come into work tomorrow. You need to rest and get in a hot bathtub for those muscle spasms. Did you get a prescription for pain?"

"Yes."

"Go home."

"Yes, ma'am. Have a good evening. I'll call you tomorrow," Sarah said.

"Need a ride?" Peter asked.

"Getting my car back might be a challenge, but I can drive. When last seen, the valets were arguing which lucky fellow was going to have to park it."

A short time later, Sarah clutched the steering wheel and looked right and left with care. Onward to visit her mother before it was too late. She recalled seeing a pharmacy at Baltimore Medical Center. With any luck, she could drop off her prescriptions and try to catch up with the social worker about her mother's nursing home placement.

She found Dr. Merrill in the ICU Conference

Room. Sarah gave the wide-eyed physician an abridged version of her day's events before asking about her mother's status.

"Unchanged. She looks good, better than you, in fact. She's not responsive to anyone or anything. The social worker came by today. I told her you were interested in Shady Rest's coma stimulation program. She's seeing if they have a bed available. You should expect to get a call from her in the next day or so."

At the bedside, Sarah held her mother's hand, and spoke in a soft voice. "I never got to tell you how much I admire you," Sarah said brushing a stray hair off her mother's forehead. "You were so brave, standing up to Aunt Ida's step-father like that. He could have killed you. My guess is, you didn't even think twice about it."

The monitor beeped steadily overhead, background music to her life now, Sarah realized.

"You fight for the ones you love, and, yeah, with the ones you love. No one can ever say you don't care. You do care, very much, under that tough exterior, you love deeply, you hurt greatly, and you never let go, do you, Mom?"

Sarah picked her mother's hand up, held her palm to her cheek, and wept. "I'm worried about Aunt Ida. I can't reach her. It's as if she disappeared. I need you to come back, Mom. I need you here with me, helping me to find Aunt Ida. I know you wouldn't give up, you wouldn't give in."

Alarm bells went off as the numbers on the heart monitor leaped to over one hundred.

A nurse ran into the room, glanced at the monitor, and pressed a reset button. She smiled at Sarah. "Power surge."

"Power surge, my ass," Sarah said after the nurse left the room. "Mom, I know you heard me. We just have to find a way to get you awake and back to me."

****

Sarah had to make the dreaded phone call to the Baltimore County Police, but put it off for as long as she could. She tried to think of anything except the idea that Aunt Ida was missing. As she climbed the back steps to her house, rivulets of sweat rolled down her face and into her eyes. The cervical collar was cumbersome and itchy.

She picked up a box on her back porch and looked at the return address. It was from her sister and weighed a ton. Self-help books, she was sure, on how to be less enabling, less co-dependent. She opened the back door and released Winston to the great outdoors and dropped the books on the dining room table. Sarah loved her sister, but she wasn't interested in getting long distance lectures on how she should be running her life. Not now. Not with everything that was going on in her life now. If Debra and Matt couldn't support her choices, so be it.

The cats and dog demanded food. "I hear you. Half the neighbors hear you." Sarah organized their meals, then her own. Eggs and toast were the best she could do at the moment.

She sat at the table, and stared at the phone. Should she call Dan? She was avoiding the inevitable. Time to call the police. She sighed, and extracted Officer Mike's business card from her wallet. The woman who answered the phone told Sarah he was off duty. She asked for the only other person she knew.

"Detective Engelman." He sounded tired.

"This is Sarah Wright. I don't know if you remember me. You were here the evening my mother fell."

"Yes, I remember you. How's your mother?"

"Not very well, I'm afraid." She gave him a quick update.

"I'm sorry to hear that. How are you holding out?"

"Not bad for someone who was hit by a van this morning." She gave him the details of the morning hit-and-run. "Suffice it to say I'm feeling sore and paranoid."

"I guess you are. You're having a terrible week. By the way, your aunt owes me a bottle of GHB. The Maryland State Crime Lab is backed up for a month of Sundays, but I still want the second one as soon as possible."

"It's on her kitchen counter. That brings me to the main reason for my call. I can't find her anywhere. I'm worried sick."

"You can't find who anywhere?"

"Aunt Ida. She left for Florida early Monday morning and was supposed to call me when she got to her hotel. She can't drive after dark, so I got worried when she didn't call. I've tried her cell phone but I keep getting her voicemail."

"Did you try the hotel?"

"Yes, and they hadn't heard from her either. Neither had the area hospitals nor the State Police. This morning, I called every single hotel, hospital, and police authority on her itinerary from North Carolina to Florida. I got zip."

"Not good."

"I want a Silver Alert issued. How do I do it?"

"You need to call 9-1-1."

Wasn't he a detective? Wasn't he supposed to detect crimes?

Or find missing people? "Can't I tell you?"

"The procedure is you call 9-1-1 and you'll get the current patrol officer."

"Why?"

"Because that's protocol. If the officer knows the victim, it could be a conflict of interest."

Conflict of interest? He'd met her aunt once. How did that qualify as *knowing* her?

"Okay, well, I guess I'd better follow the rules." Sarah nearly slammed the phone down, but didn't want to break her only connection to Aunt Ida.

She called 9-1-1.

****

The young man in front of Sarah had a crew cut, stood ramrod straight and kept calling her "ma'am." He reminded Sarah of Joe Friday, "Nothing but the facts, ma'am," from Dragnet.

His nametag said "Officer Pollack." His gaze swept her from head to toe, and stopped at her cervical collar. "Do you need medical attention, ma'am?"

Irritation tinged her voice. "I've had more than enough today, thank you."

He wrote in a little notebook and wore the expression of a person with other things to do, and other people to see. It was ten-thirty in the evening, and Sarah had the impression he was wishing the next shift had gotten this call. She recounted the facts to him.

"Do you have a recent photograph of her, ma'am?"

"Yes, this is from last year. It was my birthday. She's missing my birthday this year." She handed him a smiling photograph of Aunt Ida with Ethel. "She's the one on the right. The other one is my mother."

Sarah gave him a description of Aunt Ida's white Cadillac and license plate, including the "Mah-Jongg Maven" bumper sticker.

"Does she have any medical conditions, ma'am?" He looked around her kitchen and his gaze latched onto the clock. He seemed to be counting each tick.

"Her license is restricted. She's not supposed to drive after dark."

He jotted a note. "Is she senile or physically or mentally disabled, ma'am?"

"No, she's very sharp," Sarah said. "What about a Silver Alert? She's a senior citizen."

"The State of Maryland uses that for people with cognitive disorders." He glanced at his watch. "Ma'am, did she leave voluntarily?"

"She goes to her second home in Punta Gorda, Florida, every year. This year, she was actually a bit late in leaving."

"Do you have any evidence that her physical safety may be in danger?"

"She's not answering her cell phone, and nobody between here and Florida knows where she is," Sarah said. "It's completely out of character for her to disappear like this. Isn't that enough to worry about an accident or an abduction?"

"It's too soon to be talking foul play, ma'am."

"When exactly is it okay to talk about 'foul play'?"

"It usually takes about a month before Homicide gets involved, ma'am."

"A month? What happens in the meantime?"

"We issue a BOLO, or a Be On the Look Out, to

everyone in Baltimore County, and we send this information to the NCIC system, and, we'll follow up on every shift."

"And the NCIC system is what?"

"The National Crime Information Center, a computerized index of criminal justice information, including missing persons."

"And?"

"And, if we get or need any more information, we'll call you."

"That's it?"

"Yes, ma'am."

She closed the kitchen door behind him and locked the deadbolt. First her mother was injured and in a coma, then Sarah was hit by a van, and now Aunt Ida was missing. What the hell was going on?

Chapter Twelve

In the middle of the night, Sarah sat bolt upright in bed, drenched in sweat, heart racing. She didn't need a psychiatric nurse to interpret her nightmare. Aunt Ida was in deep trouble. She grabbed her cell phone.

"Baltimore County 9-1-1," a woman said.

"I need to speak to someone about a kidnapping."

"Who was kidnapped, ma'am?"

"My aunt, Ida Mae Katz."

"Have you received a phone call or a ransom note?"

"No. I filed a missing person report a few hours ago with Officer Pollack. He said the police would begin a follow-up investigation and report it on every shift. I have additional information that leads me to believe she's been kidnapped."

"Ma'am, did you find blood, evidence of a struggle, or suspicious circumstances that lead you to this conclusion?"

"No. I told Officer Pollack, the last time I saw Aunt Ida she was driving away in her car, on the way to her home in Florida."

"Ma'am, what evidence do you have that a kidnapping has occurred?"

"I had a dream. She told me she was in grave danger. She was pale and shaking."

"Oh, great, a 10-96!" the dispatcher said to

someone else. Then, in a loud voice, she said, "Ma'am, have you been drinking or using other mind-altering substances?"

"I was hit by a van today. I took one Tylenol with codeine five hours ago."

"Ma'am, I think you'd better go back to bed."

"You mean you won't send out an officer?"

"Ma'am, I'd hate for you to be charged with filing a false report while under the influence of drugs."

"I tell you my aunt is missing and might be a kidnapping victim, and you tell me I'm going to be charged with a crime for reporting it? Is that what you're saying?"

"Ma'am, if you have any substantiation that there's been a kidnapping, or know where such evidence can be found, then I will send out an officer. In the meantime, I suggest you go back to bed and sleep it off. Thank you for calling Baltimore County 9-1-1." She hung up on Sarah.

Sarah stared at the phone in disbelief. Shouldn't the codeine have worn off by now? Was she "under the influence"? A rush of heat ran up her neck and face. "I'm an idiot!"

Cell phone still in hand, she found her slippers and robe, tucked the phone in her robe pocket, and headed to the kitchen. Winston followed on her heels. She let him out, turned on the coffee pot and the TV.

"And I say unto you, Harry Potter is the Devil's tool to seduce our children to witchcraft," Reverend Bobby Moore ranted. "End Days are coming, I say unto you. Witchcraft is the harbinger of End Days. Read the Book of Revelations."

Sarah wanted to throw the remote at the screen, but

instead changed the station to a nice soothing infomercial for self-cleaning mops. The next time she glanced at the clock, it was a few minutes after six in the morning. She must have dozed off. Something teased at the edge of her mind and haunted her, like the familiar scent of a perfume.

Winston ran to the door, and began to bark.

"Jeez, you must have teeny-weenie bladder syndrome." She threw open the back door. "Go and get me a clue!"

He flew out the door, barking. She paused for a moment and raced after him, her bathrobe flapping in the cool early morning air. Winston ran along the edge of his invisible fence and barked. She arrived at the top of her driveway just in time to see a white van circle the cul-de-sac. She ran down the pine-tree-lined driveway, trying to catch sight of the license plate in the pre-dawn light. The Maryland truck plate began with the letter "M" and the numbers one and three. The rest of the numbers or letters were covered in dirt or mud.

"You son of a bitch!"

The van stopped, reversed, circled the cul-de-sac and came back toward her.

She froze in place. The van was so close, she could see the face of the driver, a shaggy haired man with an expression of hatred. A pine tree stood between her and the curb. She leaped behind the tree, fell onto the ground, and rolled into Aunt Ida's yard. When she came to a stop, she fumbled for her cell phone and punched 9-1-1. "Help me! Please! He's going to kill me!"

She heard a crash of metal and above her saw the sentry pine tree shudder and sway.

She clutched the cell phone to her ear, closed her eyes, screamed, and prepared to die. The sound of the engine receded. She opened her eyes, stared at the tops of the pine trees in the early morning sky, and heard a voice.

"If you are satisfied with your message, press one. If you wish to re-record your message, press two."

She had called her voicemail.

****

"Okay," Officer Mike said. "Let's go through this again."

"How many times do you need to hear this?" Sarah sneered. "A creepy looking guy with dark, straggly hair and driving a white van attempted to run me over this morning. You have physical evidence. The pine tree at the end of my driveway has a big gash in it. There are chunks of glass from a headlight all around it, and, I'm betting it's the same headlight that did this to me."

She pulled up her sweatshirt and turned around so Officer Corrigan and his tired-looking partner, Officer Pollack, could see it.

"You can cover that up," Officer Mike said.

"I'm a victim. What are you going to do about this second attempt on my life?"

"We'll take your statement and run the partial license plate number you gave us through the system, looking through the list of thousands of white vans in registered in the state of Maryland. The partial license plate and broken headlight will help narrow it down, unless he gets the headlight repaired today."

"What about the driver? Don't you have mug shots I can look through? How about a police sketch artist? I can give a good description of the guy."

Officer Pollack rolled his eyes. "Watch a lot of cop shows, do you?"

"Not lately. I've been watching my mother in a coma in an ICU. Right now, as I'm afraid for my life, I want this man arrested."

Pollack cleared his throat, just once. "I understand you called 9-1-1 last night, stating you knew Ida Mae Katz was kidnapped. The dispatcher felt you might have been under the influence of drugs at the time. Have you taken any drugs today, Ms. Wright?"

"It's *Doctor* Wright, to you, *Officer* Pollack. For your information, in case *Officer* Corrigan has not filled you in, I was hit by a van yesterday. More likely than not, it is the same white van that attempted to run me down today." She took a deep, shaky breath. "I took one Tylenol with codeine at eleven last evening. I've had nothing but coffee since then. That is a real tree with real damage. That is real glass on the ground. This is a real cervical collar. These are real bruises and scratches on my body."

The two men exchanged glances.

Officer Mike took up the saber. "Doctor Wright, do you have evidence that makes you believe Ida Mae Katz was kidnapped? Have you been in her house and seen things that look out of place? I want to work with you here, but I need concrete evidence before I can take this any further. Otherwise, I'll look like an idiot."

"I haven't been in her house since she left town. Maybe we should start there. Want to go with me? I have her house keys. She left a bottle of GHB for Detective Engelman. Can you take it to him for me?"

"Sure, we can do that. Let me call this other information into the precinct so they can get started on looking for that van," Officer Mike said. "And, by the way, we do use mug shots. They're in digital databases now, like fingerprints, however, not one hundred percent reliable. If the guy's never been arrested, he won't show up. That's when we use a sketch artist."

"Say when and I'll be there to describe the creep."

"This isn't a formal search of the house," Officer Pollack said. "We want to be with you for reassurance that everything's okay."

She retrieved Aunt Ida's house keys and left Winston outside in his electric fenced-in space. She then called to the officers and told them she'd meet them at the back door of Ida's house. Sarah walked around the fence past the now covered swimming pool, the hot tub and fishpond. "Welcome to the home of Ida Mae Katz."

She opened the kitchen door and was so overcome by the smell of bleach, she was seized by a coughing fit. "Phew," said Officer Mike. "Let's get some windows open!"

As fresh air blew in, Sarah took a deep breath and sighed in relief.

"Why would it smell so strongly of bleach in here?" Officer Pollack asked her.

"I don't know. Her cleaning lady only comes in on Saturdays. It's been days since she was here."

The granite counter was empty, as were the center island and cooktop. Everything gleamed in the sunlight.

"The smell should have dissipated by now," Officer Mike said. "Other than the bleach, is anything out of place in this room?"

"No, it looks spotless." She looked around. "Where's that bottle of GHB for Detective Engelman?"

She frowned and searched the counter, floor and drawers. "It was here when she left."

They moved on to the dining room, the den, the bedrooms and basement. Everything was in its place. "There is one other area," Sarah said.

"Where's that?" Officer Pollack asked.

"The garage. We walked past it to get into the house."

It reeked of bleach, too.

Officer Pollack raised the garage door to let in a blast of fresh air.

"Weird, don't you think?" Sarah struggled to catch her breath. "I've been in here occasionally to put things away for Aunt Ida, but never smelled bleach before."

"Tell us about the cleaning lady," Officer Mike said.

"Her name is Betty. I don't know her last name." Sarah said. "She's been working for Aunt Ida for a little over a year. She came from a vocational training organization called WorkForce. Betty's extremely hard of hearing and wears hearing aids in both ears. She also has a mild intellectual disability."

"Isn't it possible she got the days she was supposed to clean mixed up?" Officer Pollack asked. "Came the wrong day, got carried away, used too much bleach?"

"I guess so. That would be a logical explanation for the fumes in the kitchen. But the garage?" Sarah shook her head. "It doesn't make sense."

"Hey, who knows what she was thinking?" Pollack said. "Maybe she thought Ms. Katz wanted her to clean everything, including the garage."

"Now what?" Sarah asked.

"Now you lock it up and we leave," Officer

Pollack said.

Officer Mike stared at the workbench and wall above it. Every tool was in its place on the pegboard over the wooden counter and each spot was labeled with what tool went where. Shelves were neatly stacked with boxes, also clearly labeled.

"Nice tools," he said. "I have a workshop, but it's never been this neat. Okay, we need to get going."

"And I do what?" Sarah asked.

"You go about your business." Officer Mike responded. "If you see a white van without a headlight, or you see that man, do not attempt to take him on. If he comes after you again, call 9-1-1 and tell them you are in danger of imminent harm."

****

Sarah returned to her kitchen and called the office.

"General Pediatrics. How may I help you?"

"Jazmin, this is Sarah." She filled her in on the latest events. "After all this, I've decided to follow Dr. Kirby's orders and stay home today. How's Arlene's mother?"

"The Lord took her home."

Tears of sympathy filled Sarah's eyes. Her mother could be next. "I'm so sorry. When's the funeral?"

"Tomorrow, at ten in the morning, right down the street here at the Jerusalem A.B.E. Pastor James Black is officiating."

"I'll be there. Arlene needs everyone at this difficult time. Thanks, Jazmin." She ended the call and wondered if Peter would be there.

Wait a minute. That's the church in the study, she realized. When her cell phone began to ring, she almost dropped it from surprise.

153

The social worker from Baltimore Medical Center identified herself. "A bed just opened up at Shady Rest. Have you been there?"

"No, I've been busy." An understatement.

"You should visit it before you make your final decision. I'll give the administrator a call to see if she's available to meet with you."

Sarah moved as quickly as her injuries allowed, aggravated by additional aches and pains from jumping between the trees and rolling on the ground. Fear for her life had turned her into an athlete. Maybe she'd soak in Aunt Ida's hot tub. That would help her aching muscles. Later. No time to care of myself now, she thought. She dressed with care, pulling on her trusty black slacks and a fresh shirt.

The social worker called back in twenty minutes. "The administrator said you can come any time. She'll be there until five this evening. Her name is Evans."

****

Shady Rest stood on a side street in the middle of Pikesville behind a popular restaurant. Sarah found a parking space in front of the large, rambling brick building. An elderly black man sat in wheel chair by the automatic front doors. He greeted her as she entered. "Welcome to Shady Rest."

A blonde, overly made-up, truly *zaftig* woman in a low cut, tight, gold sweater sat at the information desk directly behind the man in the wheelchair. Sarah could scarcely believe her eyes. She approached the desk with caution. "Aren't you Rivah, the real estate agent?"

"Oh, honey, I got a lot of jobs. Monday through Friday, nine to five, I'm a receptionist here at Shady Rest. Weekends and evenings, I'm a realtor. Anything to make ends meet."

Sarah thought about her own financial circumstances. "I can understand that."

Leaning forward, Rivah whispered like a conspirator. "My best leads come from this place. Once grandma comes in, the family can't wait to unload the house. Even when I make the Million Dollar Club, I'm not giving up the day job." She sat back and said in a normal voice, "So what can I do for you?"

"I'm Sarah Wright. I'm looking for Ms. Evans. Is she around?"

"She sure is. She told me you might be admitting your mother to Shady Rest. Hey, does your mother own her own home?"

"Yes, but I happen to be living in it, so I won't be 'unloading' it anytime soon."

"Well, if you change your mind, here's my card." Rivah picked up a telephone receiver, and tapped at the keypad with bright red bird-of-prey nails. Her voice came over the paging system. "Ms. Evans, you have a visitor at the front desk."

Sarah waited for Ms. Evans and watched the hallway. A few elderly people made their way up and down the halls with walkers and wheel chairs. Nurses, nurses' aides, and orderlies strode back and forth on errands. The front doors whooshed open behind her.

"Welcome to Shady Rest!"

"Why thank you, Charles. It's always good to see you," said a familiar sounding woman. "Hello, Rivah."

Sarah turned to see the latest arrival. Bernice Woods stood there, looking almost as surprised as Sarah.

Chapter Thirteen

"Bernice," Sarah said. "Do you remember me?"

"Oh, my word, of course I do. How are you?"

"No broken bones. Lots of bruises and something like whiplash in my neck. I'm lucky to be alive and grateful you came along."

"What brings you here?" Bernice asked.

"My mother's in a coma; they can't keep her in the ICU any longer. I came to visit Shady Rest to see if it would be a good place for her. Are you happy with it?"

"The nursing care is excellent. There are lots of activities for the residents. I was worried it would be depressing and smell, but, it's very bright and clean."

"Maybe we should put that on a brochure," Rivah said and burst into giggles.

Bernice managed a weak smile.

A tall, elegant African American woman came into view. Her hair was pulled up in a French twist and a large streak of gray entwined along the hairstyle in an artistic swirl. Her impeccably tailored navy blue suit was accented with a pearl necklace and earrings. "Rivah, isn't there something you should be doing?"

Ducking her head, Rivah began to shuffle papers. "I think I have some filing."

"Then why don't you get to work on that?"

"Okey-dokey."

Ms. Evans turned toward Bernice and Sarah. "Ms.

Woods, so good to see you again. I trust you're well?" She extended her hand to Bernice.

"Yes, thank you, very well."

"And you must be Dr. Wright."

Ms. Evans gave Sarah a firm handshake. Sarah felt as if she was meeting a socialite instead of a nursing home administrator. "That's correct."

"Why don't we take a little tour of the facility, then we can talk in my office. Is that okay with you?"

"Perfect."

"Ms. Evans, could I interrupt you for a moment?" Bernice asked.

The administrator gave Bernice her full attention. "Of course, Ms. Woods. What can I do for you?"

"As you know, my sister-in-law's roommate just passed away. Elizabeth would like to have someone to keep her company. Could Sarah's mother could be placed in her room?"

Sarah was delighted for her own reasons, but a bit taken aback at Bernice's directness.

"I don't know how much company my mother's going to be. She's in a coma."

"No, dear, I was thinking that on the days when I can't come, you'd probably be in to visit your mother. I was selfishly hoping that in bad weather, you might be willing to drive me here. Between my sister and my niece, it's been difficult."

"If it turns out Shady Rest is a good fit for my mother, I think Bernice's idea makes sense, but I'd like to take the tour before I make any final decisions."

"Here at Shady Rest, we not only emphasize our quality of care, but our quality of caring," Ms. Evans began as they strolled down the hall. "We provide around-the-clock nursing care to chronically ill and frail elderly patients as well as individuals recovering from illnesses and injuries. We have a state-of-the-art coma stimulation program few other facilities offer."

"Is it true the coma stimulation program isn't covered by Medicare and Medicaid?"

"Because it's considered experimental, it is an out-of-pocket expense. I've seen some amazing outcomes."

"What exactly does it entail?" Sarah watched residents doing chair exercises in the activity room to the beat of a Broadway show tune.

"Daily sessions are less than a half hour, and the environment is kept quiet during the treatment. Sensory stimuli are presented in a particular order and the patient is told what to expect. If your mother has a favorite song, poem, cologne or flavor, the therapist would include them."

Sarah wondered if the flavors might include scotch and whiskey.

"Staff and family are asked to speak to the patient whenever they come into the room. Hearing is the last sense to go. People have recalled conversations they heard while in a coma."

"Are pets allowed to visit?"

"Pets-on-Wheels comes here at least once a week. Your pet would have to be certified as volunteer and go through physical and behavioral testing before he or she could come to visit. We can't allow animals with unmanageable behaviors to endanger our residents."

Winston would be staying home.

After an hour and a complete tour of the facility, Sarah asked to see Mrs. Woods' room. She waited in the hallway while Ms. Evans spoke with Bernice and

Elizabeth Woods. Ms. Evans came out of the room and invited her in.

A wizened old woman lay in one bed, her wispy white hair spread over a pillow. Her eyes were milky white, and her thin hands clutched at her blanket. She turned her head toward Sarah as she entered the room.

"Mrs. Woods, I'd like you to meet Dr. Sarah Wright."

"It's a pleasure to meet you, Mrs. Woods. Bernice tells me you're looking for a roommate."

"I could sure use the company. Bad enough I'm blind. Without a roommate, this room is like a morgue. I need a little more liveliness in here. Look around, tell me what you think."

The room was large, with two hospital beds and one bathroom, two closets, two large dressers, and two large nightstands, one empty like the bed it accompanied. The nightstand next to Mrs. Woods' bed was cluttered with belongings, including a CD player and a stack of audio books. In the center of the nightstand was a large eight by ten color photograph of Aunt Ida.

Sarah stared at the picture, her mouth suddenly feeling as if it had been stuffed with cotton.

"Isn't that a wonderful photograph?" Ms. Evans said.

"Oh, you say that about all the children," Elizabeth said with a proud smile.

"No, I mean it. That's a marvelous photograph of your daughter," Mrs. Evans said. "I've met her, so I know what I'm talking about."

"I just wish she could come here to visit me more often," Elizabeth said on a sigh. "I miss her so much."

"Well, I'm working on that as we speak," said Bernice. "Sarah, please say your mother will be Elizabeth's roommate. That way, I can impose on you to help me bring her daughter to visit more often. I'm getting too old to handle children."

It wasn't a photograph of Aunt Ida. The woman in the photograph had a flat nose and a slack jawed expression that Sarah missed at first glance. Aunt Ida was on her brain. She was seeing her everywhere.

"Well," said Ms. Evans, "She's a lovely child and even lovelier without her glasses."

Without her glasses? Of course! She was Bessie, the girl in the archived photograph. The very person she'd been searching for. It seemed like the poster and the trip to medical archives were years in the past, instead of just a few days ago. Sarah brought her attention back to the present. First and foremost, she had to attend to her mother.

"Ms. Evans and I still have a few details to work out, but I promise to have an answer to you today. Is that okay with you ladies?"

"Yes, yes," they said in unison.

"Good. I'll be back soon."

Ms. Evans and Sarah walked the short distance back to her office. Sarah felt like she was entering the honeymoon suite at an upscale hotel. Sarah complimented Ms. Evans on the décor.

"Thank you, it's my hobby. I got tired of being locked indoors for ten hours a day. Life is too short for ugly workspaces."

"Then I won't invite you to my windowless office anytime soon."

Ms. Evans sat behind her large cherry desk. "What

160

can I do to help you decide about your mother's placement?"

"My mother's retired from the federal government. She worked for the feds for over twenty years. She has an excellent pension that's being automatically deposited into her checking account. She used to take great pride in paying her bills the day after they arrived."

When she paused, Evans asked, "Did something happen to change that?"

"Five years ago, she fell under the spell of a televangelist. She allowed him to automatically deduct a thousand dollars a month from her checking account. Her finances are in a shambles. My lawyer, Sol Weinstein, is in the process of petitioning the court so I can be her guardian. I work for Hopkins, but my salary isn't in the six-figure range."

Sarah stopped, overwhelmed at the prospect of more bills.

Ms. Evans sighed. "I'm afraid your story is a familiar one. It's not uncommon for elderly people to fall victim to con artists and swindlers. Some spend much of their fixed income on magazine sweepstakes, believing they'll be the next winner. It's tragic."

Sarah's voice quavered. "How can I afford to place my mother here?"

"First of all, I commend you for taking steps to protect her. The good news is that with Medicare she's eligible for a post-hospitalization stay in a skilled nursing facility for up to one hundred days. You'll have to pay co-insurance."

"What about Medicaid when Medicare runs out? How do I find out if she's eligible for that?"

"We have a specialist here on staff who will work with you." Ms. Evans clasped her hands. "What other questions do you have?"

"What if I have problems paying the coinsurance? It could add up fast. I could be fighting with my dog for his dinner at that rate."

"Good heavens," Ms. Evans laughed. "I certainly hope you won't be eating dog food. Worst case scenario, the State of Maryland can help her qualify for charity care."

"I'm afraid I'll be qualifying for charity care." Sarah blew out a huge breath. "And doing my own coma stimulation program."

"Well, don't give up just yet. Once you get her finances under control, you may find you can afford the program. So, does that mean you've decided to place your mother here?"

"Yes. Thank you for answering my questions and for being so honest with me."

"I couldn't look at myself in the mirror in the morning if I wasn't."

"If it's okay with you, I'm going to go tell Elizabeth my mother is moving in with her. This should make Bernice a happy lady. I'll speak with the social worker and find out what the next steps are."

"Wonderful. Here are some brochures. If you have any questions I can answer, please call me. I look forward to seeing you here."

Sarah found her way back to Elizabeth's room.

"Congratulations, Mrs. Woods," Sarah announced like a game show host, "You are getting a roommate. She's not very chatty. However, I guarantee I will make up for her silence by reading books to both of you when

I come to visit. Is that a good deal?"

Elizabeth clapped her hands. "I love to listen to books."

"Sarah," Bernice said. "That's fabulous news. I can't wait until you meet Mitzi."

"Who's Mitzi?"

"Why, my niece, of course," Bernice said.

"I thought her name was Bessie?"

"Yes, her name is Bessie Mitzi Woods," Bernice replied. "The family calls her Mitzi."

Sarah stared at the photograph again. Another Mitzi? How many could there be?

"Sarah?" Bernice asked.

"What? I'm sorry, I was just wondering how many people are named Mitzi. My Aunt's cat is named Mitzi."

"Pets are such good company," Elizabeth said. "Too bad I can't keep a cat here."

"Sarah, didn't you tell me when we first met that you were looking for Elizabeth? What was that about?"

"Oh, um, ah," Sarah scrambled to come up with a reasonable response. Now that she knew these dear ladies, how could she ask them to allow Bessie/Mitzi's childhood photograph to be on a poster for a congenital syphilis study? How bizarre would that be?

"Didn't you say you work at the Johns Hopkins Medical School?" Bernice asked.

"Yes, I'm in the Department of Pediatrics."

"Oh, isn't it a small world? I graduated from Hopkins Nursing School," Elizabeth said.

"Really? I thought the Nursing School has only been around since the eighties."

"That's the baccalaureate program," Elizabeth said.

"When I graduated from the Johns Hopkins Nursing School in 1941, almost all nurses were diploma school graduates. Hopkins had a three year program, one of the most rigorous in the country."

She pushed a hair away from her face and sighed. "We trained twelve to fourteen hours a day, seven days a week. When we graduated, we could work in homes as private duty nurses, or in hospitals. I took the Maryland and the District of Columbia Nursing License Exams and passed both with flying colors."

"How'd you meet your husband?"

"He was a head resident at Hopkins. I met him on a medical surgical unit. It was love at first sight." She giggled. "We used to sneak to the clean utility room. One time, my head nurse caught us kissing. I thought I'd be fired on the spot, but she had a boyfriend who was a resident, too. We married after I graduated from nursing school and he completed his residency. We moved to Washington, D.C. Less than a year later, he got called up."

"World War II?"

"Yes. He went off to the Pacific Theater. I was twenty-one years old, all alone, and living in a new city. The Army Nurse Corps wouldn't take married women, so I went back to work." She yawned.

"You look tired, Elizabeth," Bernice said. "I think you've had enough excitement today."

"Now that you mention it, I could use a little snooze," Elizabeth said. "You're a good listener, Sarah. I can't wait for your mother to move in so we can talk some more. I have lots of stories."

"I'll be back to hear them soon."

Bernice leaned over the side of the bed and gave

Elizabeth a peck on the cheek. "Have a nice nap, hon," Bernice said. "I'll see you on Friday. I'm going to go see Mitzi tomorrow."

"Give her my love," Elizabeth said.

"I will," Bernice said.

Sarah tried not to stare at the photograph on her way out the door. She didn't want Bernice to think she was gawking at her niece. Well, if everyone has a doppelganger, Sarah had just seen her aunt's. She'd have to introduce them someday—if she could find the real Ida Katz.

Chapter Fourteen

Ida hugged the ragged quilt around her shoulders and lifted her left hand up as high as she could to combat the throbbing pain. Someone paced overhead. She heard muffled shouting, but couldn't make out the words. Her hand was numb. She lowered it with care, and brought it closer to her face for inspection.

She'd fought like a cat when the creep turned on the power saw. Ida had thrown herself at the smaller man, knocking him down. In the melee, the big oaf had cut himself in the thigh. He'd run around the garage spraying blood everywhere. The little one had duct-taped Ida's wrists to the workbench, then dragged the shrieking man into the house. They'd returned a long time later with a towel wrapped around his leg.

"Now we're really pissed," the man said as he limped over to her.

"You didn't need an excuse, you sadist," Ida said and spat in his face. Spittle oozed through his stocking mask as he reached over and grabbed her hand.

"Do it," he ordered.

The smaller man forced the bottle of GHB between Ida's lips. Liquid dribbled down her neck. The world began to spin. The last thing she saw before passing out was the pair of metal snips approaching her hand.

When she woke up, she was back in the basement, shackled to the bed, a black zip tie cinched below a knuckle. Her wedding ring was gone, along with the top of her left pinkie finger.

Again, footsteps sounded overhead. This time the door opened and the smaller one came down the stairs. "Lucky you had antibiotics and painkillers in your house. Otherwise, you'd be in a world of hurt right now. If I were you, I'd take a lot of these. I don't think the metal snips were sterile."

Ida hugged the quilt closer and glared at the smaller thug. Was that a man or a woman? The stocking distorted the person's features. Despite the deep, husky voice, and the unisex overalls, this one moved in a distinctly feminine manner.

Deep within an angry Ida began to stir. All those years ago, she'd been helpless, a child abused by an adult who should have protected her. With Ethel's help, she had survived. Now she was old and vulnerable, with no one to protect her but herself. By God, she wasn't going to go down without a fight.

"Why are you doing this to me?" She raised her voice. "What do you want?"

"All in good time, Ida. When we're ready to let you in on our little secret, you'll be the first to know," the man-woman said and began to turn away, a definite sway of the hips giving her away. It was a woman.

"How could you? Women aren't supposed to act like this. What kind of monster are you?"

The woman stopped, nodded, climbed the steps and slammed the door behind her.

****

Day? Night? Ida had no watch; they'd taken it away. She had no way of telling time, except through the sounds of footsteps overhead and the appearance of

167

meals. She thought of her senior citizen self-defense class. Purse snatchers and other would-be assailants had been covered in depth, along with ways to prevent yourself from becoming a victim, like shredding your bills and tax returns, locking your house up and having people collect papers off your lawn. But not once had they ever discussed kidnapping.

What would Ethel do? she wondered. Her street smart friend had always been ready to protect Ida, chin up, fists cocked at the slightest provocation. She'd never taken crap from anyone. How would Ethel handle this scenario?

Six sandwiches after she woke up with a zip tie on her pinky finger, Ida stopped taking her pain medication. Fearful of being too groggy or overdosing, she began to stuff the pills into the holes in the quilt, burrowing into what remained of the cotton batting. Nine sandwiches later, the stump of her pinky finger began to turn bluish black. At least it didn't hurt anymore. She hoped the color and tissue death wouldn't extend to her hand.

The door opened, and the man and the woman descended the stairs. He limped across the room and stood in front of Ida. "Time to let you in on our secret," he said and pulled off the stocking.

Heart skipping erratically, Ida gaped at the dark-haired man with the gap-toothed smile who had often worked on the electrical problems at her house. "Patrick?" she asked. "I don't understand."

The woman stepped around Patrick. "Maybe this will help." She removed her stocking mask.

Ida stared at the blonde woman without a single spark of recognition going off in her brain. She may be old, but she wasn't senile. This person was a complete stranger. "I've never seen you before in my life."

"Oh, yes you have. Once a week for a year." The woman smirked. "Oo otay, Miz Idah? Oo nee hellup?"

"Betty?" Ida whispered. Without the thick glasses, hearing aids, and what was now clearly a wig, the housekeeper was a lethal look alike for Jayne Mansfield. "How could you?"

Patrick laughed. "Well, that was fun." He slurred his words. "Time to get down to business."

He sat down on the bed. "Gimme that paper." Betty handed him a legal pad along with a pen. "Okay, lady, time for you to start writing. We're not looking for memoirs. Just your last will and testament, leaving all your worldly belongings to your beloved housekeeper, Betty Reed. Start with this: 'I, Ida Mae Katz, being of sound mind.' "

"You can't do this. I already have a will."

"You know, for a rich old biddy, you really don't know law, do you?"

"My estate is going to Ethel and Sarah. You can't change that," Ida said. "My lawyer has everything on file and knows what to do."

"Tsk, tsk. I guess you never heard about all the old men who marry young women and have a change of heart," Betty said. "It's called a 'holographic will.' You write it, we pass go, and collect a million dollars!" She laughed in a crazed cackle.

Barely able to believe her own ears—which had perfect hearing—Ida stared at the altered creature before her. Betty sounded as if she belonged in a lockdown unit for the criminally insane. She had to connect with the lunatic, get her to listen to reason.

"Why me? Why did you target me?"

"Because you're a sweet little old lady who believes the best about everyone." Betty snorted. "You chose poorly."

Patrick shoved the pad and pen toward Ida. "Start writing."

"You'll never get away with it. Sarah will identify you in court. You won't get a dime."

"Lucky for us, we already took care of the mother and we're going to take care of the daughter."

Her stomach plummeted. Ethel's fall hadn't been an accident. Now they were after Sarah. She had to stop them. But how? She glanced around the basement, hoping for something, anything to use as a weapon.

"Oh, Ida," Patrick sing-songed, "Time-to-wrida!"

She stared at his bloodshot eyes and leaned away from the man, trying to avoid the beer fumes he puffed out with each word. What would Ethel do?

"C'mon, Ida," Betty said. "We don't have all day. We've got places to go, people to kill. Start writing."

Ida gripped the pen until her knuckles turned white. What would Ethel do?

"Do hereby leave all my personal assets to my beloved housekeeper, Betty Reed," the blonde said and paced across the room.

Patrick leaned against her shoulder, breathing on her neck, "Write it!"

The image of her stepfather rose up before her eyes, obliterating Patrick's face and filling the basement with his smells and coarse voice. *"Don't you ever lock this door again. I'll kill your mother like I killed your kitten."*

But somehow his features blurred into the monster

sitting before her. "You'll do what I tell you to do."

"No," Ida screamed and jabbed the ballpoint at Patrick's eye.

****

Sarah arrived home and found Betty sitting on the top step by her kitchen door. Shirt buttoned on all the wrong buttons and half pulled out of her jeans, Betty looked as if she'd gotten dressed in the dark. Her hair stuck out at odd angles, and her glasses were awry. She looked as if she had been crying. Winston barked incessantly inside the house.

"Betty, what's wrong? You look terrible!"

"Oo nee hellup me!"

"Why don't you come inside and we'll talk." Sarah attempted to put the key in the door.

"Nooo!" Betty pulled on her arm. "Oooo must cum wit me!"

Winston was going to have to wait a few minutes more. "Okay, okay, I'm coming."

Betty half dragged Sarah over to Aunt Ida's house. They entered the kitchen and stood by the center island. "Look!" she shrieked, pointing at the kitchen floor where liquid pooled out from the freezer side of the large Sub-Zero.

"Uh-oh," Sarah said.

"Look!" Flipping the kitchen light switch up and down did nothing. No lights came on.

"Oh, I'd better call Baltimore Gas and Electric." Sarah reached for her cell phone.

Betty ran to the freezer and threw open the door. "Bad! Food go bad!"

"Okay, okay." Calling BGE was not going to get Betty to calm down. "How about if I put all the food in my freezer?" Sarah pantomimed taking the food out of the freezer.

In an instant, Betty stopped crying and smiled. "Yes."

Well, that calmed her down in a hurry. "Good, you can help me carry it over to my house."

The housekeeper gave her head a violent shake. "No! Haf to work!"

Light dawned. This wasn't Betty's only house to clean today. "Oh, you have another job to go to. I understand. I'll take care of it, then."

"Goot! Tank ooo!" Betty hugged Sarah and ran out the door.

Great, Sarah thought, now I have to lug all this frozen stuff to my house with my sore back. She found plastic grocery bags, filled them with frozen packages, and dragged them over to her house two at a time. There was so much food to move, she wondered if Ida had been saving up for a famine.

She flipped her kitchen light switch, to make sure the power was on in her house. Her power was on, but Aunt Ida's wasn't. Some fluke of BGE, she thought. Either that or Sol Weinstein had forgotten to pay Aunt Ida's electric bill. She'd give the power company a call, then if that was the case, she'd let Sol know.

Six trips later, she finished moving every single hard, cold, aluminum foil wrapped thing over. There was just enough time to take a nap before she went to visit her mother. Fully clothed, she put her head down on the pillow and fell asleep. She woke up feeling groggy and dialed her voicemail. "Message one," a female voice chirped.

"*Vot?* Is this thing working?" Gertrude asked. "Is

this you, Sarah? Look, I gotta talk to you right away! Call me at this number!" Gertrude yelled out a telephone number, then coughed and until the message ran out of time.

What on earth could be so urgent? Sarah called the number, got the voicemail. "Hi, this is Sarah. Sorry I didn't hear the phone earlier. Please try again."

Sarah called the Baltimore County Police. Yes, they had BOLO'd everyone and told every shift. No, they hadn't heard or seen anything.

She drummed her fingers on the kitchen table, got up, and rummaged in the refrigerator. Where were the pies? Oh. That's right. She took them both to work. She settled on a container of low fat, sugar-free yogurt and an apple. Too darn healthy for today, but all she had.

She thought about calling Dan. Would that make Sarah seem too desperate? After all, wasn't he already moving to Towson? Pursuing him like a hunting dog was not a good move. She didn't want him to think she was a clingy, whiny woman. Instead, she called the social worker to ask about discharge planning.

"Your mother can be transferred to Shady Rest tomorrow, probably in the afternoon. When we have a better idea of the time, we'll call you. That way you can meet her at the home and sign all the admissions documents."

No sooner did she end the call when the phone began to ring and vibrate in her hand. "*Vot* have you been doing that you couldn't call me back sooner?"

"Sorry, I didn't hear the phone before. What's up?"

Gert hacked, caught her breath and rasped. "You told me Ida Mae Katz was missing, did you not?"

Sarah gripped the phone harder. "Yes. I filed a

missing person report with the police."

"*Vot* would you say if I told you I saw her car?"

"Where?"

"At the Essen Deli."

She had to be certain before she called the police again. Not jump the gun. They thought she was crazy. She better have proof this time. "Are you sure?"

"*Vot?*" Gert's voice filled with indignation. "You calling me a liar?"

How could she undo this insult? "No, but there are a lot of big white Cadillacs in Pikesville."

"Listen, *girlchik*," Sarah could almost see Gert shaking her index finger at her. "I know it's her car because it has the bumper sticker I gave her on it— Mah-Jongg Maven!"

Sarah jumped to her feet and searched for her shoes and car keys. "I'll be right there."

"*Vot's* the hurry now?"

"I need to get over there and see the car."

"You can't see the car."

Sarah felt like she was in the middle of an old Abbott and Costello routine. "You just told me her car is at the Essen Deli."

"No, I told you I saw her car." Gert sounded annoyed. "It was parked in that parking lot across the alley where the theatre used to be."

Take a deep breath, Sarah. Stay calm. "Well, where is it now?"

Gert exploded. "How the hell would I know? It was towed away."

After ten minutes of smoothing Gert's ruffled feathers, Sarah drove to the parking lot and got the address of the impound lot off the No Parking sign, then called Officer Mike. He answered on the first ring, his voice brisk and official. "This is Officer Corrigan."

"I got a call from Gertrude Rosen saying she'd seen Aunt Ida's car being towed away from the theatre parking lot next to the Essen Deli. I think they have it at Speedy Towing."

"How do you know it was her car?"

"You can't miss a white Cadillac with a bumper sticker that says 'Mah-Jongg Maven.' Mrs. Rosen gave her that bumper sticker. She'll swear it's Aunt Ida's car and that she saw being towed away. Now are you interested?"

A long silence fell. At last he said, "Have you seen the car?"

"I'm heading for the impound lot now." Sarah pushed him a little more. "Can you meet me there?"

"Let me talk with my lieutenant. Is there a number where you can be reached?"

Sarah arrived at the impound lot and stated her case to an indifferent attendant. He wore a uniform of a gray jacket and baseball cap, both labeled with "Speedy Towing" in dark green embroidery. His greasy gray hair hung in a long ponytail over his collar. A monster trucks program played on a tiny color television in his smoke-filled booth that reeked of marijuana.

He wouldn't make eye contact. "You got proof it's your car?"

"It's my aunt's car, I just told you that. Can I look at it? She's missing."

Gaze glued to the TV, his voice a monotone, he said, "If it's not your car, you can't see it and you can't have it."

Sarah bit back her irritation and pulled out her

trump card. "What if the police say I should have it?"

"Then come back with a cop." He opened a window and a breeze blew out the remains of the reeking smoke. "Otherwise, you got no business here."

"What happens to her car if I can't get the police out here?"

The attendant turned his head and stared at her with bloodshot eyes. "We write a letter to the Motor Vehicle Administration and get the name and address of the owner. Then we send a letter to the owner of the car. If there's no response in 30 days, we junk the car."

"You junk it?"

"Lady, if we don't hear back from the owner, we got the right to do it." He turned back to the television and slammed the door to the booth.

A cold stomp around the perimeter of the impound lot fence and she found a big white Cadillac sitting at the end of a row of cars. The driver's side window had been covered with black plastic. She strained to see the front of the vehicle and make out the license plate. It was Aunt Ida's car. She returned to her car and called Officer Mike again. He was out, so she left him an urgent message. Aunt Ida would have never parked at the theatre's parking lot. She'd had her car towed once before and had no intention of going through that aggravation again.

If she didn't park her car there, who had? What had happened to her window?

And where was Aunt Ida?

****

Exhausted, sore, and frustrated, Sarah arrived home to an exuberant Winston. The cats were more subdued in their responses, electing to sit and stare at her from the counter and the tea towel on the floor. She fed everyone, including herself, then she realized she had been so caught up in finding Aunt Ida, she'd forgotten to visit her mother. I'll be spending most of tomorrow with her while she's being admitted to Shady Rest, she thought. That will make up for today. For now, she was too beat to do anything.

Then she remembered Aunt Ida's hot tub. She smacked herself on the forehead. She'd never called BGE or Sol. Time to kill two birds with one stone. She'd put on a swimsuit and robe, go over to Aunt Ida's and see if the power was still off. If it was out, then she'd make the calls. If not, then she could relax and enjoy the hot tub.

Finding a swimsuit was a challenge. Her one-piece was too painful to put it on, even with the cervical collar. The shoulder straps kept pulling down on her sore muscles, making her wince with pain. She gave up and decided to see if her mother owned any loose swimsuits she could wear.

In the top drawer of her mother's dresser lay a handgun. Well, that was an ugly surprise.

When had she gotten that? Why did Ethel feel the need to keep a weapon in the house? Was she afraid of intruders? Her mother had forced all her children to learn how to shoot rifles. Sarah had hated guns, but surprised everyone with her sharp shooting skills. When she went away to college, she gave up the sport. Sarah had no idea when her mother switched from a rifle to a .22 Ruger, but it could stay right where it was.

The next drawer was a little more helpful. In it were a variety of very dated two-piece suits. She pulled out a lime green and pink hibiscus flowered swimsuit and held up the bra to take a better look at it.

"Jeez, Mom! When and where would you have worn this? You are just full of surprises today!"

She held the top to her chest, looked in the mirror, and noticed a little straw sticking out between the bra cups. Sarah turned it inside out and took a closer look. The label said "Cole of California Top Secret." It was inflatable.

"Mom, this is too funny." She blew through the straw and watched as the cups increased in size with each breath. She decided to be generous and gave herself a D cup, then put on the suit and looked in the mirror. "Dolly Parton, eat your heart out."

Her mother was going to get an earful about this little discovery. Her cleavage could give Rivah a run for her money. Sarah sashayed back and forth in front of the mirror. Between the black cervical collar and the tropical colored swimsuit, she looked like a tawdry advertisement for a personal injury law firm.

"Robe, slippers, flashlight," she said. "I'm ready for anything." She walked the short, dark distance to Aunt Ida's house. The corner lights were on, and she could hear the waterfall running in the fishpond. Excellent. The power was back.

The fish were due for a visit. She squatted down next to the pond with a tiny handful of food and extended her hand. Jaws, the giant Koi, was being coy. The other fish rushed to the surface, nibbling the tiny balls from her hand.

"Not too much guys, you'll get sick. Aw, come on, Jaws," she said. "You know you want it. Just a little closer, now, you can do it." She leaned forward to reach closer to Jaws, stretched her arm out farther, teetering on the edge of the pond.

Something struck the back of her head, and everything went black.

****

"What if she's alive?" a woman with a husky, Lauren Bacall voice said. "I can't see her under those big-assed leaves!"

"Leave the bitch to me," a man said.

"No knives, you moron. We've been through this a hundred times. It has to look like an accident."

"You better hope your plan works," he said.

Sarah was no longer on the edge of the fishpond. She was in cold water, and it smelled like rotten vegetation. Eau de low tide. Pew. Jaws tickled her chin, nibbling at it. This was the closest the damn fish ever got to her. She couldn't see her assailants, because giant lotus leaves that grew up like trees in the fishpond obscured her vision. That meant they couldn't see her, either. Thank God the pond hadn't been winterized yet. Otherwise, all the leaves would have been cleared out.

"My plan is still good. We got the old lady. Now we got this fat bitch. And we got rid of all the evidence. Even if she survives this, which I doubt, we have an ace in the hole."

She just called me a "fat bitch," Sarah thought. Certain she'd lost a few pounds in the last week, that one really hurt.

"We have to lie low for at least a month," the woman said. "After that, the car's junk. As long as Miss Nosy is out of the picture, the police will forget about the old lady. This will be a simple case of trip and drown. Then we can put our plan into action and wait for the big bucks to roll in."

"I want to slice her up," the man said. "Eye for an eye."

"No more sharp objects," she said. "I had a terrible time cleaning up the kitchen and the garage. I almost killed myself with bleach fumes. This has to look like an accident; otherwise the cops will get wise to us!"

"I don't like it," he said.

"Tough," the woman said. "You're not the one who slaved for a year to make this happen. I set up this scam and you're not going to—what was that?"

"What?"

"That light over there," the woman said. "It's getting closer."

"Rent-a-cops maybe?"

"They must be coming to check on the old lady's house while she's out of town. Let's get out of here."

Sarah heard footsteps running away from the pond. A car engine roared, tires squealed and then there was only the sound of the pond's waterfall. She was afraid to make any movement for fear of giving away her position. Her toes were numb and she had to clench her teeth to keep them from chattering. Jaws circled her face and neck, and the smaller fish nibbled at her fingers.

The terry cloth robe weighted her down, but somehow, her head remained above the water. After what seemed an eternity, she slid across the slimy bottom to the shallow end, grabbed onto a rock and dragged herself out of the water and lay with her face hovering over the gravel. Then it struck her why she hadn't drowned. The combination of the D cup blow up bra and cervical collar had saved her life.

Chapter Fifteen

Not far from the Hopkins Medical Complex, Sarah sat in the third row on a hard pew in the sanctuary of the Jerusalem A.B.E. Church. On arrival, a deacon spotted her cervical collar and ushered her up front so she could have a good view without straining her neck.

"Brothers and sisters, thank you for coming today to Sister Bessie's Brown's homecoming to the Lord. Blessings upon y'all and upon Sister Bessie this great and glorious day the Lord has made," Pastor James Black said. "Can I get an amen?"

"Amen, brother! Amen!"

Pastor Black could have made a living as a look-alike for the actor Billy Dee Williams. Most of the congregants were already sobbing, and he'd just started speaking. People stood along the sides and in the back of the overheated church. Bessie Brown's funeral had standing room only.

One of these people was a sexual predator, Sarah thought. But how would she find him?

Dressed in bright orange robes, Pastor Black stood at a podium on a stage. Behind him were identically attired members of the choir and the organist. On the stage was an extra-large coffin, covered with white and red roses. A life-sized cardboard photo of Arlene's mother, Bessie, wearing an orange robe stood next to Pastor Black. It showed an enormous, smiling dark-

Sharon Buchbinder

skinned woman with three chins. Sarah stared at the photo, looking for a resemblance to her friend. At length, she decided Arlene had her mother's eyes.

Sitting motionless in the front row, her hair swept up in a severe bun, Arlene wore a high-necked, long-sleeved black dress. In the same pew, a boy around eleven years old sat next to her friend Jazmin.

"Please, turn to hymn one hundred and twenty-six, and join us in singing. Mrs. Black?"

He nodded toward the organist, who began to play a lively gospel tune. Mrs. Black was a beautiful woman with the skin color of a Starbucks café latte. Her braided blonde hair bounced as she leaned into the organ, raising a joyful song to the Lord. As the choir sang and rocked, Sarah hummed along.

Unlike some of her white colleagues, who darted glances around the church, Sarah felt comfortable. She'd been to similar services as a child and, in a weird way, was grateful to her mother for having exposed her to a variety of religious observances. Ethel had attended church the way other people went to the movies. As children, Sarah and her brother and sister were dragged to every holy-roller church in their little hometown and in the surrounding towns and cities. On numerous occasions, they had been the only people not jumping, dancing, or singing in congregations where people were often "taken up by the Spirit of the Lord" and spoke in tongues. By comparison, this service was tame.

A variety of odors from deodorants, perfumes, after-shave, hair products, and sweating, clapping, singing folks wafted through the sanctuary, along with the distinct fragrance of Dan's favorite after-shave. Sarah scanned the crowd, hoping he'd appear.

When the hymn ended, everyone sat down. The boy with glasses continued to stand and clap his hands, bobbing his head like Stevie Wonder. Jazmin stood to whisper something into his ear, then he sat down.

A bent-over elderly black man with short gray hair and thick wire-rimmed glasses read some passages from the New Testament. When he sat down, Pastor Black launched into a eulogy of Sister Bessie.

"What can we say about Sister Bessie that we don't already know in our hearts? She was a pillar of the Jerusalem A.B.E. Church and this community. She came to church every Sunday, sometimes twice. A Sunday school teacher, Girl Scout troop leader, and frequent visitor to the sick and the shut-ins, she walked the talk, lived her faith, and gave herself to her church."

The minister mopped his brow with a handkerchief. "Everywhere she went, she spread the word of our Lord, Jesus Christ, and she sang like an angel. We were blessed to have her voice in the choir. We will miss it. What can we say about Sister Bessie that we don't already know in our hearts? I invite family and friends to share their memories of Sister Bessie and to share the joy that she brought to us all. But first, Mrs. Black, another hymn?"

The choir sang another old hymn about the arms of God. As Sarah hummed along, she thanked God it wasn't time for her to shelter in His arms. The night before, after dragging herself out of the pond, she had made her way home. Fearful the couple who attacked her might be nearby and watching for signs of life, she was grateful she'd left the house lights off.

She had called the police and left a message for Officer Mike Corrigan, asking him to call her as soon as possible. He was the only police officer who had seemed to take her concerns and reports seriously. Then, by the light of the moon, she took a hot bath, crawled into bed with her mother's loaded gun, and her cell phone.

She called Dan. His voicemail came on. She left message after message, until she had told him everything. For the first time in over a week, she had no dreams. Her life was nightmare enough. When she awoke, she found the phone in her hand, its battery dead.

The hymn ended. Once again, the young boy continued to stand, clap his hands and bob his head. Once again, Jazmin stood and whispered in his ear. He sat down. Sarah was surprised. She had no idea Jazmin had a child. Still pretty young, Sarah wondered how old Jazmin had been when she had him.

Members of the family and the congregation climbed up the stairs to the podium to speak a few words about the dearly departed. The choir leader said he'd miss Sister Bessie's sweet soprano. The Sunday school principal cried and told the congregation how she'd be missed in the classroom. Several friends said they'd miss her at church suppers and visitations. At last, it was Arlene's turn to speak. She climbed the stairs, looking neither left nor right.

"Mama, it wasn't easy being your daughter. You leave me big shoes to fill."

She swayed and gripped the sides of the pulpit. "You've been freed from this earthly realm. Now you're home in our Lord's arms. I know you're looking down on me, watching me to see I do the right things. I promise you, Mama, I will."

She choked up, putting a tissue to her mouth.

Pastor Black reached out to pat her shoulder. Arlene twisted out of his grip and ran down the stairs, back to her seat. She sobbed and shook throughout the closing hymn, "Amazing Grace."

Sarah's heart wrenched at the sight. Soon she could be doing the same thing, placing her mother in God's hands. Not yet, please Lord. Not yet.

****

"Sarah!"

"Dan?" She slowly twirled in place on the sidewalk, trying to pick him out of the sea of black suits and dresses. She spotted him. Tanned, tall, and handsome, he was a welcome sight on any occasion, but especially now.

"I can't believe it." Sarah pushed through the surging crowd of mourners until at last she stood in front of him. The desperate woman who had spoken for hours into his voicemail was speechless with emotion. Now what should she do? Should she shake his hand? Give him a peck on the cheek? Hug him? Time and distance had made things awkward.

As if in response to her indecisive thoughts, he leaned down and wrapped his long arms around her. "I came as soon as I could."

Relief, gratitude, and love, mixed with the scent of him and memories of their intense sexual chemistry washed over her, leaving her tingling and weak-kneed. She clutched his neck and sobbed on his shoulder.

He kissed the top of her head, hugging and rocking her as he shushed her. "It's okay, you're safe now."

All the emotional tension that had been keeping her standing on her own two feet—in the face of her mother's accident, the loss of Aunt Ida, and the multiple attacks—was released with his simple assurance. She sagged against him, knowing he'd catch her, her trust in him restored with his return.

Half lifting her, he led Sarah to a bench beneath a large oak tree. She rested her head on his shoulder. She tried to speak, but words wrapped around sobs, until she was spent and exhausted.

"Feel better?"

She hiccupped, then laughed. "Now I'm starving."

"You always had a good appetite after sex," he whispered, tickling her ear.

He had always had an incredible effect on her, but how could she be simultaneously sad, fearful for her life, and sexually aroused? In public, after a funeral, no less? Damn the man. Her body screamed: Let's have sex. Now. But her brain said, Yikes. Not yet. It's way too soon.

"Let's go to the luncheon," she said with great effort.

Everyone was invited to the banquet hall next to the church. Sarah clung to Dan's arm, refusing to let go of him.

Jazmin waved to Sarah and motioned for her to join her at a table. "Well, who do we have here?" After giving Dan a long once-over, she nodded her approval at Sarah. "He have any brothers? We'll take two."

Sarah laughed. "He's an only child." She introduced Dan to Jazmin and her co-workers.

Peter waved a napkin at Dan. He had a mouthful of food and couldn't speak. Mountains of fried chicken, biscuits, greens, and mashed potatoes disappeared as he vacuumed his plate, followed by sweet potato pie.

"The ladies of the church outdid themselves," Sarah said. "Everything looks delicious."

"We pride ourselves on our cooking," Jazmin said. "This crowd ain't shy about eating. Get up to the buffet before it's all gone."

Plates piled high, Dan and Sarah returned to the table. Peter wiped hands on a napkin, introduced his wife, and told Dan what a great teacher Sarah was. "Not only was she able to teach me statistics," Peter said, "but also how to look beyond the surface of the data for more important findings."

"Like what?" Jazmin asked.

"You know the notes that the police are investigating?" Sarah whispered. "Peter and I think it's related to his research project. When I re-analyzed the data, I found an unusual number of cases of congenital syphilis among girls in this congregation." Sarah tapped the table for emphasis. "I think some creep is preying on little kids in this church."

"That's disgusting!" Jazmin said in a loud voice. "We have to do something right now!"

"About what?" Arlene asked suddenly appearing next to Sarah's chair.

Sarah hugged Arlene. "I'm so sorry for your loss. If I can do anything, please tell me."

"You would understand," Arlene said. "I know you're having a tough time with your mother."

"We're in a holding pattern," Sarah said. She introduced Dan as her "friend from out of town."

"Sarah, you should tell Arlene what you told me," Jazmin said.

Sarah shook her head. "This isn't the time to bother her with work."

Jazmin pressed on, undeterred. "Do you remember anyone in the church getting too touchy-feely with the kids? Sarah says some pervert's been messing with the girls in our church."

Arlene stiffened and stepped back. "I have no idea what you're talking about. If you'll excuse me, I have other people I need to greet." She turned on her heel and left.

Sarah bit her lower lip, patted Dan on the hand, and said, "Time for us to go."

****

A police car sat at the edge of the driveway when Sarah arrived home. She was so relieved to see Officer Corrigan, that she wasn't even annoyed by Pollack's presence. "Officer Mike! Am I ever glad to see you! Dan, this is Officer Mike Corrigan and Officer Pollack. I've told you about them."

Dan nodded and said hello.

"You called?" Officer Mike asked.

"Last night, I almost 'slept with the fish.'"

As she related the story, both officers scribbled in their notebooks. At Aunt Ida's, Sarah re-enacted the event, complete with the man and the sultry-voiced woman. Then she took them to her house to show them her "life preservers." She put her key in the deadbolt as the men stood on the top step behind her. Before she could turn the key, the door swung inward. She froze.

"I'm positive I locked the door when I left this morning."

Winston's head appeared in the gap between the door and the doorframe, happy to see everyone. He charged out the door and jumped on Dan.

"Well, hello my new best friend," Dan said.

"What's your name?"

"His first name is 'Down'!" Officer Mike said. "His second name is Winston."

Sarah was happy the silly dog was alive and well. The police officers entered the kitchen ahead of Sarah, then motioned for her to come in. Dan followed her inside.

"Did you leave the kitchen like this?" Officer Pollack asked.

Every single cabinet drawer had been pulled out and the contents spilled onto the floor. Tea towels, dishes, flatware, and glasses mingled with napkins, paper towels, soap, cereal, coffee, and tea.

"Oh, yes, my kitchen always looks like this," Sarah said, voice dripping with sarcasm. "What kind of question is that? I don't think my dog could do this much damage, even if he tried. What do you think?"

"I think you've had a B and E," Officer Pollack said.

"As in, I've been burgled?"

Dan raised an eyebrow. "Is that a real word?"

"You stay here while we check out the rest of the rooms to be sure no one's still at work," Officer Mike said. "Is there a basement?"

"Yes, and it's full of stuff, so it would be easy for someone to hide."

"Better call this one in," Officer Pollack said and pulled out his cell phone as he left the kitchen.

The room began to spin; Sarah sat down with a thud, then put her head in her hands.

"Are you okay?" Dan pulled up another kitchen chair next to her, sat down, and took one hand.

"I think so. I just got a little light-headed. I'm not

sure I can handle too many more surprises," she said. "I'm close to my rope's end."

"Did you ever get that head injury looked at?" Dan asked, reaching up to touch the back of her head.

She looked into his dark brown eyes. If eyes were the window to the soul, his was full of compassion. If she looked deeply enough, would she see love in there again? He stroked her hair with a gentle hand, evoking a memory of that same hand sliding down her neck, over her breasts, teasing her nipples—

"All clear," Officer Mike said as he walked into the kitchen.

Dan took his hand away from Sarah's head, and put his arm around her shoulder and gave her a little squeeze. She leaned against him, wishing she could have an hour alone with him.

"The rest of the house looks equally trashed," Officer Mike said. "You're going to have to figure out what's missing after the Crime Lab comes in to dust for prints. Did you have any valuables like jewelry or art?"

"No, nothing like that."

"Any guns?"

She felt sick to her stomach and it must have shown on her face.

"You had a gun?" Pollack asked.

"My mother had a .22. A Ruger. I found it yesterday when I was looking for a bathing suit. After I got knocked on the head, I came home, loaded it, and slept with it. This morning I left it in my nightstand. Do you want me to see if it's still there?"

"Why don't we wait until the Crime Lab gets here?" Officer Pollack tapped his pen against his notebook and yawned.

"Did you ever call the towing company about Aunt Ida's car?" Sarah asked. "I know it was hers. I saw the license plate."

"We're getting there," Officer Pollack replied.

Sarah yawned. "When will the Crime Lab techs get here?" She could hardly keep her eyes open.

"You can lean on me and take a nap, Sarah," Dan said. "You need to get some rest."

"Why don't you go to your aunt's house and lie down?" Office Mike said. "This is going to take a while."

****

Knowing Dan was in Ida's den, sitting in the armchair across from the couch, made Sarah feel safe enough to relax and fall into a deep sleep as soon as her head touched the pillow. She was dreaming that someone was shouting at her, saying terrible things about her. She woke up. It wasn't a dream. The yelling was real.

"What have you done?"

A red-faced man shouted at her. What was his name? Potter? Pumwhack? No, no, not those…Pollack. That's right, Officer Pollack.

"What have you done?" he repeated.

"What have I done?"

Dizzy and disoriented, she looked around the room. Dan was no longer in the room, replaced by two glaring police officers. Confused, she looked from one officer to the other, then sat upright and pushed the afghan away. "What are you talking about?"

"What did you do to your aunt?"

She looked into the officer's eyes, his face red and contorted with anger. "I didn't do anything to her.

What's the matter with you?"

"Homicide is on the way," Officer Mike said.

Officer Pollack asked, "Can you explain how a finger got into your freezer?"

Was she still asleep, simply having a very vivid nightmare? "A what?"

"A human finger. A pinky, to be exact, cut off just above the knuckle was found wrapped in aluminum foil in your freezer, along with a wedding band. The ring is inscribed 'To Ida, Love Jack.'"

The room began to spin. Her arms and legs felt like strands of wire shaking beneath the weight of a thousand angry birds. "No, no, no. That can't be."

"Where's the rest of the body?"

Sarah put her head between her knees and moaned. Bile rose in her throat, threatened to explode in a spew of vomit. "Stop it, just stop!"

"You missed a piece," Pollack shouted. "Where's the rest of the body? Did you have help?"

She snapped her head up. "Betty. We have to find Betty."

"What about her?"

"I came home yesterday afternoon and found her sitting on my back porch." Sarah felt her teeth start to chatter. "I'd been to Shady Rest Nursing Home to see about placing my mother there." Recalling the rest of the story, she moaned. "Oh, no. My mother's being transferred to Shady Rest today and I'm supposed to be there to sign the papers for her."

"Finish your story," Pollack demanded. "You found Betty on your back porch. She's your aunt's cleaning lady, right? The disabled one?"

"She looked like she'd been crying; her hair and

clothes were askew. When I asked what was wrong, she dragged me over to Aunt Ida's house."

Raggedy sobs shook her, strangling the words in her throat. "The power was out. Water had pooled on the floor beneath the freezer. I opened it and found it was filled with packages wrapped in aluminum foil. I finally calmed Betty down by telling her I'd bring the frozen food to my house. She left to go to another job; I brought everything over here and put it in my freezer."

"What's Betty's last name?"

What the hell was going on? Was it really Aunt Ida's pinky? She felt like vomiting again. "I don't know."

Saying nothing, Officer Pollack continued to stare at Sarah.

"We have to find Betty," she repeated. "She's the key."

"You have the right to remain silent," he said.

"I don't understand. What's going on?"

Officer Mike stood by the door with an unhappy expression on his face. He wouldn't make eye contact with her.

"Anything you say can be used against you in a court of law," Pollack said.

This couldn't be happening. Not now. Not in her beloved aunt's home. It had to be a terrible nightmare. "Am I being arrested?"

"You have the right to have an attorney present now and during any future questioning."

"Why won't you answer me?" Her breath came in short gasps, as if she was trying to breathe through a wet washcloth. "What's going on?"

"If you cannot afford an attorney, one will be

appointed for you, free of charge, if you wish."

"Answer me, damn it! What's going on?"

"Sarah Wright, you are under arrest for the murder of Ida Mae Katz."

Chapter Sixteen

Numb from shock, Sarah sat in a barren holding cell lined with cinder blocks at the Precinct 03/Franklin Station. They had to be wrong about Aunt Ida. She had to be alive. But where was she?

As Dan looked on, holding Winston back by the leash, and shouting, "You can't do this!" the police officers pressed her into a squad car, leaving her home under the auspices of Sergeant Detective Engelman and the Crime Lab technicians.

At the station house, she was fingerprinted, photographed and stripped of anything she might use to escape or hurt herself—such as her gold hoop earrings. Of course, they also took her purse and phone. She'd been waiting in the cell for over an hour and was getting anxious. Dan would take care of her dog and cats, but what would she do about her mother?

Aunt Ida dead? No. She didn't believe it.

Homicide Detectives interviewed her for an hour before they tired of her responses—"I didn't do it! I want my lawyer!"—and locked her up.

She felt like she was in a zoo. The painted concrete floor held a drain in the center; plastic covered mattresses and scratchy blankets had been tossed randomly around the cell. A stainless steel combination sink and toilet unit was at one end of the cell and a video camera stared down at her from the other end. As being filmed while she peed was not on her to do list, she wondered how long she could go without emptying her bladder.

The other occupant of the cell was not one to be easily ignored. With alcohol fumes radiating about her person in a cloud, the obese woman wore her bleached blonde hair in a mullet, and an eggplant colored biker outfit with a fringed leather vest and bra. A Pillsbury dough girl midriff bulged beneath the bra and over waistband of her pants. As to which numbered more—the multiple tattoos versus holes in her ears, nose and eyebrows—Sarah didn't care to determine. Biker chick moved her mattress next to Sarah's the minute she landed in the cell.

"Why don't you come over here and sit next to me?" She patted her mattress. "My name is Beverly. What's your name, hon?"

Sarah could barely understand her "Baltimorese." Her ear heard "Bebberly" for Beverly, "rat" for right and "beby" for baby, among other linguistic oddities—and more difficult to understand than Yiddish.

"Oooo, you is a beauty! Baby, I'm the best lover around—and whaddya know—it's my birthday and you is a wunnerful present! Dem police don' care what we do. We'll have us a right good time."

She finished the generous invitation with a big wet air kiss. Then, as if to demonstrate her skills, she stuck her tongue out and touched the end of her nose with the tip.

Holy crap. I have to get out of here.

Sarah lumbered to her feet, went to the glass and called out, "Hello, Officers? When can I make my phone call? I want to call my lawyer. Hello?"

"You got a 'mergency, hon? Don' you worry 'bout it none. I'll take care of you!" Beverly jumped up off the mattress and lunged at Sarah, forcing her back against the window.

"Help! Somebody, please, help me!"

Putting her face next to Sarah's, Beverly grabbed her by the shoulders and began to shake. Sarah thought she would either get drunk from the alcohol fumes or faint from fear. Her neck went into spasms.

"Is that a threat? I'm gonna kill you!"

"Help, someone!"

"I'm gonna kill you!" Beverly shouted again, then winked at Sarah.

Three police officers ran into the cell. "Beverly, knock it off." Two officers pulled her off Sarah. "Stop trying to scare her."

"Dr. Wright, come with me. You can make your phone call now," Officer Cohen said.

As the other two officers led Beverly from the cell, she blew Sarah a kiss.

In her one and only call, Sol picked up on the first ring. "It's Sarah Wright. I need your help."

"Rah Right? You'll have to speak up!"

"Where's Molly? I'm at Precinct 03—in the County. I've been arrested for Aunt Ida's murder. I didn't do it!"

"I don't handle criminal cases." The phone clicked.

"Don't hang up! Sol?" She turned to Officer Cohen. "Do I get another call if my lawyer is deaf?"

"You got your call. Back to the cell."

Sarah wondered when Beverly would be back. She crawled onto the mattress, closed her eyes, and tried to sleep to shut out the nightmare. As she was about to doze off, someone called her name. "Dr. Wright! Mr. Weinstein's here to see you."

Energized with hope, she pushed herself up from the mattress and went to the bulletproof window. Somehow Sol must have understood her on the phone. He'll get me out of here, I just know it, Sarah thought.

A tall, handsome young man with broad shoulders entered the holding cell area. He looked as if he might have played football in college. Clean-shaven with short spiky hair, he wore a brown leather jacket, a white button-down shirt and dark jeans. "Dr. Wright?"

"Yes?"

"I'm Josh Weinstein. Molly said you needed me."

"But how?"

"Molly overheard Sol on the phone with you. It's hard not to hear him when he's on the phone. As soon as she heard him say 'Rah Right,' she grabbed the extension on her desk and listened in to see what was going on."

"Let me guess—you're Molly's husband and Sol's son? So, she really is Mrs. Weinstein?" Sarah asked. "But you're so young and he is…"

"Older than most of the buildings in downtown Baltimore. I'm told I was a change of life baby though I'm not sure whose life changed more, my mother's or my father's. My mother passed away when I was just a little guy." He put his hand down to indicate a younger person.

"Sol raised me by himself and I gave him a real hard time. He spent a lot of time bailing me out of jails for a wide variety of youthful indiscretions. He knew the legal system from the outside, I learned it from the inside. Years later, when I finally got back on track, Sol set me up as a bail bondsman."

He showed Sarah his card through the glass. "My company is called 'Three Strikes Bail Bonds.' Our motto is 'One-Two-Three! We set you free!' I also attend night classes at the University of Baltimore Law School. At any rate, I'm here to see what I can do."

Not knowing where to start, Sarah let everything out in one prolonged burst of words. "The police arrested me for the murder of my aunt, her pinky finger and wedding band were in my freezer, but I didn't kill her, I swear. She's been missing for close to a week, I filed a missing person report but no one's done anything about it. My mother's in a coma in a nursing home. I was supposed to go there yesterday to sign papers. A friend was there when I was arrested, but I don't know what to do."

Feeling snotty and gritty, she wiped her face with the back of her hand. Could things get any worse?

"I can check on your house and see if your friend is there. The police may still be working the scene."

"If you see a tall, dark-haired guy hanging around, looking lost, his name is Dan. Could you tell him where I am, please?"

"Okay. I can help you with the bail part, but I can't help you with anything else. You need a criminal lawyer."

"I don't understand. What's the 'bail part'? This is all a terrible misunderstanding. It's a case of false arrest. I can't believe they have enough evidence to arrest me, much less for a conviction."

"All the police need to arrest someone is probable cause," Josh said. "Having a finger and a wedding band in your freezer and a missing person report for the same person is a good example of it. People have been convicted on the basis of less than that."

Her stomach plummeted. "If you're trying to scare me, you're doing a good job."

"Bail's not a slam-dunk in murder trials. The judge has to determine whether you're a flight risk; and he has to decide if you're a risk to the community or to yourself, or if you're a recidivist. He's supposed to apply the least, not the most restrictive measures, which some judges tend to forget."

"Please, get me out of here," Sarah said. "I have to find Aunt Ida. I don't want to make any more new friends in jail. Beverly was enough. My mother needs me. So do my pets."

Now was not the time to wonder if Dan needed her. Not in jail, anyway.

"I think I know who'd be good for this. I have to call his office and see if he's available. They probably won't do anything until tomorrow morning. Do you have any other clothes you want me to bring for your court appearance? The suit you're wearing isn't bad."

"Lucky for me, I was at a funeral this morning. Who knew I'd be best-dressed person in the slammer?"

"Well, count on staying overnight. I'm betting they'll bring you over to Circuit Court in Towson sometime tomorrow morning or afternoon. In case you do make bail, what kind of collateral do you have? Do you have any savings or possessions you can use?"

"I might as well give up now. I'm in deep financial trouble, all because of my mother. I've been going crazy trying to keep the utilities and other creditors at bay." She shook her head. "Your father's been working on getting me legal guardianship of my mother's body and property so I can take care of her. I might as well start polishing my license plate making and flirting skills now."

"Let's not get ahead of ourselves," Josh said. "What about family? Any sisters or brothers who can help you out?"

"No wealthy relatives. My sister's a nurse. My brother has a daughter in college. He has no cash."

"I'll talk to Sol and see if he has any ideas. Keep your chin up. Remember—'One-Two-Three! We set you free!' "

Sarah crawled back onto the mattress, closed her eyes and tried to sleep without much success...

The next thing she heard, "Rise and shine, Dr. Wright!" came from a chunky blonde jail deputy with streaks of blue eye shadow under her eyes. "You want some breakfast?"

"I'd like some coffee, please." She yawned and stretched and felt every ache each pain. "Would it be possible to get a pad of paper and a pen? I have something I'd like to write down."

"Your confession?"

They never gave up, did they? "No, my thoughts about this case. I think better when I can write."

The deputy gave her a doubtful look. "I'll see if it's allowed."

Alone with her thoughts, the metal toilet and video camera her only accoutrements, she didn't want to think about the day ahead. Sarah continually ran the events of the past week through her mind: Why was she under attack? Where was Aunt Ida? Why were a finger and a wedding band in her freezer? Was it really Aunt Ida's pinky?

She had to find Betty to help corroborate her story. If only she could reach someone at WorkForce. The housekeeper was crucial to finding Aunt Ida.

"Here's your coffee," the deputy chirped. "Your lawyer called. He said he'd meet you at Circuit Court."

"What about a pad of paper and a pencil?"

"Nope. You're not a deaf mute, so you're not entitled to have them." She gave Sarah a smug little smile. Sarah finger spelled b-i-t-c-h in sign language after she was alone.

The officer returned a short while later. "Sheriff's transport is here for you; time to put on your jewelry." She approached Sarah with clanking manacles and shackles.

"I'm shocked," Sarah said. "I can't believe you think it's necessary to treat me like a murderer." When the woman only gaped at her, she said, "Let me re-phrase that. I won't run away."

"Yeah, that's what they all say." The deputy placed the matched set of jewelry on Sarah's wrists and ankles, then led her in a shuffling walk to the female sally port.

A hot flush of humiliation crept up her neck and face. A Sheriff's Deputy signed for Sarah, took her by the arm and led her to a waiting van. "Am I the only person you have?"

"You're a regular celebrity. Get limousine service, complete with a bucket of champagne."

"What do you mean? I haven't been on the news, have I?"

"The question is what news haven't you been on? Television crews are at the courthouse now. CNN might even be there. They're calling this a 'high anus' crime."

Sarah grimaced. "It's pronounced 'hay-nous.'"

If the gods were on her side today, perhaps Marian had been working so hard, she'd not had time to turn on the TV or radio news. Perhaps, she and all of the staff of the Pediatrics Department had gone camping in Tibet. Yeah, that's right. A great big camping trip with no electricity and a whole clan of Yetis.

Her life was ruined.

When the van stopped and the rear doors opened, and a swarm of reporters, microphones on long poles and cameras with blinding lights surged forward. Cringing, Sarah clung to the Deputy's arm while questions flew at her like verbal rocks.

"What made you attack your aunt, Dr. Wright?"

"Why'd you do it, Dr. Wright?"

"Will you plead insanity?"

"How about a few words for CNN, Dr. Wright?"

The deputy took her to a detention area in the basement of the courthouse and signed Sarah over to another deputy. A distant murmuring sound turned out to be the rumble of hundreds of prisoners' voices. The new deputy, a flat-faced white man with no discernible emotions, placed her in a barred cell with a motley crew of women who made her long for Beverly. Sarah tried her best not to look anyone in the eye, but it was difficult when a muscular cellmate in a denim shirt began to sniff her.

"She's in heat," the body-builder shouted out to the vast amusement of the assembled female miscreants.

Just take me now, Lord.

As if in answer to her prayer, a deputy walked over to the cell and called her name. "Sarah Wright?"

She could hardly hear him over women yowling

like cats. "That's me!"

"Your lawyer's here to see you."

A short shuffling walk later, she was in a small room, looking through a grate at a man in a navy blue pinstripe suit, red tie, and light blue oxford button-down shirt. He was taller than Sarah by about three inches and had the powerful build of an athlete. His brown hair was neatly styled and his ruddy face was clean-shaven. He opened a leather portfolio embossed with gold initials and holding a Mont Blanc pen in the clip. On one hand, a diamond encrusted Rolex twinkled, matched only by the large gold signet ring on the other.

"You must be Dr. Wright. I'm your defense attorney, Will Rutler." He motioned for her to be seated. "Let me tell you how this goes. I'm here for the limited purpose of getting you out of jail."

"Mr. Rutler, this is a huge mistake, I didn't do it. "

"We don't have time for your editorial comments and we're not here to discuss the trial. Tell me about yourself. How long have you been in Baltimore? Do you have roots here? I need to be able to establish for the court that you are neither a flight risk, nor a risk to yourself or the community. Are you with me so far?"

Sarah nodded and took a deep breath.

He raised his eyebrows and stared at her. "Well?"

"I live with my mother, have been living with her since she had a DUI and broke both legs. I took care of her full-time for a year, then accepted a position at Hopkins. I'm in Pediatrics, doing child abuse and neglect research. She—my mother—is in a coma. "

"Tell me about her."

"What does she have to do with this?"

"Let me be the judge of that. You said she's in a

coma. How'd that happen?" He took notes as he spoke.

"Last week, after drinking and using GHB, she fell on a patch of ice and has been in a coma ever since. She's in a nursing home now and I was supposed to sign her transfer papers yesterday, but I got arrested. I swear, she has nothing to do with Aunt Ida's disappearance."

"One more time, tell me about your mother," he said, with more patience than she could have found were the circumstances reversed. "I know you're upset, but you have to talk to me or I can't help."

Sarah spent the next ten minutes telling Mr. Rutler about her mother while he took copious notes but remained silent. At length, he closed his leather folder. "When we go into the courtroom, say nothing. I'll do the talking. Got it?"

"But—"

"No buts! This isn't the time to tell them about anything else. This isn't the trial. You stay quiet." He glared at her. "Are we clear on that?"

"Yes. I have one question for you."

"Shoot."

"How much is this going to cost? I have no money. I'm struggling to pay my mother's bills. I can't afford huge legal fees."

He flashed a blinding white smile. "We'll settle up later. Right now, stay calm and let me do the talking."

"All rise!" the bailiff announced. "Circuit Court for Baltimore County is now in session; the Honorable Judge Stein presiding!"

Everyone stood when the black-robed judge entered the courtroom.

"You may be seated. We have here before us the

State of Maryland versus Sarah Leah Wright on a charge of first degree murder," Judge Stein said. "This is a bail hearing. The pretrial release officer has reviewed the case. Ms. Baker, what is the recommendation?"

A perky blonde woman in a black pants suit stood. "Your Honor, the Pretrial Release Office has reviewed the case and we concur. Due to the totality of the circumstances, if Dr. Wright wasn't the murderer, then she knew about it and aided and abetted the murderer or murderers. Because of the heinous nature of the crime, it is recommended bail not be granted for the defendant."

Oh. My. God. I am doomed.

The prosecuting attorney continued. "The State of Maryland has the sworn testimony of two police officers that they were present when the finger and wedding ring of Mrs. Ida Mae Katz were discovered. The ME tells us Mrs. Katz' body was cut up with a table saw, which would have been a very messy affair. The house and garage were thoroughly cleaned with bleach, making the use of Luminol impossible. This is the sign of a very intelligent criminal and premeditation."

The blonde attorney picked up a piece of paper. "Furthermore, a police officer is prepared to testify that it was obvious that a table saw, metal snips, and other tools were removed from the workbench in the garage. The cover-up speaks volumes about a person familiar with the forensics of crime detection."

A very intelligent criminal?

Premeditation?

A cover-up?

"Upon searching the garbage pail in the defendant's kitchen, the Crime Lab found a white handkerchief smeared with blood. Preliminary analyses lead us to believe the blood is a match for Mrs. Katz' blood."

Sarah thought back to the rag Winston dragged into the house and closed her eyes. She was doomed.

And the nails continued to be tapped into Sarah's coffin. "9-1-1 records show that the defendant made numerous phone calls, claiming Ida Mae Katz was missing, in an obvious attempt to point the finger at a phantom kidnapper."

Had she cried wolf? Sarah wondered. What should she have done? Ignore all the signs? Gone about her business? Pretend nothing was wrong?

"Furthermore, the defendant's fingerprints were found on a CD in Mrs. Katz' car, which was abandoned in a parking lot. The defendant, Sarah Wright, is a Registered Nurse with a PhD in Public Health. We are prepared to prove she had motive, ability and the mental state to kill Mrs. Ida Mae Katz."

With that, the blond attorney sat.

Sarah felt as if she'd been slammed with a baseball bat. She stared at Judge Stein with his thin face, dark brown hair and receding hairline. From his perch on the bench, his dark eyes seemed to bore into her.

"Do you have anything to say, Mr. Rutler?" Judge Stein said.

"Your Honor, with all due respect to Ms. Baker, we're here to determine conditions for bail and we all know a person is of greater value when they are out and able to participate in their own defense. She's innocent until proven guilty."

Sarah wanted to stand up and applaud for Will Rutler, but her hands were still manacled.

"Mr. Rutler, while I agree the evidence is circumstantial, it is overwhelming. Having a finger and a wedding band in a freezer, along with a bloody handkerchief from the victim in one's home is more than enough." Judge Stein began to scribble something on a piece of paper. She wanted to scream, "I didn't do it!" but kept quiet as instructed.

Others had not followed directions, however. Behind her, loud whispers ebbed and flowed. The Judge looked at the bailiff, who walked over in Sarah's direction and spoke to someone standing behind her. "If you don't keep quiet, you will be removed from the courtroom, do you understand?"

"Yes," a man's voice said. The voice sounded familiar, but she couldn't place it. She didn't want to turn and look for fear of being reprimanded by the intimidating judge.

The bailiff walked back to stand guard by the Judge's bench and stared at the offender.

A sheaf of papers was handed to Mr. Rutler from behind. He opened them, nodded, then closed them. "Your Honor, I'd like to request bail for my client."

"Bail? This is a first degree murder case and you're asking for bail?" Judge Stein said.

"Yes, your Honor. The evidence is circumstantial and there are no forensics to place her at the scene. Nothing but conjecture says she's the one who committed the crime." Rutler frowned in the direction of the State's Attorney. "My client is not a flight risk, nor is she a risk to herself or the community. Her ten-year-old car barely gets her back and forth to work. She doesn't even have a current passport. She has a clean record, not even a traffic ticket. She is a productive citizen employed at a prestigious medical institution."

He paused and looked around the courtroom. "Most importantly, she has an elderly mother who's in a Pikesville nursing home in a coma. My client is the sole support of her mother and has been granted guardianship of her mother's body and property." He waved the sheaf of papers. "Dr. Wright is not leaving town. Your Honor, we want the least restrictive measures to assure her appearance at trial."

She'd been granted guardianship of her mother? When did that happen?

"The State of Maryland disagrees, your Honor." The State's Attorney shot out of her chair. "We have reason to believe Dr. Wright has motive and means to disappear if she's granted bail."

What was she now, Houdini?

"Your honor, I repeat, my client has no previous record," attorney Rutler maintained. "She's a hard-working citizen who has devoted her life to caring for people. She's a pediatric nurse and her research helps children. She's not a flight risk."

"What about her inheritance?" Ms. Baker said.

"Counselor, you know as well as I she doesn't have access to that money."

What inheritance? What money? What the hell were they talking about?

Judge Stein watched the two attorneys as if it were a tennis match then said, "I've heard enough. Bail is granted at one million dollars."

"One million dollars! Where am I going to get one million dollars?"

The judge and Rutler glared at Sarah. She closed her mouth.

Judge Stein said, "You don't need the entire amount. You only need ten percent or one-hundred thousand dollars in cash for a bail bondsman to post a corporate surety. If you don't have the cash, then you go to jail."

"We have the money, Your Honor," a man said from behind Sarah.

She turned briefly to see who'd spoke. Josh Weinstein and standing at his side, holding a large leather briefcase was his father, Sol.

Standing next to Sol, was Dan.

Chapter Seventeen

"Could someone explain what's going on?" Sarah asked as she clutched Dan's hand.

Josh led the way to a counter outside the courtroom. "You need to sign some papers, then you can leave."

"No, not just that. What happened in there? Where'd this money come from? Oh, and here's a good one—what's this nonsense about an inheritance?"

Rutler looked at Sol. "You'd better tell her before she finds out from the press."

"Not here," Sol yelled. "Too many big ears."

"Let's go to lunch at Squid Pro Quo," Rutler suggested. "We can talk there. Are we squared?"

"Just some papers to sign," Josh said. "Then we can go."

Sarah signed a mountain of papers and Josh spent a few moments with the Clerk of the Court. While she waited for Josh to tell her what to do, Beverly walked through the metal detector, still in the leather biker outfit. Beverly smiled and waved at her as if they were old friends. Sarah smiled and waved back. A chubby, woman with a bleached blonde beehive followed Beverly through the metal detector. She scowled at Sarah, grabbed Beverly's hand, and dragged her into a courtroom.

"Who's that?" Dan asked.

"Long story," Sarah advised. "Best told over a large drink."

As they walked the few short blocks from the Circuit Court house to San Sushi, Two, Josh told Sarah and Dan its nickname was Squid Pro Quo because of all the lawyers and judges who ate there. The owner was walking around the restaurant greeting customers. Paintings of fish and geisha girls covered the walls.

"Hey, Vandi, what's good today?" Rutler asked.

"We got some great white tuna, beautiful ahi, spicy tuna roll. You name it, we make it."

"Give us a round of miso soup and then we'll order some sushi and sashimi after that. We need to talk. Can you put us in a quiet corner?"

"Take the big booth in the front of Thai One On."

After ordering a drink, Sarah went to the ladies room, grateful for a porcelain toilet that wasn't out in the open for all to see. She washed her hands and splashed some cold water on her face. Her black eyes matched her cervical collar. She gave up and returned to the table where the soup was waiting.

She slid in next to Dan, and he gave her knee a squeeze, then left his hand resting on her leg. Shudders of pleasure ran up her thigh, and she practically groaned with the effort to restrain herself from grabbing his hand and sliding it under her skirt. She took a big sip of hot tea and pushed away the erotic fantasy. Later, after a long hot shower and a lot of rest.

"Okay, gentlemen, some explanations, please," she said in a squeaky voice.

Dan gave her an odd look and smirked. She felt his hand sliding along her thigh. She was going to have to have a few words with him when they got alone. She put her hand on top of his and interlaced her fingers with his. "First, is it true I was made my mother's guardian?" Sarah asked, attempting to stay focused.

"Yes," Sol yelled.

"Dad," Josh said. "Lower your voice. We're not deaf."

"Okay," Sol said in a normal indoor voice. "I was able to get your petition pushed through quickly because I called in a favor. Will and I spoke yesterday, and he thought it would strengthen your case for making bail."

"It worked, didn't it?" Will said.

"They don't call you the 'Pit Bull' without good reason, Will," Sol said.

"Mr. Rutler, how did you know I didn't have a current passport and that my car was over ten years old? I don't recall telling you any of that this morning."

"Sarah, before I take a high profile case like this, I like to know something about the client. Sol and Josh were key referrals. I would have taken you on their say-so alone, but that doesn't mean I don't do my homework. I have a private investigator on retainer."

She nodded. That made sense. "Okay, fair enough. Now, what's all this about an inheritance, and why didn't you want to talk about it at the courthouse?"

"There's no need for the media to get this information from us," Sol said. "It'll come out soon enough at the trial. Sarah, you know Ida had no surviving family. Her husband died and they had no offspring. She always thought of you and your mother as her family."

"Yes, I love her, too."

"Ida was a wealthy woman."

213

"I know she was comfortable. She had a new Cadillac every other year and a second home in Florida. Her husband left her a nice nest egg."

He gave her one of those patient, speaking to a child smiles. "Sarah, Ida wasn't just 'comfortable.' She was a multimillionaire. She left everything to you and your mother."

****

The rest of lunch passed in a blur.

Mom and me sole heirs? How could that be? The figures were incomprehensible. Now she understood why Mr. Rutler hadn't been worried about being paid.

Dan whispered in her ear, sending frissons of pleasure up her neck. "Think you can loan me a few bucks? I'm a little tapped out."

She looked up at him and fell into those chocolate brown eyes. God, it was nice to have him back in her life, even if she was indicted for murder. As soon as she could get him alone, she was going to show him how much she'd missed him.

Sol was talking to her, but all she could hear was "Blah, blah, blah, money. Blah, blah, blah, Sarah." She needed to get some sleep so she could think straight.

"What do I do now?"

Rutler answered. "Get some rest. Then you need to make appointments with Sol and me to go over our legal strategies."

****

When they walked out of the restaurant, Dan explained the latest obstacles in her life. "Your house and Ida's are crime scenes," he said. "And, they've impounded your car. The police allowed me to take the cats and Winston after I argued with them that it wasn't fair to send them off with Animal Control."

Aghast, Sarah asked, "They were going to send them to the pound?"

He nodded. "If it hadn't been for that one guy—Mike?—I don't think they would have let me take them."

Dan put the key in the car door and a large, gray dog's head popped up.

"Winston! I can't believe you brought him," she said and laughed. The dog danced and jumped as Sarah pushed him into the backseat of the car.

"He looked sad and lonely, so I brought him with me for the day."

"It's nice to see you boys are bonding," she said. "What about the cats. Are they okay?"

Winston poked his head between the two front seats and licked Sarah's face.

"I got you a room at the Extended Stay Inn in Cockeysville. They allow pets. The cats are there already and settled in."

Sarah's cell phone chirped. There were four hang-ups and three messages in her voice mail.

"Sarah, this is Marian Kirby. Call me. It's urgent!"

"Sarah, this is Peter. Call me, it's urgent!"

"*Vot* is wrong with you? Don't you ever answer your phone? It's Gert. Call me!"

Sarah turned to Dan. "Your mother called."

He grimaced. "I didn't tell her anything, honest. I haven't even told her I'm in town."

The last message was just the sound of someone crying.

She punched in her work number.

"General Pediatrics, this is Jazmin. How may I

help you?"

"Jazmin! It's Sarah! I've gotten urgent messages from Marian and Peter. What's going on?"

"Dear Lord, it's been one terrible week. First Arlene's mother passes, now you've been arrested. It's on every channel. Is that for real? I don't like the sound of it. Dr. Kirby and Dr. Peter are furious upset."

"This is all a big mistake. I swear I didn't kill my aunt or anyone."

"I'm no fan of the police. My brother was arrested on account of being black. You're a good person, Dr. Wright. But, you know how folks talk. They're saying you shouldn't be allowed to come in here anymore."

Sarah was stunned. "Did Dr. Kirby say that?"

Jazmin's silence spoke volumes.

"Is she around? I need to speak with her."

Marian answered on the first ring. "Sarah, whatever you do, do not come to work today!"

Her throat closed over. "What's going on?"

"The whole hospital is in an uproar about your arrest and the murder charges. Parents are flipping out."

Of all the people, she never expected Marian to turn on her like this. "I'm not a murderer."

Marian sighed. "If you come here during clinic hours, we can't guarantee your safety. Your face has been on every television in the hospital, not to mention on the front cover of the newspapers. One caption said 'Butcher Cuts Up Aunt!' Stay home."

"Marian, let me work. My mother's in a coma, my aunt is missing, I've been run over, hit on the head, nearly drowned, and locked up for a crime I didn't commit. Don't take everything away from me, please, I'm begging you."

After a long pause, she said, "I'll have Jazmin leave a laptop in your office for you to pick up tonight after all the outpatient departments are closed. Peter can come to your house to work on the project. Try not to be seen. We can't afford this kind of publicity."

"I'm innocent until proven guilty, Marian. Marian?"

The connection was broken.

She called Peter next. He wasn't in, so she left a voice mail message.

"I'm calling your mother," she told Dan. "Do you want to speak with her?"

"Do I have to? I have no idea of what to say."

She tried Gert's number.

"Hello? Who's this?" Loud music from Oklahoma blared in the background. "Hold on a minute. Where is the *fercockta* remote controller for this thing? Here we go. Who is this?"

"Mrs. Rosen, it's Sarah Wright. You called me?"

"Yes. *Vot's* the story with your aunt?"

"What do you mean?"

"I mean did you find the *fershtinkina* car?"

"Oh, yes, I did. Thank you. It was in an impound lot in Towson."

"*Nu*, so any word from Ida?"

Sarah was momentarily speechless. "Have you been watching television, Mrs. Rosen?"

"Yes, I've been watching TV all day. Why?"

"Have you seen the news?"

"*Ach*, no, it's too depressing. I only watch musicals on cable."

"Are you sitting down?"

"Yeah, why?"

"The police think my aunt has been murdered."

"*Vot?* No, that can't be. That's horrible. Do they know who did it?"

"They think I did it. I was arrested yesterday and just got out on bail today." She stopped, unable to say another word. Her mouth wouldn't work.

Dan reached over and held her hand. Tears dripped off her nose.

Gert's voice grew gentle. "So did you do it?"

She choked back a sob. "No, I swear I didn't kill Aunt Ida. I love her."

"Sarah, Jews have been accused of terrible crimes throughout history. Russians soldiers started pogroms by telling ignorant peasants Jews used the blood of Christian children in their matzah for Passover. Accusations don't make it so."

"You're going to hear some terrible stories about me in the next few weeks. Please don't believe them, I would never hurt anyone on purpose, much less my aunt."

"*Oy!* Anyone tries to tell me lies about you and I'll kick them in the *tukhis!*"

"Thank you." She gave Dan a watery smile. He gave her a questioning look.

"I got a few more questions. One, do you have a good lawyer?"

"Yes. His name is Will Rutler. They call him the 'Pit Bull.' "

"Good." She coughed. "Two, when will you have the service for Ida, and will you be sitting *shiva?*"

"I don't know. It depends on when they release her remains, I guess. What's *shiva?*"

"Jewish mourning. Tell you what, I'll give the

rabbi a call and see what I can arrange. How about a memorial service? You don't need any remains with that. We Jews don't do viewings; we have short services and shorter funerals." Gert took a drag on her cigarette. "We sit *shiva* on hard stools or benches for a week in a *shiva* house where we cover all the mirrors. We wear slippers instead of shoes, we don't cut our hair, we tear our clothing and we don't work. People come and pay their respects."

"I can do that. Yes, I'd like you to call the rabbi. Please give him my telephone number. And, thank you. Thank you for having faith in me."

"You can't fool an *alter cocker* like me. I know you're telling the truth."

Sarah teared up. "I wish you could talk to the police."

"*Nu*, so who says I can't?"

Dan pointed at the phone and nodded.

"Someone wants to talk to you, Mrs. Rosen." She handed Dan the phone.

"Hi, Mom!" Dan said and pulled the phone away from his ear. Sarah could hear his mother shouting, "*Vot* are you doing in town?"

"It's a long story," he said. "How about if I tell you when I see you? I'll call you when I know what I'm doing. Maybe we can get a bite to eat at a nice deli. I think you'll like it. It's called the Essen Deli."

****

A short time later, Dan opened the door to the hotel room. "After you."

The cats stared at Sarah from the couch, eyes glinting in the low light. A galley kitchen to the right was set up with cat and dog bowls and a vase of flowers sat on the end of the counter.

"For me?" She put her arms around him and gave him a fierce hug. He hugged her back and just as she turned her face up for a kiss, her phone rang. The Caller ID showed Baltimore County. "I'm sorry," she said. "I think I'd better take this."

"Where are you?" Officer Mike said. "I need to talk to you."

"I have nothing to say to you except this: Go to hell!"

Dan stared at Sarah. "Who is it?"

"Watch your language," Officer Mike said.

"Watch yourself. I trusted you, Mike. You put me in jail. What kind of justice is that?"

"I need to speak with you in person."

"Sarah—" Dan said.

"Get a court order or arrest me." Sarah shouted. "This is harassment. I told you my aunt was missing and you did nothing, except to say she was an adult. The next thing I know you're accusing me of murdering her. Have you looked for her housekeeper, or the creep in the white van that tried to run me down? What about the people who tried to drown me?"

She took a long shuddering breath. "You've done nothing, nothing and nothing. It was easier to pin the supposed murder on me so forgive me if I say I don't trust you."

"Dr. Wright—"

"I'm in mourning. Don't bother me."

Sarah slammed the phone shut, leaned back against the door, slid to the floor, and sobbed.

Dan knelt down in front of her, lifted her chin, and looked her in the eyes. "You should have let him talk to you, Sarah."

She pulled away and glared at him. "I thought you were on my side. Are you against me, too?"

"No, but you don't seem to be thinking clearly," he said. "Next time, see what he has to say before you start yelling."

"You're a great Monday-morning quarterback."

He looked stung. "What are you talking about?"

"You always have a better way to do something. No matter what, I can't ever do anything right, can I? But you, Mr. Perfect, you have the One Right Way. Your way. Maybe it's time we just accept the fact that I'll never be good enough for you. Go ahead. Walk out. It's what you're good at."

"I'm a perfectionist? How about you, Ms. Control Freak? Your life is completely unmanageable and there's nothing you can do about it. The only thing you can control is you. Not your mother, not Aunt Ida, not the police, not the criminals. You and I are a lot more alike than you want to believe. We both want it our way, because we're smart, and we think we know what's right."

Sarah opened her mouth to argue, but before she could speak, he pulled her into his chest and kissed her hard on the lips. When she pulled away, he said, "I am not leaving you. You can kick, scream, shove, and push me away all you want, but I'm not going anywhere. We have a second chance to make things right in our lives. How many people can say that? We'll get through this. Together."

She collapsed into his arms and sobbed. "I'm sorry, so sorry."

"Shhh," he said and held her tight.

The cats climbed onto her lap, and Winston leaned against her. "Dan?"

"Yes?"

"I'm squished. Can you help me up?" As Dan helped her to her feet she sniffled and said, "I really missed you. I even missed our fights."

"I missed making up," he said sliding his arms around her waist. "Why don't you show me how much you missed me?"

She pulled on his tie and began walking backward toward the bathroom.

"Let's start by getting this thing off. Then, if you don't mind helping me get undressed, I'll see what I can do about that."

She pulled his shirt out of his pants and began to unbutton it.

"To hell with that," he said and yanked the shirt over his head, buttons popping off in every direction.

She worked at his belt and zipper while he unbuttoned her blouse.

"Careful of the neck," she said. "It's still tender."

He stroked her hair, "I promise to be gentle with your neck. But the rest of your body's going to get a work-out." He nibbled at her shoulder, and began kissing his way down to the base of her neck. "Time to take this off."

Her bra fell away, and his lips bounced moved her breasts. "Eeny." Kiss. "Meeny." Lick. "Miny." Nip. "Moe!" His lips landed on her left nipple. He licked and sucked her breast while his hands stroked her back.

Sarah gasped as his hands slid between her legs. "Get out of those pants so I can torture you."

"Oh, I like this new side of you," he said, giving

her nipple a playful bite. "Do you have a little whip to go with that attitude?"

"What do you say we take this party to the shower?"

Sarah closed her eyes as Dan drizzled shampoo on her hair, then massaged her scalp with long, slow, firm strokes. His fingers traced soap bubbles down her neck to the base of her throat, and rubbed lazy circles around her nipples. She returned his caresses with increasingly firm strokes on his back, then his buttocks, and between his legs.

He moaned as she fondled his penis. Up then down. Up again. He stilled her moving hand and pulled her in for a long hard kiss, pressing his erection between her legs. He slid deep inside her and stopped moving.

"What's wrong?" she asked.

"Nothing. I want to enjoy the moment."

He pressed his lips onto hers, his tongue deep in her mouth. It felt like all the air was sucked out of the steamy shower stall room. He stayed still, holding onto her until she couldn't take it any longer.

"Don't stop, please, don't stop!"

At last, he resumed his long, slow love-making, each stroke driving her further up the spiral of passion until she climaxed and shuddered to a halt. Weak-kneed, she fell against his chest and gasped for air.

"I can't move," she said. "You've ruined me for all other men—again!"

He toweled her off, kissed her shoulders and back, then kissed each tender scrape and bruise on her body. As he turned her to face him, he kissed her breasts and kissed his way down to her belly-button, pushing her against the sink. He lifted her up on the counter, leaned her back against the mirror, and pressed his face between her legs.

He licked her thighs, teasing his way upward, making slow circuits, playing with her, until she yanked his head down, and whispered hoarsely, "If you don't take care of me right now, I'm going to scream my lungs out."

They made love all morning. They spoke about the time apart, and the void in their lives that hadn't been filled by anyone else.

Dan was the first one to use the "L" word.

Sarah sobbed, telling him over and over again how sorry she was that she had driven him away and that she couldn't bear to lose him again.

He kissed her tears away and made slow, gentle love to her. When they came together, she screamed, "I love you!"

As he fell back on his pillow, panting, he said, "Could you repeat that please? I don't think the guy in the next building heard you."

A sudden pounding on the wall next to the bed let them know someone had heard them. Dan responded by banging the headboard with his fist.

Sarah put her face in the pillow, laughing until she was forced to come up for air.

"I love you, I love you, I love you, and I'm not letting you out of my life again," she said and gave him a playful jab in the belly.

"Oh, that's good, because I thought I'd have to handcuff you to me to prevent you from escaping again. Oops. Sorry, bad choice of words."

She kissed the tip of his nose and said, "I have no

plans to escape." She glanced over at the clock. "Oh my God! I have to get over to Shady Rest."

"I thought you'd want to get out of your jail house outfit, so I ran by Nordstrom's and picked you up a change of clothes."

"I think I'll keep you."

****

"Now you can tell all your friends, Rivah," Sarah said as Rivah stared at her with her mouth agape.

Sarah and Dan headed toward Ms. Evans' office dodging dietary staff with meal trays. Ms. Evans was working at her computer, looking as elegant as always. Sarah tapped on her door and introduced Dan.

"Ah, Dr. Wright. I see you're out from under your emergency."

"Yes. I made bail, if that's what you mean."

"What?"

"It's okay. Let me summarize for you. The police found Aunt Ida's finger in my freezer. I was arrested for her murder, which, by the way, I did not commit. I spent the night in cell with a drunken, amorous lesbian biker. I was set upon by a pack of media hyenas. Through the efforts of two outstanding attorneys, the Pit Bull and Sol Weinstein, I made bail to the tune of one million dollars. Now, here's the punch line."

"Ms. Wright—"

Dan grabbed her arm, "Sarah, you're doing it again!"

She shook Dan's hand off her arm. "No, wait, you have to hear this. My mother and I are the sole heirs of my aunt's multimillion-dollar estate. So, while you may be concerned an alleged murderer has arrived at Shady Rest just in time for dinner, you can rest assured that every penny of my mother's care will be paid. How do you like that news?"

"I had no idea," Ms. Evans said.

"You're kidding, right?"

"Sarah, you have to calm down," Dan said.

"You mean you haven't been watching TV or reading the newspapers?"

"I'm so overwhelmed with work I haven't read a paper in weeks," Ms. Evans said. "The television gathers dust in my home."

"I feel like a total jerk. Please forgive me," Sarah said and covered her face with her hands. She didn't have a chip on her shoulder. It was a log.

"I tried to tell you, Sarah," Dan said. "You may feel like everyone's staring at you, but they're not." He put his arm around her shoulders. "She's having a rough time, Ms. Evans."

Ms. Evans gave her a compassionate look. "The papers can wait."

"No. I want my mother all squared away, just in case there are any other crises in my life," Sarah said. "I want her cared for even if I'm not around to do it. At least now she can afford to have the coma stimulation program."

"She's being well taken care of by our nursing staff. Mr. Weinstein's secretary called and said he'd take care of everything. He sent copies of your guardianship papers over to us, so all we need is your signature on some forms."

Dan squeezed her hand, "It sounds like Sol's taking care of everything for you. You can take a breather."

"You'll get to meet my mother," Sarah said. "She's not very talkative right now, but that could be a good thing."

Sarah took care of the paperwork and went to visit her mother and Elizabeth.

"Hey, ladies. Guess who's coming to dinner?"

"Who?" Elizabeth asked.

"An old friend," Sarah said. "Dan, this is Elizabeth Woods."

"I can't see you, Dan. Come over and take my hand," Elizabeth said. "Smooth hands, long fingers. Are you a surgeon?"

"Wow, that's impressive," Dan said. "Vascular surgery."

"Good guess. Your hands are too soft for manual labor, and Sarah's in the medical field."

"Nice to meet you," he said.

"I think it's time you met my mother," Sarah said and pulled the privacy curtain aside. Despite the feeding tube, her mother appeared normal, as if she was sleeping and not in a coma. Rosy color bloomed in her cheeks, and she breathed in a natural rhythm.

Sarah sat in the chair beside the bed and took her mother's hand. It was warm. "Mom, I'd like you to meet Dan. Dan, this is my mother." Her mother's hand jerked. "I guess you wonder where the heck I've been. It's a long story, but hey, you've got some time on your hands."

She told her mother about Aunt Ida and the arrest while Dan held Sarah's hand and squeezed it from time to time. "You know what, Mom? The most amazing thing to me was people's reactions to me after the arrest. The people I trusted most turned their backs on me. The people I expected to be least supportive were right there for me. I guess this is God's way of showing us who our real friends are."

"I know exactly what you mean," Elizabeth called from the other bed. "When we found out Mitzi was developmentally delayed, they called it 'feeble-minded' in those days, a lot of our so-called friends disappeared. Having trouble in your life sure clears out all the suckers, but the ones who stay are good as gold, like my sister-in-law, Bernice."

"She's very kind," Sarah said and stood up and went over to Elizabeth's bedside.

"Yes, she's been a wonderful to me and to Mitzi. Diabetes is taking its toll on me. My kidneys are bad, and I don't know how much longer I'm going to last. I'm worried about Mitzi. Bernice isn't getting any younger, either, even though she won't admit it. I wish I could be sure Mitzi would be taken care of when I'm gone." Elizabeth was crying.

Sarah handed her a tissue from the box on the nightstand, picked up the framed photograph of Mitzi, and held it so Dan could see it, too. "Mitzi needs a fairy godmother."

Chapter Eighteen

Elizabeth almost smiled at Sarah's choice of words. How many years now had she lived thinking the same thing? Fifty? Sixty? A lifetime. As soon as she had realized the extent of Mitzi's illness, an anvil of guilt and regret had been placed around her neck. Regret that she had stolen a defective baby. But she loved Mitzi.

Guilty that she felt regret over stealing a sick infant. The irony of it all. She should have just left the baby there. Her need to have a child had overridden all her moral upbringing and professional training, like some irresistible animal instinct. She had paid the price of her choice over and over again.

After she had seen the specialist at Hopkins, she had gone home in a state of panic. Her wish to have a baby was fulfilled, only to find out the child was damaged, infected with syphilis. Telling her husband was unthinkable. The only thing she could do was treat the baby herself. Thanks to his military connections, John had ample quantities of that new wonder drug, penicillin, right there in his office. He had patients lining up to be treated for everything from hammertoe to cellulitis.

His practice had taken off, and his stockpile was so large, he never even noticed the missing bottle, needle, and syringe. She knew how to sharpen the needle and inject medications. It wasn't any different from when she'd worked in the hospital.

But the mother was another story.

Had she ever been told she was infected? Using the cover of a unit nurse's reunion at GWU, she had spent a week at the Washington, D.C. hospital, bribing medical records librarians to search for the mother's name, address, anything so she could track her down. She wasn't sure how she'd do it, but somehow she would let her know, make amends. Yes, she'd make the ultimate sacrifice and return the child. She had found Ida's full name and address at the time of birth, but had hit a dead end at the Florence Crittendon Home. The matron had slammed the door on her face after telling her the records were closed.

Elizabeth went home, held the baby, and cried herself to sleep, crushed with the burden of her multilayered sin. She turned to God and prayed for his help. When nothing came of her prayers, she decided that these were the wages of her sins and that she must pay the dues.

Until the morning she picked up the Baltimore Sun and saw the marriage announcement of Ida Mae Jacobs and Jack Katz, a builder in Pikesville.

"John, I think it's time we moved to the suburbs," Elizabeth said at breakfast. "I'm tired of city life. Crime rates are rising. It's noisy. The air is full of smoke."

"Where did you have in mind? I'm feeling crowded here, too," he said.

"How about Pikesville? I see there's a restricted development going in there, called Colonial Village."

"A restricted community? I won't live anyplace that doesn't allow Jews and Negroes. I worked with some fine physicians who were Jewish and met some of those great Tuskegee fliers during the war. No. I won't abide that."

"Oh, of course," she said, knowing full well his feelings. "I read that another builder is working out there. His name is Katz."

"A Jew? That's more like it. I'll make the call. I need new office space, too."

"John?"

"Hmmm?" He sipped his coffee and read the paper.

"Do you think your sister, Bernice, would like to live out there? I know you two are close and she's been so wonderful with Mitzi, I'd love to have her with us."

He put his coffee cup down.

"Let me meet with Katz first. After that, I'll take a look at our finances and see if I can afford a second house for my sister. I love Bernice, but I don't think she should live with us. A couple has to have some privacy."

John came home with a big smile on his face and a signed contract for two houses on the same plot of land, side by side. "Jack drove a hard bargain, but so did I, Little Mother!"

Elizabeth hugged John and had cried for joy—almost forgetting the original reason why she wanted to move out of the city. As the Woods settled into the new homes, Elizabeth's urge to divulge her burning secret faded.

"It's God's will," she whispered at night to Mitzi. "I was chosen to be your mother."

Two weeks after they moved into the new house, the doorbell rang. A tiny woman with long black hair falling in waves and curls over her shoulders stood on the front porch. Her aqua blue dress had a full skirt and a plunging neckline, showing ample cleavage.

She smiled and said, "Hello, Mrs. Woods. I'm Ida Mae Katz. Welcome to the neighborhood!"

Elizabeth's world shimmered and shuddered to a halt. She took a deep breath. "What a surprise!" She trembled as she took the heavy basket out of Ida's hands. "Won't you come in? Things are still in boxes, but I think we can find the kitchen table."

Elizabeth saw her reflection in the hall mirror. Her red hair was piled up on top of her head with curls in the front. She wore a yellow summer dress with short sleeves and a collar, cultured pearls and matching earrings, the picture of the physician's wife. She ordered herself to remain calm. *I'm a trained nurse. I can handle this.*

"It looks like you have everything under control," Ida said. "You're very organized for someone who just moved in. I was in boxes for a year."

"Old habits," Elizabeth said, hoping her voice didn't break. "I'm a nurse. I like everything in its place."

"Really? Where did you work?"

Elizabeth busied herself with the kettle, turning her back to Ida, and pulling teacups out of a kitchen cupboard. "I trained at Hopkins. But then I got married."

"So you didn't go overseas?"

"No. I was very tempted. I almost wished they had instated the draft for nurses." *It would have kept me out of GWU,* Elizabeth thought. *But God had a plan. He wanted me to save Mitzi. Otherwise, why would I have been there?*

"Ah," Ida said. "Your husband wanted you to stay at home."

"Exactly. Sugar for your tea?"

The ladies settled in the kitchen since the dining room was still filled with china barrels and wood crates. "Do you have children, Mrs. Katz?"

"Call me Ida, please. No, no children—yet. It's just Jack and me." She sipped her tea. "And you? Any children?"

"A daughter. She's napping."

"How old is she? What's her name?"

Elizabeth struggled to remain calm. "She's four. Her name is Bessie."

"A beautiful name." Ida smiled. "I would love to have a daughter."

The pause in the conversation stretched out to an uncomfortable length. Elizabeth didn't know what to say. She knew that if was ever there a time and place to confess to Ida, this was the moment. Instead she said, "Tell me about Pikesville."

"We have our own police sub-station, with twelve officers on duty around the clock." Ida chattered on and on. Elizabeth thought she'd never leave.

Finally, as Elizabeth walked Ida toward the front door, Mitzi began to cry. Panic struck Elizabeth. What was she thinking? If Ida discovered the child was hers, Elizabeth would be sent to jail. Hadn't she just been told they had a dozen police officers? She felt light-headed, dizzy with the terror of being discovered.

"Sounds like someone wants her mother," Ida said. "I'll be on my way." Elizabeth never invited Ida back to her home.

****

Back in the present, listening to Sarah read, Elizabeth still felt the pain of the decision to place Mitzi at the Asylum and Training School for the Feeble Minded. She was less than ten miles away from her real mother, but Mitzi might as well have been hidden away in another country. Sixty years later, the folly of it all hit Elizabeth again. The rusty anvil of guilt turned into despair. She was going to go to hell, she was sure.

Mitzi's real mother was dead. Murdered. There was no hope of confessing her sins to Ida Mae Katz now. Who would take care of Mitzi? Elizabeth had to tell someone. Who could she trust to do the right thing?

****

By the middle of the third chapter in the romance novel, Elizabeth was asleep. Sarah gave her mother a kiss goodnight and headed out the door with Dan. "I need to run by the office this evening to get that laptop."

"Oh, I see. A few quickies with me and it's back to work for you." Dan pushed his lower lip out in a pout. "I guess I'll go visit my mother while you run downtown."

"That's a good idea. She'll be happy to see you. Can you take me by the rental place so I can get a car since the police have impounded mine?" She paused. "I wish I could find Betty. I know she's key to getting these charges dropped."

"The housekeeper?"

"Yes." As she told him everything she knew about Betty, an idea occurred to her. She pulled out her cell phone, dialed information, asked for WorkForce.

"Hi, this is Sarah Wright. I'm calling on behalf of my aunt, Ida Mae Katz. I need to reach a woman she hired through your agency. Her name is Betty; I don't know her last name. It's urgent that I reach her."

A woman said, "What's the full name and address of her employer?"

Sarah gave the woman the information.

"I'm sorry, we have no record of placing anyone with an Ida Mae Katz."

"Maybe you know her by sight? Two hearing aids, thick glasses, mousy brown hair? Sort of dumpy, usually wears blue jeans and sweatshirts."

"When did she begin work with your aunt?"

"About a year ago."

"Oh, I wasn't here then. They were using a lot of temp workers. Do you want the administrator to call you?"

"Yes, please, I'd appreciate it."

"No luck?" Dan asked.

"Dead end."

****

At nine in the evening, Sarah had no problem getting a good parking space in the Outpatient Garage. She waved her identification card at the security guard and walked toward her office. The halls were devoid of the usual crowd of milling people, except for an occasional cleaning lady. Right outside her door, she smelled a familiar fragrance. Sarah was positive it was the same scent as before. She glanced around. The hall was empty.

Sarah put the key in the lock and pushed the door inward. The only light in the office was coming from the monitor of the desktop computer, silhouetting the shape of a woman. Sarah reached to turn on the overhead light.

"Please don't turn the light on," Arlene said.

Sarah closed the door and pulled the visitor's chair next to the desk chair. Her friend's face was puffy, a pile of tissues sat in her lap, and the sleeves of her sweater were rolled up, exposing white bandages on her wrists. The scent of perfume filled the office. Sarah finally remembered the name of the scent: Obsession. "What's wrong?"

"I'm sorry."

Puzzled, Sarah couldn't imagine why she'd apologize. "For what? You're welcome to use my office. You heard about me, didn't you?"

"Yes, it's terrible what they're saying." She sniffed and dabbed at her nose.

"I didn't kill my aunt. I hope you believe me. I love her." Sarah was weepy, too.

"I know what it feels like to be unjustly accused. The weight of it burdens your heart and soul. Makes you lose sleep at night and hardens your heart. It's such a terrible sin that it's in the Ten Commandments, 'Thou shalt not bear false witness against thy neighbor.' "

"Thank you. That means a lot to me."

"What are you doing here at this hour?"

"Picking up a laptop. Jazmin was supposed to leave it in my office. Marian told me not to come during normal business hours. Didn't want me to 'frighten people.' Maybe I'm being harsh. Maybe it was for my own good."

"Yeah, 'for your own good,' how many times did I hear that in my life? Mama must have said it to me about twenty times a day. Even more, after my big sin!"

Sarah didn't say anything. She didn't know where this was going.

"You were at Mama's funeral. Did you think it was perfect?"

"Well, I don't know about 'perfect,' but a lot of friends spoke well of her."

"Oh, no. Mama was perfect. She never did anything wrong in her whole life."

She saw that the burden of grief was heavy for Arlene. "You were right, those are big shoes to fill."

"Well, they don't fit. I'm throwing them back. I'm ready to tell the truth to everyone in the world. Mama's dead and buried. I can't hurt her with this anymore. It's killing me. I've been told, we're only as sick as our secrets. I guess that makes me a very sick person. It's time I got well."

Arlene reached over and grabbed Sarah's hands. "I need to tell you something. Something terrible."

"I'm here as long as you need me," Sarah said.

"Thank you." Arlene took a deep breath. "It started with the 'God's Children' club, a group of misfits. We were fat, ugly, slow, whatever nasty label other people put on us. He told us we were all God's children and took us in for weekly group therapy. Some of us were 'special.' He met with us privately, in his office. It was a beautiful space, full of nice things. He gave us juice and cookies. I loved those chocolate chip cookies. His wife made them."

She paused and Sarah waited, afraid to speak.

"He said I was perfect, just the way I was. I was fat and wore thick, ugly glasses. He was tall, thin, and handsome. He said he'd be there for me. My father had left when I was three years old. I didn't have any brothers or sisters. Mama raised me alone. He said we were his chosen ones."

She blew her nose. "There was a full-length picture of Jesus in his office, holding his hands out to a group of children. They were throwing down their crutches and going to him. It was beautiful. On the top of the picture it said, 'Suffer the Little Children.'

"At first, we just talked about school, my daddy, my mama. Then he started telling me how perfect I was. He said 'God doesn't make junk!' I was only eleven years old, fat and ugly and I desperately needed to believe what he said."

Arlene rubbed her right hand on the bandage on her left wrist.

"One day, after my cookies and juice, he told me to stand up. I remember feeling woozy, but I did what he asked. He told me to stand in front of the full-length picture of Jesus, to close my eyes, and be very, very still. I could feel him touching my hair, my glasses, and my clothes, but it was like it was happening to someone else. Then he told me to open my eyes."

She clutched her wrist and her hands shook.

"The full-length picture of Jesus was gone. Instead, there was a full-length mirror, with my naked reflection. I started to cry. He told me not to weep because God made me perfect, just the way I was. He touched my skin and told me I was the color of cocoa, and my hair was like silk. He told me God made my body, and what I did with it was a gift. I felt special and beautiful."

She closed her eyes and sobbed. "He said it was our secret, not to tell anyone because they wouldn't understand."

She opened her eyes. "I was twelve years old when I found out I was pregnant. I went to my mama, because she taught me to tell the truth. Always. I told her the truth and she beat me. She called me a liar. She said I was a whore."

Arlene looked directly into Sarah's eyes. "She sent me away. She wouldn't let me have an abortion. She said it was God's punishment. She said, 'These are the wages of sin!' She sent me to live with my aunt in Connecticut in a little town in the middle of nowhere. My aunt beat me and said Jesus told her to do it."

She looked down at her lap. "After I had the baby, I stayed there for a little while. Then I came home because I found out I had syphilis and my baby had congenital syphilis. He was blind, partially deaf, and brain damaged. I knew I needed to get help. Mama let me come home under the condition that I never speak of the circumstances of my pregnancy. Shortly after I came home, we moved to Randallstown."

Arlene took a deep breath. "That was ten years ago. I have lived with my lie every single day for ten years. I'm tired of lying. My mother made me lie. She called me a whore and a liar."

Sarah's heart pounded against her chest as if it wanted to get out. Something terrible was coming. She knew it. "Arlene, why are you telling me this?"

"I couldn't tell Dr. Peter, he's a man. I don't trust men. I trust you. You know what it's like to be falsely accused. I knew you'd understand."

"Why did you know I'd understand?"

"Because of the poster in the hallway. As soon as I saw it, I knew who it was. I didn't have the nerve to come right out and tell you because my mama was still alive, but she's gone now. I can tell you who the sexual predator in that congregation is."

"Who is it, Arlene?"

"Why, it's Pastor Black."

"Pastor Black? Where was his wife?"

"His wife? Oh, she was there, too. She brought the cookies and juice to our special sessions. She made videotapes of everything."

Sarah felt ill. She had seen the Very Reverend and his wife just days ago. They had seemed so normal. Was that the face of evil? Not the twisted monsters of our nightmares, but the pleasant, banal visages of everyday evil, right in our own backyard? How had Arlene had the strength to be near them, much less at a celebration of her mother's life?

"Arlene," Sarah said, hugging her. "I'm so sorry."

Arlene sobbed so hard she shook the chair and Sarah. At a loss for words, her thoughts kept returning to the day of Arlene's mother's funeral and the questions she'd asked that made Arlene almost run away. She should have known that something was up. The answer had been right under her nose all along.

What kind of mother denies their own child's pain and fears? What kind of mother believes the worst of her daughter? Did the need to be the perfect "pillar of the church community" overpower Bessie's need to be a good mother to Arlene, the "fallen woman" who was really just a child? Arlene's mother had sent her away to punish her and to ensure she continued to be disciplined.

Sarah's mother had sent her away to save her. For one of the first times in her life, Sarah saw with stunning clarity how much her mother loved her. Savaged by her husband, she did the best she could at the time with the resources she had. At least Sarah had been sent to live with a grandmother who adored her.

Variations on the theme of motherhood swirled in Sarah's mind. Culture, religion, and society differences gave external structure to the role of women, but within those man-made constructions, women created their own realities, their own relationships with each child. The environment compressed the mother-child into configurations as varied as snowflakes. Sarah had a sudden insight.

"The young man sitting between you and Jazmin at the funeral—he's your child?"

"His name's Darnell. We sat in the front row so Pastor Black and his wife would be forced to see him during the entire service. I'm not hiding my son anymore."

"Are you willing to go to the police with this?"

Arlene nodded. "They have to pay for what they did. I don't have the strength not to go through with it. Do you see these bandages?"

"I noticed them earlier."

"Every time I feel the shame overwhelm me, I cut myself. The pain helps me to stop thinking of the shame, but my therapist told me someday I'd go too far. I might die from my cutting. Then, who would look after Darnell? When I saw your poster, I realized they hadn't stopped. They just kept doing terrible things to girls like me whose only sin was to want to be loved."

Sarah took a deep calming breath. "Arlene, what do you want me to do?"

"Can you call that woman detective for me and tell her we need to see her right now?"

"We may have to go to the police station. Are you okay with that?"

"Yes. I can do anything now. No one else should have to suffer like I have."

Detective O'Grady wanted Arlene to come in to make a statement. As Sarah organized herself to leave, she picked up the laptop and put some files in her backpack. She looked around her office, knowing it could be the last time she'd see it. The computer was still on and Arlene was in her office, getting her coat. Sarah moved the mouse to log out. The screen saver of tropical fish disappeared, and the document Arlene had been working on came back into view.

A detailed account of everything Pastor Black and his wife did to Arlene, including the denial that the child was his appeared on the monitor. They told Bessie Brown she needed to pray for Arlene because she was a sinner. They also told her the child needed to be disciplined. Bessie Brown had beaten her twelve-year-old pregnant daughter with belts, hangers, and broomsticks. While her mother beat her child, Pastor Black and his wife held Arlene down and said prayers to drive out Satan. Sarah recalled the first message Arlene left: Satan pretends to be an angel.

Sarah printed out the document, put it in an envelope, and handed it to Arlene in the hallway. "I think you'll need this. It will speak when you can't."

A smile played at the corners of Arlene's lips. "Oh, it's speaking volumes right now."

"How so?"

"I posted it on every website, discussion group and bulletin board I could find on the Internet. The world needs to know what they did. People need to protect their children from these predators. Even if they try to flee, by this time tomorrow, that bastard and his evil wife shouldn't be able to get another church-related job in the United States, if not the world. "

At the police station, with the little detective's quiet questions, Arlene's statement took several hours. Sarah sat with her and witnessed an amazing transformation. With each hideous revelation, Arlene became stronger and more certain of herself. By the end, she didn't really need Sarah there. She was Superwoman, able to take on sexual predators all by herself. After Arlene's story came out, other victims would come forward. Perhaps the demons that drove the young woman to self-mutilation would be exorcised, and her healing could begin.

Sarah hummed a little tune to herself as she waited for Arlene to go to the ladies' room, then called Peter and left a message on his voicemail. "We got our man—and woman. Call me when you get a chance."

Just as she finished, her phone rang with an unfamiliar number. "Hello, this is Ralph Harlow," said a man with a deep voice. "I'm the administrator of WorkForce, Inc. Is this Sarah Wright?"

"Yes, it is. Thank you for returning my call."

"I hope I'm not calling too late, but it seemed urgent. I've been at an all-day strategic planning retreat and just got your message. What can I do for you?"

"I'm trying to track down a woman my aunt hired through your agency about a year ago. I understand there was a lot of staff turnover during that time."

"What was the woman's name?"

"All I have is a first name—Betty. Ida Mae Katz hired her as a housekeeper and paid her in cash. Betty has mousy brown hair, two hearing aids, eyeglasses, and deaf speech. Sound familiar?"

Sharon Buchbinder

"Well, I started here about a year ago. The only Betty I recall was a temporary secretary. She left shortly after I arrived. I don't think it's the same person, because this Betty had brassy blonde hair, no hearing aids, no glasses and a voice like Lauren Bacall."

Sarah's breath caught in her chest. "Did you say Lauren Bacall?"

"Yeah." He chuckled. "I'm a film nut. I love all the Bogie and Bacall movies."

"Mr. Harlow, this is probably a long shot, but do you recall Betty's last name?"

"Freed? Something like that?"

This was the lead she needed. "Do you have any idea of where she went?"

"No, I never got a call for a reference from anyone. She just sort of disappeared. Sorry I can't be more helpful."

"You've been terrific. Thanks, Mr. Harlow. Have a great night."

She tried to reach Officer Corrigan.

"Whom shall I say is calling?"

"Dr. Sarah Wright." A long pause in the conversation told Sarah that her call wasn't welcome.

An ice cold tone confirmed her hunch. "What is it you want to tell him?"

"Tell him Lauren Bacall is Betty Freed, F-r-e-e-d. It's important."

"Okay, Dr. Wright, I'll get right on that." Was the dispatcher being sarcastic?

Arlene came out of the ladies' room. "What's next?"

Sarah gave her a hug. "Leaping over tall buildings on your way home, Superwoman."

****

On her return to the hotel, Sarah found Dan was still out, but Winston was happy to see her. She walked around the parking lot and urged him to hurry up. She needed to get some sleep. An old-time telephone rang in Sarah's purse and she fumbled to get to the cell. Only family members had that ring tone. She pulled the cell up to eye level and almost dropped it from surprise. The Caller ID said: Ida Mae Katz.

"I knew you were alive!"

"Oh, I wouldn't count me out just yet," said a man with a familiar voice.

"You!" Sarah shouted. "Where's Aunt Ida?"

"If you ever want to see the old lady alive again, you'll follow my instructions."

Chapter Nineteen

Sarah put the key in the door and it swung inward before she could turn the deadbolt. Panic rose up in her chest, urging her to run, but the thought of keeping Aunt Ida safe pressed her feet forward. The man had said he'd kill the older woman if Sarah didn't do exactly as she was told. She flipped the light switch. Nothing happened.

"Hellup me, hellup me!"

It was Betty, screaming in pain.

"Hang on Betty, I'm coming. The lights are out, I can barely see in here."

As her eyes adjusted to the light of the full moon filtered through the kitchen windows, she made out the figure of Betty sprawled on the floor. Her back was to Sarah, so all she could make out were the other woman's jeans, sweatshirt, and bright yellow rubber gloves. The cleaning woman's leg twisted out at an awkward angle.

Winston at her side, Sarah knelt on the floor. "Betty, what happened?"

"Hellup, I fall, can't geddup." She moaned. "Hurt."

"I'm going to have to call for help. I don't think I should move you."

"That's right, don't move her." The man from the van stood behind the kitchen door, wearing a yellow slicker and an eye patch. When he limped forward,

Sarah saw he held a gun in one hand and a bottle in the other one.

"Who are you? What did you do to Betty? Why are you doing this? Why—"

The man's face twisted in a snarl. "Why don't you shut up?"

"What have I have done to you? I don't even know you."

"I told you to come alone. Get rid of the dog."

Holding her hands up to show she was unarmed, Sarah stood and led Winston to the back door. "Go on out and do your business, Winston." As she said the words, Sarah made the sign for "Help!"

The man closed the door and stood in front of it, blocking her exit. "What'd you tell him with your hands?"

"It's the sign for 'go to the bathroom.' " Sarah stepped toward Betty's prone body.

"Don't move, girlie."

Sarah stood with her back pressed to the kitchen counter and her hands down at her sides. She pressed her right hand against thigh, searching her pocket for her cell phone. Her stomach plummeted. It wasn't there. She had to do something.

"At least let me help Betty."

"Hellup me, hellup me…"

"No." He took a long swig from the bottle and the moonlight fell on the label. Johnny Walker Black, one of her mother's favorites.

"Is it money you're after? Just tell me what you want."

"Just tell me what you want!" He mimicked in a falsetto voice. "You sound like that old lady. Here's the deal. I want you and your old bitch of an aunt dead and you're gonna do it."

"What?"

"Are you deaf? You're going to knock the old lady off."

"Why would I do that?"

"Well, after you kill her, you're going to feel so guilty about killing your poor old aunt, you won't be able to live with yourself." He smirked and took another swig from the bottle. "And, you're going to write all of that in your suicide note."

"What are you talking about? I didn't kill my aunt. It was you. You killed her. Why? Why would you kill a dear old lady like Ida Katz?"

The man snickered. "You want to tell her?"

"Who are you talking to?" Sarah asked.

"He's talking to me, stupid," said a woman with voice just like Lauren Bacall. Betty rolled over on the floor, stood up, and stretched.

"I'm so sick and tired of wearing these freaking hearing aids!" She reached into her ears and yanked out the flesh-colored pieces of plastic and threw them on the floor.

"And these glasses!" She pulled the thick eyeglasses off her face and threw them down.

"And this godawful itchy wig!"

She yanked the wig off, threw it on the floor along with the other pieces of her disguise, and dug at her scalp with gloved hands. Static electricity made her brassy blonde hair stand up off her head.

"Whew, that feels so much better. Give me some of that, will ya?" She reached for the bottle and took a long pull.

The man laughed, and she put her arm around his waist. "Now, aren't you glad we had a back up plan, baby? Isn't this fun? Miss Smarty Pants P-H-D doesn't look so brainy right now, does she? She looks stooopid."

Sarah stood with her mouth open, astonished by the transformation. At last, she found her voice. "You're Betty Freed."

"Reed, you moron, not Freed."

Sarah pointed at the strange man, the one who had tried to run her down with the white van. "Who's he?"

"This is my husband, Patrick Reed, recently of the Maryland State Penitentiary." She smiled up at him. "While he was there, he studied to become an electrician. Rehabilitation is a beautiful thing. I noticed you and Ida have a lot of trouble with your electricity."

"He turned the power off at Aunt Ida's?"

"Yup, just long enough for me to pour some water on the floor so you'd think the meat in the freezer would go bad. 'Food go bad!' Remember that?" Betty cackled. "I shoulda been an actress. The year I spent working at WorkForce with those morons finally paid off. God, I'm good!"

Sarah's mind reeled with the shock of their relentless attacks. "You knocked me on the head and tried to drown me."

"That wasn't planned. Patrick has a little impulse control problem, right, Hon?"

She smiled at Patrick. He grinned back. "I liked cutting the old lady. I'd be happy to knife this one, too." His lip curled. "She owes me."

"Now, darling we've been over this a million times. That wouldn't be suicide. It has to be a suicide to make the plan work."

She'd had enough. They were crazy. "I have no intention of killing myself."

"Why do you think he's wearing a slicker and I'm wearing these rubber gloves? We're going help you kill yourself. You see, I'll hold your hand, and you'll hold the gun. I'll help you pull the trigger. By the way, thanks for the gun. That was a real find."

Her voice cracked. "What did I ever do to you to deserve this? What could my aunt possibly have done to offend you so badly, you'd want to kill her?"

Betty smirked. "We have reasons. A couple million of them."

Patrick snickered.

Sarah stared at the two felons through tear-blurred vision. "Why are you doing this?"

"Let me spell it out for you. When Ida Katz called WorkForce for a housekeeper, I was working there as a temp. I took the call. She was chatty, told me all sorts of things about her house and what she needed. I decided to take the job myself. So, I picked out one of the institutionalized inmate's files, used her social security number and became her."

Such a simple plan, it staggered Sarah's mind. Steal the identity of a vulnerable person unable to speak or advocate for herself, and use that as a cover identity. All Betty needed was access to the data, which she had by virtue of her role as a temporary employee. So simple, so easy, so evil.

Betty took a swig of liquor. "Piece of cake. I use my real first name. That way I don't forget what my name is supposed to be when people talk to me. The beauty of using a disabled person's identity is she'll never find out what I've done. And her caregivers never had a clue. Dumbasses." Betty brayed and chugged from the bottle.

Betty snorted. "I know people better than psychologists do. I never steal from a mark until they trust me completely. Ida truly believed I was deaf, half-blind, and slow-witted. I heard all her phone conversations and read every important piece of paper in the house. I found out how wealthy the old gal was and the fact she was leaving it all to you and your alkie mother."

Poor sweet little Ida. Believed the best of everyone. Not Ethel. Her mother had been suspicious of Betty from the start. The cleaning lady's inability to understand sign language had been a big red flag to Ethel. Sarah's stomach knotted. "Did you attack my mother?"

"That woman is hard-headed. She wouldn't come outside until we tied the damn dog to a bush and started beating him. Once he started yelping, she flew out there to save him. I yanked that cane right out of her hand. The rest, as they say, is history. Don't worry. We'll get over to Shady Rest and finish her off after we're done with you."

Biting her lip, Sarah struggled to keep her emotions under control. Her mother hadn't gone out to stash her bottles. She'd rushed out to save Winston. Once again, she had underestimated her mother and the intensity of her love. She would never, ever make that mistake again. She heard herself speaking with a southern accent that only came out when she was enraged.

"I still don't understand how you expect to get Aunt Ida's money. You're not making any sense."

"You are dumber than a rock. I'll speak slowly so you can read my lips. By the time we're done tonight, Ida will have no living benefactors. All that money shouldn't go to waste, right?"

The brassy blonde snickered and swigged at the bottle. "We decided her beloved housekeeper, Betty, was much more deserving. And Ida Katz has agreed. In fact, she's in our basement, waiting to do her final paperwork. Just as soon as we get rid of you and your mother, so she has no reason to keep fighting us."

"Yeah," Patrick said. "Then I get to kill the old bag. I can't wait to get even with her for poking that pen in my eye."

"You'll never get away with this!"

Betty glanced at the kitchen clock. "Oh, look at the time. You need to write your suicide note, missy."

Patrick grinned at his wife and took another swig from the bottle.

"Let's see, where's a paper and pen?" Betty looked around. "There's a piece of paper right next to you on the counter. I bet there's even a pen."

Sarah turned around and stared at the counter, looking for a weapon. The knife block was gone, along with every other small appliance on the counter. Everything had been taken by the police.

Stall for time. "You have to tell me what to write. I've never written a suicide note."

"Tsk, tsk. All that education and you can't write a suicide note?" Betty laughed and hiccupped. "Okay, here's what you write: I killed my aunt. I can't live with myself. Please forgive me. Sign your name." She hiccupped again.

"I can't see to write. I need better light."

"Patrick, you have a flashlight, don't you?" He handed Betty the bottle, fished in his pockets, and handed Sarah a penlight.

"Stop dragging your feet and write the note."

She wrote for a few minutes and then stopped. "How do you spell psychopath?"

Patrick pointed the gun at her shoe. "Write the note or I'll shoot you one piece at a time, starting with your foot."

"No. Don't shoot. I'll write the letter."

Sweat running down her back, Sarah started over, writing in tiny print everything they had told her, minus her confession and suicide note. In the distance, she could have sworn she heard a dog barking. Her pulse raced and she took her time finishing the note.

"C'mon," her nemesis snarled. "We ain't got all day."

The yapping grew louder. Please, God, let that be Winston with help.

She turned to hand him the note and the kitchen door crashed into Patrick's back, knocking him onto the floor face first. The gun flew out of his hands and landed at Sarah's feet. The blessed sound of Winston's baying filled the kitchen.

"Goddammit," Patrick shouted over the din.

Betty fell on her butt and started laughing so hard she couldn't stand. "Hellup, I fall, can't geddup!"

Winston stood on Patrick's back, growling and snapping at him like a feral dog. A violent struggle between man and beast ensued. Howling yelps of pain filled the small kitchen as thuds of human fists connected with canine flesh.

Sarah shrieked, "Don't hurt my dog."

Enraged and out of control, Patrick didn't' stop. The moonlight revealed him on his feet, pounding at Winston, punching him over and over and over again.

The dog twisted left and right, trying to avoid the brutal kicks. The dog couldn't last much longer. She had to do something, anything. What could she do? The gun. Where was the gun? She scrabbled at the floor and found the .22.

Winston's howling had become a high-pitched whine, like the sound of a crying baby. If she didn't do something, the sadist would kill him. She had no choice.

An ear-splitting blast filled the room, and Patrick fell to the floor, shrieking. Sarah's ears rang. She looked down at her hands. She'd only wanted to stop him. Had she killed him?

Dan ran into the kitchen. "Sarah."

Sidearm drawn, Officer Mike pushed Dan and pointed his weapon at Sarah.

She dropped the Ruger, put her hands on her head and yelled, "I know where Aunt Ida is."

She raced through the story, emphasizing that the elderly woman needed medical attention.

"You can put your hands down," Officer Mike said. He turned and called out the door. "Hey, Pollack, get in here. We have the location of a kidnapping vic."

Dan went to her side and put his arms around her. "Shh. It's okay, you're fine."

She held on for dear life. "What made you come?"

"I went back to the hotel and you and Winston weren't there. I found your cell phone on the ground in the parking lot. When I saw Aunt Ida's name in the phone log, I had a feeling you'd come home to look for her." He patted her back. "I saw Winston running down the street, and I knew something had to be wrong. I called 9-1-1. They told me to wait outside, not to do anything. Winston had other ideas."

Betty and Patrick were handcuffed and kept at separate ends of the kitchen. Patrick lay on his side, moaning and cursing while Officer Mike examined him. Officer Pollack was on his cell phone.

Officer Mike rose to his feet. "Remember when I called you the other day and wanted to speak to you?"

"Yes. I was awful. I'm sorry." Sarah glanced at Dan. "Someone told me I should have listened to you."

"I wanted to tell you that while we wrapped up the crime scene inside your aunt's house, another officer found a white van with a broken headlight a block over toward Stevenson. It was gone by the time we got the list."

"And?" Sarah asked.

"That van was registered to an electrical contractor, Patrick Reed, a career criminal recently released from the Maryland State Penitentiary. Officer Pollack and I have been making extra patrols of this neighborhood to see if he'd come back. We didn't see the van tonight."

"Getting to be a liability," Betty said in a slurred voice. "We got a car." She hiccupped.

"Shaddup," Patrick said, his voice muffled by the floor.

Betty cackled, hiccupped, and fell over.

"I don't think either of these two is in any condition to make a statement. Nice shot. You got him in the butt. He'll live. What have they been drinking?"

"I think they found my mother's private stock of Johnny Walker Black," Sarah said. "The bottle's over there on the floor. I don't think they knew she'd added GHB to her whiskeys. They don't seem to be used to that particular blend."

Mom, the mixologist, Sarah thought. Ethel's house special probably helped save Sarah's life. The brew evened the odds a bit when the drug hit Betty and turned her into an uncoordinated pile of giggles.

Officer Mike shook his head. "Going to be hard to write this one up."

"Did you ever get my message from the non-emergency dispatcher?" Sarah asked.

"No, I haven't been back to the precinct this evening. What was it about?"

"I spoke with the administrator at WorkForce, the agency that placed Betty at my aunt's home. Seems no one knew anything about the placement, nor did my description of Betty match anyone they knew. However, the administrator recalled a Betty Freed worked there as a temp about a year ago. He said 'she had a voice just like Lauren Bacall.' Guess who?"

He shook his head.

Sarah pointed at the passed out blonde on the floor. "Officer Mike, meet Betty Freed—Reed, aka, Lauren Bacall, aka, Betty, the 'disabled' housekeeper. The drunk with the gunshot in the butt is her husband, Patrick Reed."

"The clowns who tried to drown you," Dan said.

Then Sarah told Officer Mike about how Betty stole someone's identity and took the job. She pointed out the hearing aids, eyeglasses, and wig on the floor.

"Betty decided stealing jewelry from Aunt Ida was small potatoes compared to the millions of dollars she could have if she kidnapped Aunt Ida and forced her to handwrite a new will, leaving everything to her 'beloved housekeeper, Betty.' They were already halfway to getting me convicted of Aunt Ida's murder."

"Did they attack your mother?" Officer Mike asked.

"Yes. They lured her outside by beating Winston. That's why he was tied to the tree with the clothesline. After they got rid of me by staging my suicide, they planned to finish my mother off at the nursing home." Sarah shuddered at the thought, wondering what they had in mind. An air bubble in her IV? A pillow over her face? And what about Elizabeth? Would they have left her alone? She doubted they'd leave any loose ends.

Additional police officers arrived. Winston, battered, bloody, and limping, attempted to greet each one. EMTs appeared with stretchers to transport Betty and Patrick.

Officer Pollack shouted from the door. "They found Ida Katz."

Chapter Twenty

The room telescoped to black tunnel vision despite the lights now blazing in the room. Sarah's legs buckled, and she whispered, "Is she alive?"

Dan grabbed her before she hit the floor. "Let's get you to a chair."

Now at Sarah's side, and helping Dan lift her to a kitchen chair, Officer Pollack's granite brow furrowed and his lips thinned.

As if intuiting bad news, Winston placed his head on her knees and whined. Sarah feared the worst. What good would it be to be vindicated, deemed not a murderer, but still lost Aunt Ida? "Is she d—" She couldn't bring herself to say the word.

Pollack shook his head. "She's alive, but weak."

The breath whooshed out of her lungs. Sarah rested her forehead on Winston's to keep the blackness away. Where there was breath, there was life. She lifted her eyes up and connected with the officer's gaze. Was that regret she saw in his eyes? Regret that she wasn't the murderer he had made her out to be? Or regret that he hadn't listened to her from the start? She wanted to believe it was the latter.

"Where are they taking her?"

"Hopkins ED."

Officer Mike seemed to be in charge. She directed her plea to him. "Can I go to her? Please?"

He nodded and motioned to Pollack. "There's a ton of uniforms outside. Get one to take her to the ER."

She grabbed Dan's arm. "We can't just leave Winston here; he needs an emergency room, too."

He lifted the Weimaraner up in his arms and the dog whimpered. "It's okay, boy. We'll get you fixed up." He nodded at Pollack. "Get her to Hopkins. I'll catch up later."

****

Half an hour later, Sarah limped into the ER with a uniformed officer at her side. A nurse rushed forward to usher her to a room. All but one cubicle was empty. She stepped through the gray curtains and froze, and an impression of déjà vue enveloped her. Not again. Dear God, not again.

Electric warming blankets covered Aunt Ida up to her chin. Her pale face dappled with bruises in various stages of purple, yellow and green, she looked as if she had been used as a punching bag. Sarah's stomach rolled at the thought of her tiny aunt enduring such abuse. A plastic intravenous bag hung overhead and the tubes from them wormed beneath the blankets. Multiple monitors beeped at irregular intervals. A shiver of apprehension ran up her spine.

"Hang in there, Aunt Ida, you can make it."

She closed her eyes, unwilling to think of losing another person who meant so much to her. First her mother lost in a coma because of those bastards, now her aunt. Where was the justice? How could those crooks ever pay for their crimes? Betty and Patrick had taken away Sarah's loved ones, yet those monsters were alive and well. They'd probably go to prison, but was that a reasonable trade?

Sarah sat down in a chair beside the hospital bed and held Aunt Ida's hand beneath the covers. She closed her eyes, bowed her head and whispered, "*Shema Yisrael, Adenoi Elohenu—*"

A feeble voice joined in, "*Adenoi Echod.*"

Sarah's eyes flew open. "You're awake, oh, thank God, you're awake."

Aunt Ida favored her with a weak smile. "Who could sleep through that racket?"

****

Despite looking as if she'd gone ten rounds with a professional boxer, Aunt Ida insisted on going home on the third day of her hospitalization. Her left eye was swollen, and her neck had finger-shaped black and blue marks. The plastic surgeon had put in over fifty stitches in her face and scalp. The doctors were reluctant to sign the discharge papers, until Sarah pointed out that she'd get just as good care in the comfort of her own home.

Aunt Ida took no chances. She whispered, "Get me out of here before they change their minds, Sarahlei."

"You have to rest, Aunt Ida. No senior citizen self-defense classes for you for a while." Sarah squeezed her good hand. "How did you survive this ordeal?"

The older woman smiled. "When we were young, your mother never took crap from anyone. She was nobody's doormat. I just kept thinking: What would Ethel do? Then I'd do it."

Sol Weinstein stopped by as Sarah was packing up Ida's flowers and balloons from well-wishers. "Nu, you bullied your way out of the hospital?"

"And you wouldn't?" Aunt Ida said. "I hear you came to Sarah's rescue with the bail. I knew I could trust you to use my money the right way."

"Your money? Are you kidding? That would be unethical." He yelled and flashed his big white smile. "Sarah's my client, too. She gave me one whole dollar to keep me on retainer. I used my own money. I knew she was innocent."

Sarah gave Sol a big hug. "And the rest is history."

"Will Rutler got all the charges dismissed. Your record is squeaky clean." Sol shook his finger at her. "Now, let's see if you can keep it that way."

Aunt Ida patted the arm of the wheelchair. "Get me out of here, before the nurses think it's time to poke me again. Sol, give me a push. Sarah's got her hands full."

"I have my hands full with you, Aunt Ida. You're the one we need to keep out of trouble."

****

Aunt Ida insisted that her memorial service not be cancelled. "When else will I have a party like this?"

The rabbi was delighted to hear that the dearly departed was still among the living and was pleased to officiate at what would now be a celebration of life. He said, "I have a blessing for everything!"

"Look at this crowd. It must be the food that's bringing them in," Aunt Ida said. All of Aunt Ida's friends had sent trays from Essen Deli. There were bagels, lox, matzo ball soup, whitefish salad, tuna salad, rugelach, kugel, and latkes. Even in Aunt Ida's spacious kitchen, refrigerator space was running low.

"They're here to see you," Sarah said. "Everyone's so happy that you're alive and well,"

"It's a double *chai*," Gert said. "Ida's been saved and you and Dan are back together."

A group of Aunt Ida's friends from her senior citizen self-defense class, Mah-Jongg, and every other social group clustered around Aunt Ida, demanding that she tell her story over and over again.

Jazmin, Arlene, and Darnell arrived with a flower arrangement from the Pediatric Fellows and a card from Marian. Arlene took Sarah aside and told her the police had executed a search warrant and found a large collection of graphic videotapes hidden in a false wall in Pastor Black's study. Pastor and Mrs. Black were in jail on multiple counts of child molestation, abuse, and rape. Loyal congregants were holding fund-raisers for legal fees.

Molly and Josh Weinstein arrived and Winston, covered in stitches and bandages, greeted them with glee. Peter and his wife, Joanna, arrived with another bouquet of flowers. Sarah thanked them and went to the kitchen to search for a vase. She found a plastic milk bottle, which would have to do.

The front doorbell rang again. Sol Weinstein strolled in accompanied by Will Rutler. The noise level in the house went up by a couple hundred decibels. She brought a tray of food out of the kitchen and wandered around, hoping people would help her get rid of the excess food. Even Winston had his limits with leftovers.

Officers Corrigan and Pollack arrived and offered their apologies. "Listen, I'm really sorry I had to be so harsh," Officer Pollack said. "We have rules and regulations we have to follow. I didn't want to arrest you, but Detective Engelman said there was probable cause. He was worried you'd take off."

"I know you were only doing your job. So was Detective Engelman."

"Speaking of the devil," said Officer Corrigan.

"Please accept my congratulations on your Aunt's rescue. And the charges being cleared," Detective Engelman said and shook Sarah's hand.

"Thank you, Detective Engelman."

"Call me Rob, please."

Officers Corrigan and Pollack waggled their eyebrows at each other.

Heat rose from Sarah's neck and cheeks.

"Hey, Sarah," Dan said and slid his arms around her waist from behind. "Hello. Glad you guys could make it."

The uniformed officers said they had to get back to work. On cue, Detective Engelman grabbed the pager at his waist, looked down, and said, "Me, too. Gotta run. Nice to meet you."

"You know, I'm perfectly capable of taking care of myself," Sarah said. "I don't need a bodyguard."

Sarah loved Dan, but she couldn't take it if he turned back into that overbearing know-it-all again.

"Hey, I was just being friendly," Dan said and nibbled her ear.

Everyone agreed that a miracle had happened and that life had given Ida, Sarah, and Dan a second chance. As the last of the diehard senior citizens filed out the front door, the backdoor bell rang. Bernice Woods stood on the back porch, holding the hand of a woman who wore thick glasses.

"I waited until the crowd died down. I didn't want to do this in front of hundreds of people," Bernice said.

"Please come in," Sarah said as she glanced at the heart-shaped birthmark on the woman's cheek. "There's only a few of us here now. Ida, Sol, Dan, me."

Sarah led Bernice and the woman into the living

room. Ida looked up with a puzzled expression.

Bernice cleared her throat. "Once upon a time, a desperate young woman made a terrible choice, thinking she was doing the right thing. She compounded that error so many times over that she continued to hide the mistake beneath more lies and secrets. Shame clouded her judgment."

Sarah watched Ida clench and unclench her hands as tears trickled down her bruised cheeks. What was going on?

Bernice continued, "Shame and fear of going to jail kept her a prisoner of her own secrets. I don't know if you will ever be able to forgive my poor, misguided sister-in-law. She's near death and wants you to know that she's sorry."

Bernice took a deep shuddering breath.

"Ida Mae Katz, I'd like you to meet your daughter, Mitzi."

****

The parking lot at Shady Rest was half-full of cars. A breeze stirred the overhead tree branches, showering Sarah, Dan, and Aunt Ida with red, orange, and brown leaves.

"Are you sure you're up to this?" Sarah asked.

"I have to do it," Aunt Ida said.

"Okay, let's go," Sarah said.

"Welcome to Shady Rest," Charles said.

Bernice stood by the front desk. "She's waiting."

Sarah led Aunt Ida down the cheerful hallway, into Ethel and Elizabeth's room. Bernice trailed behind them.

"Hello," Sarah said.

Elizabeth looked terrified. Bernice whispered hello

to Elizabeth and held one of her bony hands. She clutched the photo of Mitzi with her other hand and stared at Sarah with blind eyes.

"Is Ida Mae Katz with you?" Elizabeth asked.

"Yes, I'm here. Sarah, please get me a chair. I want to sit down."

Sarah pulled a chair next to Elizabeth's bed.

Tears streamed down the sides of the bed-ridden woman's face. "I can never make it up to you, Ida. I sinned. I never told you, even when you came to my house that day and welcomed us to the neighborhood. I should have told you then, but—"

Aunt Ida took Elizabeth's skinny hands into her own bruised ones, her pinky now a stump. "Elizabeth, I need you to listen to me. I've made mistakes, too. We were young. Victims of circumstances beyond our control. Foolish. It's time to clear the slate, to give ourselves a second chance."

"I'm sorry," Elizabeth whispered, her hand shaking. "So sorry."

"I have to tell you something. Sarah, sit down. You need to hear this." Ida pulled an envelope from her pocket. "Sol was to give this to you upon my death. It will be easier if I tell both of you at the same time. Sarah, you've heard some of this before."

Sarah pulled up a chair at Ethel's bedside. "Hey, Mom," she said and leaned down to give her a kiss. "We're all here." She held Ethel's hand and waited for Aunt Ida to speak. Dan stood behind Sarah's chair, his hands on her shoulder.

Aunt Ida cleared her throat, and began to read from her letter. "Now that Ethel's in a coma, unable to talk, I feel I should speak for her. I want you to know how

265

very much your mother loves you. She was afraid if she said how much she loved you, she would lose you, too."

Sarah squeezed her mother's hand and sniffled.

"Sarah, your mother and I met when we were girls, children really," Ida continued. "My mother was born into a wealthy family. My real father died when I was a baby and my mother remarried a controlling and abusive alcoholic. She had tuberculosis. My stepfather addicted her to morphine in order to control her money and to ensure she would be too ashamed to go to anyone in our religious community for help."

"Oh my God," Elizabeth said. "What a monster."

"He raped me on my twelfth birthday and forced himself on me almost nightly thereafter. I became pregnant. He sent me away from Baltimore to Washington, D.C., to the Florence Crittendon Home for Unwed Mothers. That's where I met Ethel. What a strong, smart young woman she was. She kept my spirits up and held my hand when I cried. The doctors at G.W.U. discovered not only did my stepfather give me a child, but also syphilis. They treated me, but by the time it was discovered, I was four months pregnant. Even though he was a monster, and I knew the child was damaged, I wanted the baby."

Elizabeth sobbed and clutched Mitzi's photo to her breast.

"One day Ethel and I convinced the matron we needed to go outside for a walk. My drunken stepfather appeared and told me my mother was dead. He killed her with an overdose of morphine, expecting to inherit all her money. Instead, he discovered she left it all in a trust for me. He accused me of knowing I would inherit her estate and threatened to kill me. When he rushed to attack me, your mother stepped between us and told him to stop. He pushed her. She hit him in on the chin with both fists. He fell over, smashed his head on the sidewalk and died."

Aunt Ida took a deep breath and wiped her nose with a handkerchief. "Sarah, your mother was braver than I thought I could ever be."

Sarah squeezed her mother's hand tighter.

"After that, I helped Ethel escape from the home so she could run away and get married," Aunt Ida said. "To this day, I regret helping her. Her husband was an alcoholic, too. He beat Ethel so badly she lost the twin boys she carried. The sight of their little bodies devastated her. That's why Ethel always said she was 'drinking with the boys.' When she lost the twins, he sobered up and promised to reform. He kept his word, even going to St. Elizabeth's Hospital to fight his demons. A year after his release, he began drinking again."

Elizabeth's sobs had subsided to snuffling.

"When I delivered Mitzi at GWU hospital, I nearly bled to death. I had to have a hysterectomy. Just before they put me under anesthesia, I saw her. She had dark hair and a little heart-shaped birthmark in front of her left ear, just like me. That was November 27, 1942. The worst part was when they told me my baby died shortly after delivery. They told me they buried her in the hospital rose garden."

Elizabeth had begun to sob again, her shoulders shaking with each breath.

Aunt Ida pushed on, despite tears rolling down her cheeks, and words catching in her throat. "Things are not always what they seem. Sometimes we cannot bear to share our secrets, because of the shame."

Elizabeth sobbed and shook, her head turned away from Ida. Aunt Ida took her hand, and said, "Listen to me. Right now. You must hear me." Her tone was firm, but kind. "I forgive you, Elizabeth Woods. I forgive you because I've made mistakes, too. I cost my best friend her twin boys because I thought I was doing the right thing. I, too, have lived with the guilt and shame of causing another person to lose something most precious to her. We are human. We make mistakes. If nothing else, we must learn to forgive ourselves, and to forgive other people."

Sarah wept and stroked her mother's head. She strode over to Aunt Ida and hugged her.

"Thank you. I know this was hard for you to do."

"No, Sarahlei. After my ordeal, it's impossible for me not to do this. We've all suffered. It's time to let the healing begin."

"Thank you," Elizabeth said.

"One more thing," Aunt Ida said.

"What?" Elizabeth asked.

"Mitzi will be cared for the rest of her life. I set up a trust fund. She'll have anything she needs. My one stipulation is that her family must remain intact."

Sarah said, "Don't you want to be in her life?"

"Yes," Ida said. "I expect to be part of her family. Can you live with that, Elizabeth and Bernice?"

"Yes, oh yes," Elizabeth said. Bernice nodded agreement.

A grunting sound came from Ethel.

"Mom?" Sarah said. "Was that you?"

"Sarah, I think your mother's coming to," Dan said

moving closer to her bedside.

Aunt Ida walked over and stood by her old friend.

"I'm sorry, Ethel," Aunt Ida said. "No more secrets. It's time for us to be honest with everyone, including ourselves."

Ethel opened her eyes, blinked several times, lifted her hand, and signed, "I love you, Sarah."

"I love you too, Mom." Sarah leaned over the bed and gave her mother a fierce hug. "I knew you'd come back. Thank you for everything you've done for me. As soon as you're up to it, we're going to make up for lost time and have a lot of very long conversations. Maybe you'll even tell me a few secrets."

Epilogue

The room shimmered with candles and the scent of white lilacs, the first of the spring from Aunt Ida's yard, filled the room. A string quartet, which had been playing a medley of classical rock songs, stopped playing, and then commenced the wedding march. A small cordon of wheelchairs sat in the front row, advance guard of the women from the nursing home. Ethel looked regal with her hair pulled up in a French twist. Elizabeth sat next to her in a daffodil yellow dress, her white hair coifed into a soft pageboy.

Aunt Ida wore a beautiful aqua blue gown that set off her skin tones. Her signature bun was decorated with white and purple lilacs. As Sarah walked down the flower petal strewn aisle on the older woman's arm, she could see Dan's handsome face and broad smile welcoming her. At one point in her life, she thought she would never be heading toward the flower bedecked wedding canopy, with her true love waiting for her.

Family and friends had come in from all over the country, filling every seat in the room and lining the walls with a standing room only crowd. Sarah had been concerned about overburdening the facility, but Ms. Evans had been insistent that the couple use the Shady Rest Community Room for the affair.

Not that it had been a totally easy last six months.

Between trying to decide where to have the event,

who to invite, who not to invite, and who would be insulted if they didn't invite them, the planning had been like a roller coaster. On top of everything else, Dan had been adamant about one particular detail: Winston had to be the best man.

Wearing a black bow tie, the large gray dog was the first to enter, carrying a small basket in his mouth. A tiny satin pillow holding two rings rested within the basket. When everyone was in place, a hush fell over the crowd.

The same rabbi who had officiated at Aunt Ida's celebration of life had returned for the couple's wedding vows. At Sarah's request, the rabbi began with the Story of Ruth, the first recorded convert to Judaism, ending with, "And Ruth said, 'Entreat me not to leave thee, or to return from following after thee: for whither thou goest, I will go; and where thou lodgest, I will lodge: thy people shall be my people, and thy God my God.' For this is the power of love, amen."

The rabbi nodded at Dan. "Sarah Leah Wright," Dan said. "You are the strongest woman I have ever known, aside from Aunt Ida."

Giggles came from the crowd and he smiled. "I know I can be a pain in the neck. I'm hoping you can look past that and see how much I love you. I want to be with you the rest of my life. For richer or poorer, good health and bad, forever and ever. Will you marry me?"

Smiling with her eyes full of tears, Sarah looked around the room at her friends and family and thought of Aunt Ida's words: Never give up hope.

"Daniel Rosen," Sarah said. "You are a pain in the neck—but so am I. We were destined to be together. It is *beshert*. Life, birth, kidnapping, death threats, and arrests, I want you by my side. Yes, I will marry you."

"By the power vested in me by the State of Maryland, and through the power of God and love, I now pronounce you husband and wife."

A glass shattered.

"*Mazel tov!*"

Dan leaned down and gave Sarah a passionate kiss.

Sarah closed her eyes. The room and the crowd disappeared as she responded with equal fervor.

"Get a room!" Sol yelled.

"Better yet, get me grandchildren!" Gertrude shouted.

The room erupted in whistles, applause, foot stomping, and barking.

A word about the author...

After working in health care delivery for years, Sharon Buchbinder became an association executive, a health care researcher, and an academic in higher education. She had it all—a terrific, supportive husband, an amazing son, and a wonderful job. But that itch to write (some call it an obsession) kept beckoning her to "come on back" to writing fiction. Thanks to the kindness of family, friends, and critique partners, she is now published in mystery and romance.

When not attempting to make students, colleagues, and babies laugh, she can be found herding cats, waiting on a large gray dog, fishing, dining with good friends, or writing.

You can find her at www.sharonbuchbinder.com